HUMAN-MACHINES

HUMAN-MACHINES

AN ANTHOLOGY OF STORIES ABOUT CYBORGS

EDITED, WITH AN INTRODUCTION
AND NOTES BY

Thomas N. Scortia and George Zebrowski

VINTAGE BOOKS

A Division of Random House

New York

LIBRARY OF CONGRESS CATALOGING IN PUBLICATION DATA
Main entry under title: Human machines.
Bibliography: p.
CONTENTS: Scortia, T. N. and Zebrowski, G.
Introduction: "Unholy marriage".—Endore, G. Men
of iron.—Dann, J. I'm with you in Rockland. [etc.]
1. Science fiction, American. I. Scortia,
Thomas N., 1926–   II. Zebrowski, George, 1945–
PZ1.H883   [PS648.S3]   813'.0876   75-13382
ISBN 0-394-71607-8

Manufactured in the United States of America

ACKNOWLEDGMENTS

"Men of Iron" by Guy Endore. Copyright © 1940 by The Black and White Press. Reprinted by permission of the author's agent, Barthold Fles.

"I'm with You in Rockland" by Jack Dann. Copyright © 1972 by Random House. Reprinted from *Strange Bedfellows* by permission of the author.

"Masks" by Damon Knight. Copyright © 1958 by *Playboy*. Reprinted by permission of the author and his agent, Robert P. Mills, Ltd. Afterword to "Masks" appeared as part of "An Annotated

*We would like to thank the following
for their aid and advice:*

Janet Kafka
Pamela Sargent
Frank M. Robinson
Gail Winston
Ron J. Julin

For Robert Heinlein,
who taught us both.

Contents

INTRODUCTION
"Unholy Marriage":
The Cyborg in Science Fiction

Machines have always fascinated people. Indeed, men and women of the twentieth century have developed a relationship with their machines that approaches the proportions of a love affair. It is not uncommon for the driver to love his automobile, or for that matter, the writer to love his typewriter. From their primary purpose as an extension of man's limited muscular and intellectual capability, machines have become in our society symbols of power and virility, often assuming sexual symbolism in the minds of men. (See Jack Dann's disquieting "I'm with You in Rockland" later in this book.) Who can doubt the sexual nature of the motorcycle between the cyclist's legs, man or woman? Detroit in its search for new buyer motivations in years past has acknowledged this sexual overtone to the point of designing Buick bumpers with mounded chromium buffers that were known in the trade—rightly enough—as "breasts." Rarely does the operator of a complex machine, be it a bulldozer or a computer, refer to his charge as an "it." More often than not, the machine is a "she," implying the capricious nature of machines in the eyes of male operators.

Behind all of this sexist symbolism and anthropomorphism is the tacit belief that machines have personalities, even souls, and that the man-machine combination is more than a purely physical interaction. At times the biological word "symbiosis"—a joining together of two organisms to make a greater whole—seems appropriate to describe the emotional nature of this union. As more and more sophisticated machines are built with feedback devices allowing the operator to adjust the performance of the machine dynamically in midtask, the resemblance to a true symbiosis becomes clearer. After all, the quest for greater efficiency dictates that the man-machine combination should be as intimate as possible, that the characteristics of the union should approach those of a single organism.

In the quest for a condition transcending humanity, it was logical that people should conceive the idea of becoming a part of their machines. It was inevitable in the latter part of the twentieth century—with its pacemakers, artificial heart valves and mechanical sense expanders—that the concept of the cyborg be born. Cyborg, a portmanteau word compounded of cybernetic and organism, was coined in 1960 by Manfred Clynes who, with Nathan S. Kline, wrote: "self-regulating man-machine systems . . . need(s) to function without the benefit of consciousness in order to cooperate with the body's own autonomous homeostatic controls. For the artificially extended homeostatic control system, functioning unconsciously, . . . [Manfred Clynes] has coined the term Cyborg."[1]

The basis for the cyborg idea is not new to man, who has been modifying himself for centuries with peg legs, hand hooks and glasses. Even animals on occasion modify themselves and extend their operational capabilities with external materials. The North American crayfish (otherwise known as the crawdad), lacking a natural balance organ, orients itself by the pressure of a minute grain of sand on the nerves

1. Manfred Clynes and Nathan S. Kline, "Cyborgs and Space," *Astronautics*, September 1960, p. 27.

in a pit in the head, sealed by a membrane grown after the bit of sand has been introduced. (A favorite high school laboratory trick is to rear the crayfish in an environment where only iron filings are available and then disorienting the mature crustacean by holding a magnet above the animal; the poor creature, convinced that "up" is now "down," invariably turns on its back.)

"Crocodiles have been found," writes D. S. Halacey, Jr., "with a considerable weight of stones in their stomachs . . . ballast to permit the amphibians to cruise lower in the water and thus not be as vulnerable."[2] In the same manner many birds ingest small stones and gravel, but for a completely different purpose: to assist in the grinding of food grains in the stomach.

What is new in the cyborg concept is the idea of unconscious feedback and self-regulation. The key word in Clynes's definition is "homeostatic," implying a symbiosis that operates and is self-regulating without the conscious control of the human partner. It also implies a degree of feedback between man and machine *in both directions* so subtle that the distinctions between flesh and metal in the resulting organism is, for practical purposes, lost. Such a concept must inevitably pose many unsettling philosophical questions, the very center of which is the age-old one: "What is human?" The classical view of evolution changes dramatically as humanity learns how to alter itself at will and is able to communicate that knowledge to subsequent generations. With the advent of the cyborg, man will have come full circle. Having learned feedback control from biological systems and having applied the concept to his technology, he will have returned to a philosophy of whole systems in which there is no functional distinction between flesh and the machine. One can only speculate on what will be the intellectual impact of such an idea in the future. The psychological

2. D. S. Halacey, Jr., *Cyborg: Evolution of the Superman* (New York: Harper and Row, 1965), p. 12.

impact on the individual in such a symbiosis is the subject of a number of stories in this collection. Two outstanding ones, "Masks" and "No Woman Born," present two completely different human adjustments to this transhuman state.

A few writers (including the two editors) have dealt with two fundamental problems in the acclimatization of the brain to a cyborg existence. The adult human has become adjusted to the myriad somesthetic signals of his body—the awareness of limbs, of joints articulating; the sensations of wetness and temperature in the gastrointestinal tract; the minute pulsations of the viscera–all of the tiny signals of pressure and pain that tell us we are living in a self-repairing and self-monitoring organic body. So automatic is our subconscious awareness of these signals that in their absence the brain manufactures bogus impulses. In medicine the phenomenon of the "phantom limb" is well known. Amputees sense the existence of the lost limb for months, and in many instances this awareness of a nonexistent member never disappears. How much more traumatic must it then be to the disembodied (and functionally specialized) brain to be constantly aware of sensations from a phantom body?

A second and even more profound change in the cyborg existence stems from the absence of the human endocrine system. While the mind has from childhood learned appropriate emotional responses that echo endocrine secretions in response to stimuli, this conditioning in itself is not autonomous. There is ample evidence of this in endocrine pathology, where emotional responses and even the whole subtle fabric of personality may become distorted through endocrine imbalance or the withdrawal of a vital secretion. The loss of primary androgen secretions from the testes in the male, for example, results in depressed libido and sexual response. (It is probable that these functions would disappear completely, were it not for the androgen secretions of the adrenals.) Depressed adrenal secretions, as a second example, produce a placidity and a depressed physical and emotional response to emergency situations. Profound personality changes have been clinically observed in both of the above situations as well as in instances where other ductless glands have increased or decreased their activities.

The biochemistry of the brain is not yet well understood. Many psychiatric dysfunctions, especially schizophrenia, now appear to result in part from disturbances in the biochemistry of the central nervous system. (Phenylpyruvic oligophrenia, or phenylketonuria, a psychopathological condition characterized by the atypical secretion of phenyl pyruvic acid in the urine, has been known for years.) Such basic biochemical functions as the maintenance of the sodium-potassium electrolyte balance in blood and interstitial fluids, or the maintenance of acid-carbon dioxide balances, undoubtedly affect the functioning of the central nervous system and consequently, this ephemeral thing we call personality.

In many stories in this collection the authors are not concerned with the total transplantation of a human nervous system into a mechanical environment. Rather they are concerned with the consequences of less far-reaching couplings of human and machine. The harbingers of such matings exist today in such devices as pacemakers and experimental strength-augmenters, but more subtle techniques are needed to replace the crude galvanic muscle responses upon which these devices are based. If true cyborgs come into being, they will result from sophisticated myoelectric techniques: the direct mating of electrical stimulus and nerve impulse.

This step seems rather simple to most laymen who hold a common misconception: that nerve impulses and electric currents are identical. This misconception leads the uninformed to believe that the mating of electrical systems with nervous systems is a relatively simple matter. Actually electrical currents are very rapid flows of free electrons through a metal conductor (or more properly, the rapid exchange between metallic atoms of loosely bound outer valence shell electrons), while nerve impulses, proceeding at a speed two orders of magnitude slower, involve electron-exchange oxidation-reduction reactions within the fluid of the cell and at its dendrite-neuron plate conjunction with the next cell. Because nerve impulses are chemical in nature, initiated between cells by a constantly regenerated material called acetylcholine, the mating of electrical and nervous systems requires unexpected subtleties. Until a number of formidable technical problems have been solved, effective myoelectric techniques and fully integrated cyborgs cannot be developed.

The cyborg may well display an unexpected synergism wherein the resulting organism has capabilities greater than the sum of the separate capabilities. Halacey writes: "For wooden leg, substitute an artificial limb of plastic and metal, powered with electronic muscles and controlled by the wearer's own nerve signals, amplified by miniature transistorized equipment. For iron lung substitute implanted artificial heart or other internal organ . . . For steam shovel operator substitute military technician who operates weapons of war simply by 'thinking about them.'"[3] In the same way that billions of brain cells produce the complexity giving rise to consciousness and the sensation of a subjective interior in human beings, so the cyborg will become a different kind of human being, with enhanced perceptions and even satisfactions different from our own. Potential for fulfillment will be greater, environmental adaptability better and quicker. Access to stored learning through direct computer hook-ups will give a broader command of the whole body of human knowledge.

The development of cyborgs will be speeded by new developments in medical research and by the miniaturization techniques from the space program. Cyborg techniques in turn will certainly affect the development of medicine and

3. Halacey, op. cit., p. 13.

the progress of space technology. (See Scortia's "Sea Change.") Some cyborgs will be specialized; others will be designed to amplify generally existing human abilities. In every instance man will consciously change in some fashion. Clynes and Kline[4] have termed this ability of man to change himself "participant evolution."

Paralleling this development of man-machine symbiotes will be the extension of present computer technology to develop machines capable of inductive reasoning and, more importantly, possessing feedback systems of sufficient subtlety that self-repair and ego-awareness are possible. The fusing of such machine intelligences and quasi-intelligences with human intelligence in a cyborg union might yield a quantum jump in capability. One may well postulate a whole new race of cyborg geniuses. Certainly the crude machine model of the cyborg that has historically dominated our thinking would become meaningless. Self-modification and a new form of evolution might be possible, leading to dramatic changes in the nature of the human race.

We might postulate an even more daring development in this long evolution. The pairing of human and machine intelligences could come about only through a thorough mechanistic understanding of the functioning of the human brain and a thorough mechanistic description of that function we call personality and ego awareness. Such a mechanistic description places within grasp the duplication of such functions in a machine, and leads, of course, to the development of true machine intelligence.

If we *are* willing to admit a purely mechanistic basis for personality and ego awareness (a disconcerting metaphysical concept to many), we may speculate that the human personality could be duplicated in a machine. While organic systems, even in a cyborg union, would have a finite mortality, the personality (one might use the word "ego" or even "soul" with equal facility here) duplicated in the machine

4. Manfred Clynes and Nathan S. Kline, op. cit.

might live forever. Such a duplicated personality would be identical to the organic personality with all of the memories and conditionings of the latter. Each personality, organic and mechanical, would probably be convinced of its own uniqueness as an individual.

This is the ultimate development of the cyborg concept, where even the organic member of the partnership has been supplanted by a machine duplicate. Such a machine duplication poses many vexing philosophical and religious questions (as in J. J. Coupling's "Period Piece"), not to mention a bewildering array of purely legal questions. If both the organic intelligence and the machine duplicate exist side by side, which is the true "John Doe"? Since each is identical to the other, the pragmatic answer is that both are the true "John Doe." (From this point, of course, each will change as each separately undergoes different experiences to evolve along separate lines.)

If the organic John Doe dies and the mechanical duplicate lives on, are we justified in saying that John Doe is dead? The mechanical entity is aware of *being* John Doe, and except for the accident of materials in which the John Doe personality is lodged, that awareness is completely justified. Do John Doe's social and legal commitments, normally voided with his death, continue in force? Can we speak of a "soul" as distinct from a personality, a soul that departed with the death of the organic John Doe? If so, may we now speak of the mechanical John Doe as having a "soul"?

If there is a continuity of personality and memory, can we say that John Doe is dead? Communication theory mathematically treats the process whereby patterns (messages) are transmitted both spatially and temporally. Such a concept may certainly be applied to the transmission of an organic intelligence through time, an intelligence that exists as a coherent pattern imposed on organic matter that itself is constantly replaced throughout a lifetime. If personality is a pattern that exists independently of the organic molecules that for the moment carry the pattern, then the imposition of that pattern on nonorganic materials represents a true continuity of the message (personality).

Consider some of the moral problems that would arise from such a situation. If the organic John Doe commits a crime before the machine personality comes into being, is the machine personality guilty of the crime committed by the organic personality, particularly if the organic personality ceased to exist with the creation of the machine personality? If we argue for the continuity of personality, then a good case may be made for the moral guilt of the machine. At this point the metaphysical arguments of the Middle Ages seem childishly simple by comparison.

Participation in a man-machine symbiosis should have profound psychological consequences. The evolution of social attitudes is slow and painful. It was only a generation ago that the bespectacled schoolchild was ridiculed as "four-eyes." Even in today's so-called permissive society, the man or woman who deviates physically or socially beyond a certain point is the target of attack. The monkey pack still tears apart the monkey with the pink ribbon. How much more then will the early cyborg be the target of such thinking, even if the adaptation is conservative?

What about the human himself? Since the cyborg presumably will have talents superior to the unmodified human in one or several areas, how will he view himself? What psychological changes may we expect in a person with even the most unobtrusive modification? In "Masks" Damon Knight has tellingly explored such changes in the ultimate cyborg, the completely disembodied brain in a mechanical body. In his postscript after this story, he notes the profound effect of the loss of the endocrine systems. Implicit in the story are the effects of highly refined senses and even of special senses. One may well ask if in creating an extremely modified cyborg, we may not truly be creating a monster by human standards? (Of course, in bandying that word about, it is well to remember that the original Latin meaning of "monster" was "omen" or "portent.")

To summarize, a cyborg would be a human-machine self-regulating (homeostatic) system whose mechanical portions would be wedded to the biological ones in an integral, systematic fashion, as far-reaching as the way in which the human heart is wedded to the rest of the body. The enhancements would become part of a total living creature. The total system would be such that nature *might* have produced it but did not—except in the general sense in which Clynes and Kline view man's "participant evolution" as a continuing process of nature in general and man as a kind of *deus ex natura*.[5] Nothing vitalistic or unphysical is involved in this process—only the recognition that new qualities are born from complex new relationships.

Often developments such as the advent of the cyborg are viewed with a simple-minded Faustian suspicion which precludes a creative view of the subject. Dangers always exist within the body of a new technological movement. (See Kurt Vonnegut's "Fortitude.") But dangerous consequences are magnified by human ignorance; creative development requires understanding and imagination. The cyborg concept, like other basic innovations, signals a turning point in the direction of human change. As with so many self-fulfilling prophecies, the very existence of the idea inspires human efforts to make it a reality.

The cyborg appeared in science fiction well before the coining of the term. The stories in the following pages by C. L. Moore, Henry Kuttner and James Blish appeared in the thirties and forties. Before this there were stories of machine men by Neil R. Jones, John W. Campbell, Jr., Edgar Rice Burroughs and others. (The cyborg theme is quite closely related to those of robots and artificial beings.)

The early fifties saw the publication of Bernard Wolfe's monumental and neglected novel *Limbo*, which described a

5. Op. cit.

world where sound human limbs and sense organs were voluntarily replaced by sophisticated prosthetic devices superior to the organic counterparts. A whole society grows up centered about the wholesale cybernetization of humanity, complete with a political philosophy (voluntary amputation and replacement as a moral substitute for war), a system of aesthetics, and even an elaborate series of sports centered around specialized cyborg capabilities. Vonnegut's *Player Piano*, while not a cyborg novel, appeared at about the same time and foresaw the coming age of computerization, automation and cybernetic approximations of human functions —the first overt example of technology approaching the complexity and sophistication of biological systems. Another outstanding novel using cyborg concepts was C. M. Kornbluth and Frederik Pohl's *Wolfbane*, which described the incorporation of human minds into a totally alien system.

Anne McCaffrey's stories of the cyborg starship Helva, collected in *The Ship Who Sang*, are direct descendants of the stories by Blish, Moore and Kuttner. More recently, Joseph Green's *The Mind Behind the Eye* depicts the cybernetic takeover of a brain-damaged giant alien by human beings. Arthur Clarke's Nebula-winning novella "A Meeting with Medusa" describes a cyborg probe designed to explore the upper reaches of Jupiter's atmosphere and nearby space.

Halacey describes the use of cyborgs in the exploration of space: "There are those scientists who suggest the creation of cyborgs from scratch, tailored to the specific planet they voyage to. This would involve tinkering with the genes in the tiny egg cell and the much tinier sperm that fertilizes it."[6] (James Blish exploited this concept brilliantly in his "pantropy" stories of the fifties, published as *The Seedling Stars* (New York: Gnome Press, 1957). "A second approach," Halacey continues, "is to surgically alter an earth being to accommodate him to the terrific gravity he will

6. Halacey, op. cit.

encounter, the gases he will breathe and so on. A third and more acceptable solution is the use of an earthman 'amplified' electronically where necessary, doctored with drugs, deep frozen, and properly shielded to keep out harmful radiation." Such techniques could develop a great variety of human beings with specialized adaptations to explore space or to live in the oceans.

It is clear that cyborg technology encompasses biological engineering, prosthetics, space technology and dozens of other fields. Many books have been written to discuss possible applications of electronic cybernetic equipment to amplify human capabilities. Several of these are listed in the Recommended Reading section in the back of this book.

What does the science fiction writer contribute to these innovations? Traditionally, literature serves to focus and communicate experience in order to develop in the reader an imaginative perception, a gain in experience beyond his normal sphere. Science fiction certainly participates in this function, seeking to convey a future or an alternate experience that grows from an imaginative postulate developed through character and plot; it offers "what if" experience and explores the special human significance of that experience.

One of the interesting questions raised by writers considering the probable path of future human change is the problem of one's relationship to one's body. Fiction, with its special tool of choosing a character's point of view, seeks to create the illusion of internal states, perceptions, and thoughts—to create experience, but experience refined and selectively observed. Using the cyborg concept, stories such as "Masks" and "No Woman Born" probe the nature of self-identification and body experience—in effect asking us *who we are*.

Both "Masks" and "No Woman Born" describe the severing of ties with the racial mainstream and all of its implicit drives. Knight and Moore are also asking: "Can we become other than human and find satisfaction? Will things human matter any more?" It's interesting to note that each author comes up with a different answer. Both remain concerned with the most primary interest of fiction: change.

Many writers have considered physics and biology in terms of their ability to change the human body and personality. Some look forward to the improvement of humanity; others view such projects with dread. The thoughtful, of course, see the potential for misuse and understand that unintentional miscarriage can occur, pointing out the need for constant critical examination and evaluation in the application of such dramatic new techniques.

What would the experience of a cyborg human be like? What new insights would be possible into our basic humanity and life as intelligent beings? The stories in this collection seek to explore these questions. The validity of the authors' answers wait on history, but (to paraphrase Halacey) within these pages you will meet ordinary people seeking out extraordinary destinies, extraordinary people seeking out ordinary destinies, and extraordinary people seeking extraordinary destinies. The extraordinary in every story is some variation of the cyborg state.

Thomas N. Scortia, SAUSALITO, CALIFORNIA
George Zebrowski, JOHNSON CITY, NEW YORK
MARCH 1975

Men of Iron
Guy Endore

"Men of Iron" is a transition piece. The process whereby the protagonist and his machine are hybridized is a mystical one, and more than any other writer in this book, Endore sees the machine as a conscious personality, one whose power exceeds that of its human operator. In this he echoes the fear and awe of machinery of the early exploited worker at the dawn of the Industrial Revolution. The fear of industrial dehumanization, the subject of so many writers and the target of Chaplin in *Modern Times,* becomes reality; Endore even suggests a perverse satisfaction and fulfillment in this final capitulation.

We no longer trust the human hand," said the engineer, and waved his roll of blueprints. He was a dwarfish, stocky fellow with dwarfish, stocky fingers that crumpled blueprints with familiar unconcern.

The director frowned, pursed his lips, cocked his head, drew up one side of his face in a wink of unbelief and scratched his chin with a reflective thumbnail. Behind his grotesque contortions he recalled the days when he was manufacturer in his own right and not simply the nominal head of a manufacturing concern, whose owners extended out into complex and invisible ramifications. In his day the human hand had been trusted.

"Now take that lathe," said the engineer. He paused dramatically, one hand flung out toward the lathe in question, while his dark eyes, canopied by bristly eyebrows, remained fastened on the director. "Listen to it!"

"Well?" said the director, somewhat at a loss.

"Hear it?"

"Why, yes, of course."

The engineer snorted. "Well, you shouldn't."

"Why not?"

"Because noise isn't what it is supposed to make. Noise is an indication of loose parts, maladjustments, improper speed of operation. That machine is sick. It is inefficient and its noise destroys the worker's efficiency."

The director laughed. "That worker should be used to it by this time. Why, that fellow is the oldest employee of the firm. Began with my father. See the gold crescent on his chest?"

"What gold crescent?"

"The gold pin on the shoulder strap of his overalls."

"Oh, that."

"Yes. Well, only workers fifty years or longer with our firm are entitled to wear it."

The engineer threw back his head and guffawed.

The director was wounded.

"Got many of them?" the engineer asked, when he had recovered from his outburst.

"Anton is the only one, now. There used to be another."

"How many pins does he spoil?"

"Well," said the director, "I'll admit he's not so good as he used to be . . . But there's one man I'll never see fired," he added stoutly.

"No need to," the engineer agreed. "A good machine is automatic and foolproof; the attendant's skill is beside the point."

For a moment the two men stood watching Anton select a fat pin from a bucket at his feet and fasten it into the chuck. With rule and caliper he brought the pin into correct position before the drill that was to gouge a hole into it.

Anton moved heavily, circumspectly. His body had the girth, but not the solidity of an old tree trunk: it was shaken by constant tremors. The tools wavered in Anton's hands. Intermittently a slimy cough came out of his chest, tightened the cords of his neck and flushed the taut yellow skin of his cheeks. Then he would stop to spit, and after that he would rub his mustache that was the color of silver laid thinly over brass. His lungs relieved, Anton's frame regained a measure of composure, but for a moment he stood still and squinted at the tools in his hands as if he could not at once recall exactly what he was about, and only after a little delay did he resume his interrupted work, all too soon to be interrupted again. Finally, spindle and tool being correctly aligned, Anton brought the machine into operation.

"Feel it?" the engineer cried out with a note of triumph.

"Feel what?" asked the director.

"Vibration!" the engineer exclaimed with disgust.

"Well, what of it?"

"Man, think of the power lost in shaking your building all day. Any reason why you should want your floors and walls to dance all day long, while you pay the piper?"

He hadn't intended so telling a sentence. The conclusion seemed to him so especially apt that he repeated it: "Your building dances while you pay the piper in increased power expenditure."

And while the director remained silent the engineer forced home his point: "That power should be concentrated at the cutting point of the tool and not leak out all over. What would you think of a plumber who brought only 50 percent of the water to the nozzle, letting the rest flood through the building?"

And as the director still did not speak, the engineer continued, "There's not only loss of power, but increased wear on the parts. That machine is afflicted with the ague!"

When the day's labor was over, the long line of machines stopped all together; the workmen ran for the washrooms and a sudden throbbing silence settled over the great hall. Only Anton, off in a corner by himself, still worked his lathe, oblivious of the emptiness of the factory, until darkness finally forced him to quit. Then from beneath the lathe he dragged forth a heavy tarpaulin and covered his machine.

He stood for a moment beside his lathe, seemingly lost in thought, but perhaps only quietly wrestling with the stubborn torpidity of his limbs, full of an unwanted, incorrect motion, and disobedient to his desires. For he, like the bad machines in the factory, could not prevent his power from spilling over into useless vibration.

The old watchman opened the gate to let Anton out. The two men stood near each other for a moment, separated by the iron grill, and exchanged a few comforting grunts. Then they hobbled off to their separate destinations, the watchman to make his rounds, Anton to his home.

A gray, wooden shack on a bare lot was Anton's home. During the day an enthusiastic horde of children trampled the ground to a rubber-like consistency and extinguished every growing thing except a few dusty weeds that clung for protection close to the house or nestled around the remnants of the porch that had once adorned the front. There the children's feet could not reach them, and they expanded a few scornful coarse leaves, a bitter growth of Ishmaelites.

Within were a number of rooms, but only one inhabitable. The torn and peeling wallpaper in this one revealed the successive designs that had once struck the fancy of the owners. A remnant of ostentatiousness still remained in the marble mantelpiece, and in the stained-glass window through which the arc-light from the street cast cold flakes of color.

She did not stir when Anton entered. She lay resting on the bed, not so much from the labor of the day as from that of years. She heard his shuffling, noisy walk, heard his groans, his coughing, his whistling breath, and smelled, too, the pungent odor of machine oil. She was satisfied that it was he, and allowed herself to fall into a light sleep, through which she could still hear him moving around in the room and feel him when he dropped into bed beside her and settled himself against her for warmth and comfort.

The engineer was not satisfied with the addition of an automatic feeder and an automatic chuck. "The whole business must settle itself into position automatically," he declared. "There's altogether too much waste with hand calibration."

Formerly Anton had selected the pins from a bucket and fastened them correctly into the chuck. Now a hopper fed the pins one by one into a chuck that grasped them by itself.

As he sat in a corner, back against the wall and ate his lunch, Anton sighed. His hands fumbled the sandwich and lost the meat or the bread, while his coffee dashed stormily in his cup. His few yellow teeth, worn flat, let the food escape through the interstices. His grinders did not meet. Tired of futile efforts, he dropped the bread into the cup and sucked in the resulting mush.

Then he lay resting and dreaming.

To Anton, in his dream, came the engineer, declaring that he had a new automatic hopper and chuck for Anton's hands and mouth. They were of shining steel with many rods and wheels moving with assurance through a complicated pattern. And now, though the sandwich was made of pins, of hard steel pins, Anton's new chuck was equal to it. He grasped the sandwich of pins with no difficulty at all. His new steel teeth bit into the pins, ground them, chewed them and spat them out again with vehemence. Faster and faster came the pins, and faster and faster the chuck seized them in its perfectly occluding steel dogs, played with them, toyed with them, crunched them, munched them . . .

A heavy spell of coughing shook Anton awake. For a moment he had a sensation as though he must cough up steel pins, but nothing appeared save for the usual phlegm and slime.

"We must get rid of this noise and vibration before we can adjust any self-regulating device," said the engineer. "Now this, for example, see? It doesn't move correctly. Hear it click and scrape. That's bad."

Anton stood by, and the engineer and his assistant went to work. From their labors came forth a sleek mechanism that purred gently as it worked. Scarcely a creak issued from its many moving parts, and a tiny snort was all the sound that could be heard when the cutting edge came to grips with a pin.

"Can't hear her cough and sputter and creak now, can you?" said the engineer to the director. "And the floor is quiet. Yes, I'm beginning to be proud of that machine, and now I think we can set up an adjustable cam here to make the whole operation automatic.

"Every machine should be completely automatic. A machine that needs an operator," he declared oratorically, "is an invalid."

In a short time the cams were affixed and the carriage with the cutting tool traveled back and forth of itself, never failing to strike the pin at the correct angle and at the correct speed of rotation.

All Anton had to do was to stop the machine in case of a hitch. But soon even that task was unnecessary. No hitches were ever to occur again. Electronic tubes at several points operated mechanisms designed to eject faulty pins either before they entered the hopper or after they emerged from the lathe.

Anton stood by and watched. That was all he had to do, for the machine performed all the operations that he used to do. In went the unfinished pins and out they came, each one perfectly drilled. Anton's purblind eyes could scarcely follow the separate pins of the stream that flowed into the machine. Now and then a pin was pushed remorselessly out of line and plumped sadly into a bucket. Cast out! Anton stooped laboriously and retrieved the pin. "That could have been used," he thought.

"Krr-click, krr-click," went the feeder, while the spindle and the drill went *zzz-sntt, zzz-sntt, zzz-sntt,* and the belt that brought the pins from a chattering machine beyond, rolled softly over the idlers with a noise like a breeze in a sail. Already the machine had finished ten good pins while Anton was examining a single bad one.

*   *   *

Late in the afternoon there appeared a number of important men. They surrounded the machine, examined it and admired it.

"That's a beauty," they declared.

Now the meeting took on a more official character. There were several short addresses. Then an imposing man took from a small leather box a golden crescent.

"The Crescent Manufacturing Company," he said, "takes pride and pleasure in awarding this automatic lathe a gold crescent." A place on the side of the machine had been prepared for the affixing of this distinction.

Now the engineer was called upon to speak.

"Gentlemen," he said fiercely, "I understand that formerly the Crescent Company awarded its gold crescent only to workmen who had given fifty years of service to the firm. In giving a gold crescent to a machine, your President has perhaps unconsciously acknowledged a new era . . ."

While the engineer developed his thesis, the director leaned over to his assistant and whispered, "Did you ever hear of why the sea is salt?"

"Why the sea is salt?" whispered back the assistant. "What do you mean?"

The director continued: "When I was a little kid, I heard the story of 'Why the sea is salt' many times, but I never thought it important until just a moment ago. It's something like this: Formerly the sea was fresh water and salt was rare and expensive. A miller received from a wizard a wonderful machine that just ground salt out of itself all day long. At first the miller thought himself the most fortunate man in the world, but soon all the villages had salt to last them for centuries and still the machine kept on grinding more salt. The miller had to move out of his house, he had to move off his acres. At last he determined that he would sink the machine in the sea and be rid of it. But the mill ground so fast that boat and miller and machine were sunk together, and down below, the mill still went on grinding and that's why the sea is salt."

"I don't get you," said the assistant.

Throughout the speeches, Anton had remained seated on the floor, in a dark corner, where his back rested comfortably against the wall. It had begun to darken by the time the company left, but still Anton remained where he was, for the stone floor and wall had never felt quite so restful before. Then, with a great effort, he roused his unwilling frame, hobbled over to his machine and dragged forth the tarpaulin.

Anton had paid little attention to the ceremony; it was, therefore, with surprise that he noticed the gold crescent on his machine. His weak eyes strained to pierce the twilight. He let his fingers play over the medal, and was aware of tears falling from his eyes, and could not divine the reason.

The mystery wearied Anton. His worn and trembling body sought the inviting floor. He stretched out, and sighed, and that sigh was his last.

When the daylight had completely faded, the machine began to hum softly. *Zzz-sntt, zzz-sntt,* it went, four times, and each time carefully detached a leg from the floor.

Now it rose erect and stood beside the body of Anton. Then it bent down and covered Anton with the tarpaulin. Out of the hall it stalked on sturdy legs. Its electron eyes saw distinctly through the dark, its iron limbs responded instantly to its every need. No noise racked its interior, where its organs functioned smoothly and without a single tremor. To the watchman, who grunted his usual greeting without looking up, it answered not a word but strode on rapidly, confidently, through the windy streets of night—to Anton's house.

Anton's wife lay waiting, half sleeping on the bed in the room where the light of the arc-light came through the stained-glass window. And it seemed to her that a marvel happened: her Anton come back to her free of coughs and creaks and tremors; her Anton come to her in all the pride and folly of his youth, his breath like wind soughing through treetops, the muscles of his arms like steel.

I'm with You in Rockland

Jack Dann

In the following story, Dann writes of a reversible cyborg union, one in which the final fusion through myoelectric linkage has not taken place. Yet the strength augmenter he describes has homeostatic features in the sense that it has sophisticated feedback mechanisms. We spoke in the introduction of the sexual potency associated with the powerful machines. Here is the ultimate expression of this identification, a full machine augmentation carried to its logical sexual conclusion.

I'm with you in Rockland
*   where we wake up electrified out of the coma by*
*   our own soul's airplanes*
I'm with you in Rockland
*   in my dreams you walk dripping from the sea-*
*   journey on the highway across America in tears*
*   to the door of my cottage in the Western night*
*   —ALLEN GINSBERG, "Howl"*

Flaccus decreased the pressure on the accelerator pedal and the speedometer needle drifted back to 100 m.p.h. That's better, he thought. The evening rain was making the road slippery. He glanced at the hitch-hiker sitting beside him and pressed his back into the cushioned seat, his arm resting on his leg, the steering stick held loosely between his thumb and forefinger. His eyes were half-shut. He could feel the cement being sucked under the car, inches below his feet. He could almost feel his feet melting into the floor as he tried to merge himself with the car.

Like this, he could drive his best. He didn't need to look to the side to judge distance; he could feel it. He was walking with a new body and it was better and stronger than his own. But it was not enough. The car could not satisfy Flaccus; it could only remind him of a stronger, better body.

* * *

Flaccus had worked up a good sweat piling up steel beams for the last two hours. He was wearing an exoskeletal harness, a light metal framework equipped with sensors that picked up his every movement and transmitted them to artificial muscles. With the harness, Flaccus could support 2,500 pounds in each hand.

Flaccus moved smoothly through his work, dipping and pushing, lifting and pulling, his motions smooth and easy. He imagined that his muscles rippled as he swayed back and forth. He stretched out his arms. The harness felt good. It was all around him, thin, light strips of body armor, giving him all the power and security he needed. He was soft tissue surrounded by a steel and plastic carapace. Fifty feet away from him stood the new construction project, a jagged framework of plastic and steel.

"Of course I love you," Flaccus said as he stared out the window at the New York skyline. The recent temperature inversion had put an invisible lid on the city. The air, saturated with pollutants, would be difficult to breathe. And the media would play up the increase in deaths by asphyxiation and emphysema. The extreme humidity put Flaccus's nerves on edge.

"Well, you certainly don't show it," Clara replied, pulling her synthetic silk nightgown together.

Flaccus continued staring out the window. He could see her reflection: she was wearing another frilly nightgown. He hated lacy, flowery nightgowns. And Clara had grown to be just the type of woman to wear them. He looked through the reflection of her face at a string of lights near the river. The heavy smog softened the city, merged the sharp interplay of shadow and light into a gray sea. Only the brightest lights were in sharp focus.

"I just can't. I can't love you that way; that's the way I am. I don't mind if you get a lover. I realize you have needs, but I cannot satisfy them."

"But I don't want a lover; I want you." She put her arms around Flaccus's waist. Flaccus ignored her, pretended that he couldn't feel her hands massaging his stomach. He felt the city all around him. He could feel himself blending into the gray smog, drifting down to the cement below. The apartment was a prison, keeping him from the outside, forcing him to play games with this trapped stranger.

"Could you put some heat on? I'm really freezing."

Flaccus turned off the Headway Control and passed two cars ahead of him. The luminescent road divider slithered back and forth and Flaccus tightened his grip on the stick. The thin metal bands on his hand reflected the road lights. Flaccus increased the air flow and turned the heat up a bit.

Shouldn't have picked up a hitch-hiker, he told himself. But what the hell; he was celebrating. He glanced at her: brown hair to her shoulders, tanned face, hook to her nose. Her blouse rippled as she allowed her body to find a more natural position. Knee touching dashboard, hand resting on her lap.

Force yourself. Try to talk to her, you need to talk. You've got to talk. But he had forgotten her name, or maybe he had never asked. Well, you could ask her, he thought. You could say, "What's your name again?" Then you could add, "I never can remember names," and take it from there. Instead, he ignored her.

Try a tree, he thought. That might be easier. If you could feel comfortable around a tree, that would be a start. He chuckled. The girl raised her eyebrows—obviously a studied habit—and huddled against the door.

The trees formed a wall on each side of the highway. They appeared preternaturally green in the artificial light. Although he could see city exits every mile, Flaccus still felt he was in the wilds. He did not like being outside New York.

Who the fuck cares, he thought. You don't need New York. You need a vacation. A guideway exit sign blinked on and off above the highway. He took the next exit. Flaccus could not concentrate on his driving; he was too aware of the girl.

He stopped at the check-in station, inserted his credit card in the roadside meter, and then followed the car ahead onto the access ramp. He stopped the car, cut the engine, and pushed a dashboard button to activate the guide arm.

"Better on the guideway," the girl said. "I mean I don't care which way you take, just as long as we're in the general direction."

Answer her. He thought of moving his hand to her lap, but lit a cigarette instead. She was too young; no, that's not it, he thought. He thought of her breasts pushing into his face. Masturbation would be better.

He watched the car ahead. A small retractable arm emerged from its side and clamped onto one of the guideway's two side rails. Then the car accelerated and merged into the traffic on the main guideway.

Flaccus remembered he was wearing the harness. He could feel it coiled tightly around his body, waiting for a signal to transmit to its own muscles. But for the last twenty minutes Flaccus had forgotten about it. It was his own strength that pushed and balanced the steel beams; it was his own firm, gentle touch that directed everything to its proper place—girders, huge plates of glass, heavy machinery. He did not need anything but himself. But he felt a claustrophobic fear of being swallowed when he thought of the harness wrapped around him. He shrugged it off and tried to get back into the rhythm of his work. For Flaccus, the harness had to be his freedom.

*   *   *

"Come on," Clara said, "just sleep with me tonight. We don't have to do anything, just be close together." She pulled him away from the window and helped him into her bed. He was still thinking about the outside. The cool, recirculated air was giving him a headache. He wanted to sweat; he would much rather be at work.

Clara pushed herself against him, resting her leg on his thigh. Her body had become flabby, soft where it was once hard. He let her touch him; it was better than listening to her cry for half the night. Flaccus tried to get an erection. Clara knew how to touch him, but he couldn't respond. He tried thinking about other women. He imagined himself in a car with a brown-haired girl. She was begging him to stop, throwing her head back and moaning. But he was so strong, so hard. He often fancied himself in a car making love.

Clara was beneath him; he supported his weight with his elbows. Was she pretending too? he asked himself. He had to do it now. He could do it. She positioned herself under him. If I can get in, he thought, I'll be all right. He became soft. She said, "Come on, please . . ."

Think about the harness, think about working on the buildings. You're strong, powerful. You've got to do it. Think of the girl in the car, her breasts pushing against you. You're enclosed in steel, crushing out her life.

"God, it's cold," the hitch-hiker said. She had just awakened after sleeping fitfully for an hour. "Christ, you can see your own breath." She raised the temperature without asking for permission.

Flaccus turned the dashboard lights up and looked at the girl shivering beside him, her arms pulled close to her chest for warmth.

"How can you stand it so cold?" she asked.

It would be easier in the car, Flaccus told himself. Especially now. It would be much more erotic if he could just

touch her, squeeze her breasts, without talking and playing
seduction games.

He reached over and touched her breast. She examined
the thin metal bands on his hands, but didn't stop him.

"Did you hurt your arm in an accident?" she asked.
Flaccus did not answer. She rested her head on the window
and closed her eyes. "Why don't you put the seats down?"
she asked. She made no move to be near him when he
reached over to fondle her other breast.

Flaccus didn't want her to move closer. He just wanted
her to be still while he touched her. And he would not ask
her name. She was just there; that's how he wanted it.

And she obliged. She waited a proper amount of time
before she removed her blouse and began conversation.
"You didn't tell me why you put the temperature down so
low. I think I've got pneumonia now." She removed her
pants.

Flaccus cleared the windows and watched the shadows
draw patterns on her face and chest. With his finger he
followed the shafts of light that intermittently cut her into
pieces. She touched herself, but did not try to touch him.

It was almost quitting time. In five minutes some two
thousand workers would be going home for dinner, but
Flaccus would not be one of them. He waited around while
the other harness workers discharged their equipment in the
construction hut.

Flaccus stayed out of sight long enough to make Tusser,
the Keeper, properly impatient. When Flaccus finally entered the hut, Tusser was swearing and pacing back and
forth. Flaccus told him that he would lock up. He knew the
alarm system and had once served some time as a Keeper.
When Tusser was hungry he did not mind bending rules
for his friends.

As soon as Tusser left, Flaccus turned off the alarm
system. He took off his harness, lowered it over the support

hooks where it hung from the wall like a skeleton in a dungeon. He did not remove its power package. Flaccus then took off his workclothes and slipped back into the harness. He felt strong and real again, and also clean, as if he had just washed and rested. He put on his street clothes. There were a few bulges, but they were not very obvious. The harness was now a part of his muscle and bone; it was as familiar as his skin. Flaccus would remember to keep his hands in his pockets when he left the hut.

It was the weekend. Flaccus would have three days grace. The only people on the premises would be the night watchmen, and they would not notice that anything was wrong.

Clara was asleep. Flaccus touched her, grew bolder, kissed her. She moaned and started to awaken. Flaccus got up and walked to the window to watch the city. The smog covered everything with a gray gel. Flaccus imagined his building was a steel stick wound round and round with gray cotton candy.

"Are you going to put the seats down or do you want to do it like this?" The hitch-hiker leaned toward Flaccus. "Either way, I don't care, but let's just do it." She turned on soft music, but blanked the screen.

The windshield fogged a bit, then cleared. Flaccus watched the dividing lines in the road. Straight for the city, he thought. He felt a surge of power. Straight for the city. He repeated it to himself. There were cars all around him, all moving at the same speed. But he could not see very far: everything was covered with smog or fog. Smog meant the city.

"Come on," she said, reaching for his crotch, touching the fleshy part of his leg. She found a metal band and traced her finger along its edge. Flaccus pushed her hand away.

* * *

"And that's all of it," Clara said, lighting a new cigarette with an old one. "I've been seeing him for about six months, and I just didn't know how to tell you before. So I'm going to stay with some friends for a while until I decide what to do. Is that all right with you?"

She had chosen to talk to him in the living room, rather than the bedroom. Her hair was piled high on her head and her make-up was rather heavy. Flaccus suddenly found her desirable.

"I think this is for the best. It's what you wanted all along, isn't it?" She paused, her breathing was heavy. "Doesn't what I'm telling you upset you?"

Flaccus could find no reason to set her mind at ease.

Flaccus could take her now. He was strong enough. The harness was no longer an extension of Flaccus: it was Flaccus. Gently, he touched the hitch-hiker's shoulder, then squeezed, crushing it between his fingers. The girl screamed and fainted. Flaccus shook his head wildly, looking for a way out. He jerked at the door latch, but it broke apart in his hand. He smashed the window and looked down at Clara.

She was breathing heavily and making stupid little noises. "Put it in," Clara said, her teeth clenched. She reminded him of the Cheshire cat, smiling and leering up at him. He could feel himself disappearing until there was nothing left but his penis, and that getting smaller and smaller until it too disappeared.

Masks

Damon Knight

Damon Knight is one of the most formidable talents in science fiction. We are indeed tempted to say "among all of the practitioners of the short story." His syntax, his word sense, his complete and conscious control of every conceptual step in the creative process could well serve as a model for all aspiring writers. "Masks" is one of the most highly polished pieces ever to come from this brilliant writer's typewriter. Rather than comment on it, we refer you to Knight's own remarks following the story. They give a rare insight into the workings of the creative process.

The eight pens danced against the moving strip of paper, like the nervous claws of some mechanical lobster. Roberts, the technician, frowned over the tracings while the other two watched.

"Here's the wake-up impulse," he said, pointing with a skinny finger. "Then here, look, seventeen seconds more, still dreaming."

"Delayed response," said Babcock, the project director. His heavy face was flushed and he was sweating. "Nothing to worry about."

"Okay, delayed response, but look at the difference in the tracings. Still dreaming, after the wake-up impulse, but the peaks are closer together. Not the same dream. More anxiety, more motor pulses."

"Why does he have to sleep at all?" asked Sinescu, the man from Washington. He was dark, narrow-faced. "You flush the fatigue poisons out, don't you? So what is it, something psychological?"

"He needs to dream," said Babcock. "It's true he has no physiological need for sleep, but he's got to dream. If he didn't, he'd start to hallucinate, maybe go psychotic."

"Psychotic," said Sinescu. "Well—that's the question, isn't it? How long has he been doing this?"

"About six months."

"In other words, about the time he got his new body—and started wearing a mask?"

"About that. Look, let me tell you something, he's rational. Every test—"

"Yes, okay, I know about tests. Well—so he's awake now?"

The technician glanced at the monitor board. "He's up. Sam and Irma are with him." He hunched his shoulders, staring at the EEG tracings again. "I don't know why it should bother me. It stands to reason, if he has dream needs of his own that we're not satisfying with the programmed stuff, this is where he gets them in." His face hardened. "I don't know. Something about those peaks I don't like."

Sinescu raised his eyebrows. "You program his dreams?"

"Not program," said Babcock impatiently. "A routine suggestion to dream the sort of thing we tell him to. Somatic stuff, sex, exercise, sport."

"And whose idea was that?"

"Psych section. He was doing fine neurologically, every other way, but he was withdrawing. Psych decided he needed that somatic input in some form, we had to keep him in touch. He's alive, he's functioning, everything works. But don't forget, he spent forty-three years in a normal human body."

In the hush of the elevator, Sinescu said, ". . . Washington."

Swaying, Babcock said, "I'm sorry, what?"

"You look a little rocky. Getting any sleep?"

"Not lately. What did you say before?"

"I said they're not happy with your reports in Washington."

"Goddamn it, I know that." The elevator door silently opened. A tiny foyer, green carpet, gray walls. There were three doors, one metal, two heavy glass. Cool, stale air. "This way."

Sinescu paused at the glass door, glanced through: a gray-carpeted living room, empty. "I don't see him."

"Around the ell. Getting his morning checkup."

The door opened against slight pressure; a battery of

ceiling lights went on as they entered. "Don't look up," said
Babcock. "Ultraviolet." A faint hissing sound stopped when
the door closed.

"And positive pressure in here? To keep out germs?
Whose idea was that?"

"His." Babcock opened a chrome box on the wall and
took out two surgical masks. "Here, put this on."

Voices came muffled from around the bend of the
room. Sinescu looked with distaste at the white mask, then
slowly put it over his head.

They stared at each other. "Germs," said Sinescu
through the mask. "Is that rational?"

"All right, he can't catch a cold or what have you, but
think about it a minute. There are just two things now that
could kill him. One is a prosthetic failure, and we guard
against that; we've got five hundred people here, we check
him out like an airplane. That leaves a cerebrospinal infec-
tion. Don't go in there with a closed mind."

The room was large, part living room, part library, part
workshop. Here was a cluster of Swedish-modern chairs, a
sofa, coffee table; here a workbench with a metal lathe,
electric crucible, drill press, parts bins, tools on wallboards;
here a drafting table; here a free-standing wall of bookshelves that Sinescu fingered curiously as they passed. Bound
volumes of project reports, technical journals, reference
books; no fiction except for *Fire* and *Storm* by George Stew-
art and *The Wizard of Oz* in a worn blue binding. Behind
the bookshelves, set into a little alcove, was a glass door
through which they glimpsed another living room, differently furnished: upholstered chairs, a tall philodendron in a
ceramic pot. "There's Sam," Babcock said.

A man had appeared in the other room. He saw them,
turned to call to someone they could not see, then came
forward, smiling. He was bald and stocky, deeply tanned.
Behind him, a small, pretty woman hurried up. She crowded
through after her husband, leaving the door open. Neither
of them wore a mask.

"Sam and Irma have the next suite," Babcock said. "Company for him; he's got to have somebody around. Sam is an old air-force buddy of his, and besides, he's got a tin arm."

The stocky man shook hands, grinning. His grip was firm and warm. "Want to guess which one?" He wore a flowered sport shirt. Both arms were brown, muscular and hairy, but when Sinescu looked more closely, he saw that the right one was a slightly different color, not quite authentic.

Embarrassed, he said, "The left, I guess."

"Nope." Grinning wider, the stocky man pulled back his right sleeve to show the straps.

"One of the spin-offs from the project," said Babcock. "Myoelectric, servo-controlled, weighs the same as the other one. Sam, they about through in there?"

"Maybe so. Let's take a peek. Honey, you think you could rustle up some coffee for the gentlemen?"

"Oh, why, sure." The little woman turned and darted back through the open doorway.

The far wall was glass, covered by a translucent white curtain. They turned the corner. The next bay was full of medical and electronic equipment, some built into the walls, some in tall black cabinets on wheels. Four men in white coats were gathered around what looked like an astronaut's couch. Sinescu could see someone lying on it: feet in Mexican woven-leather shoes, dark socks, gray slacks. A mutter of voices.

"Not through yet," Babcock said. "Must have found something else they didn't like. Let's go out onto the patio a minute."

"Thought they checked him at night—when they exchange his blood, and so on. . . ?"

"They do," Babcock said. "And in the morning, too." He turned and pushed open the heavy glass door. Outside, the roof was paved with cut stone, enclosed by a green plastic canopy and tinted-glass walls. Here and there were concrete basins, empty. "Idea was to have a roof garden out here, something green, but he didn't want it. We had to take all the plants out, glass the whole thing in."

Sam pulled out metal chairs around a white table and they all sat down. "How is he, Sam?" asked Babcock.

He grinned and ducked his head. "Mean in the mornings."

"Talk to you much? Play any chess?"

"Not too much. Works, mostly. Reads some, watches the box a little." His smile was forced; his heavy fingers were clasped together and Sinescu saw now that the fingertips of one hand had turned darker, the others not. He looked away.

"You're from Washington, that right?" Sam asked politely. "First time here? Hold on." He was out of his chair. Vague upright shapes were passing behind the curtained glass door. "Looks like they're through. If you gentlemen would just wait here a minute, till I see." He strode across the roof. The two men sat in silence. Babcock had pulled down his surgical mask; Sinescu noticed and did the same.

"Sam's wife is a problem," Babcock said, leaning nearer. "It seemed like a good idea at the time, but she's lonely here, doesn't like it—no kids—"

The door opened again and Sam appeared. He had a mask on, but it was hanging under his chin. "If you gentlemen would come in now."

In the living area, the little woman, also with a mask hanging around her neck, was pouring coffee from a flowered ceramic jug. She was smiling brightly but looked unhappy. Opposite her sat someone tall, in gray shirt and slacks, leaning back, legs out, arms on the arms of his chair, motionless. Something was wrong with his face.

"Well, now," said Sam heartily. His wife looked up at him with an agonized smile.

The tall figure turned its head and Sinescu saw with an icy shock that its face was silver, a mask of metal with oblong slits for eyes, no nose or mouth, only curves that were faired into each other. ". . . project." said an inhuman voice.

Sinescu found himself half bent over a chair. He sat down. They were all looking at him. The voice resumed, "I said, are you here to pull the plug on the project." It was unaccented, indifferent.

"Have some coffee." The woman pushed a cup toward him.

Sinescu reached for it, but his hand was trembling and he drew it back. "Just a fact-finding expedition," he said.

"Bull. Who sent you—Senator Hinkel."

"That's right."

"Bull. He's been here himself; why send you? If you are going to pull the plug, might as well tell me." The face behind the mask did not move when he spoke; the voice did not seem to come from it.

"He's just looking around, Jim," said Babcock.

"Two hundred million a year," said the voice, "to keep one man alive. Doesn't make much sense, does it. Go on, drink your coffee."

Sinescu realized that Sam and his wife had already finished theirs and that they had pulled up their masks. He reached for his cup hastily.

"Hundred percent disability in my grade is thirty thousand a year. I could get along on that easy. For almost an hour and a half."

"There's no intention of terminating the project," Sinescu said.

"Phasing it out, though. Would you say phasing it out."

"Manners, Jim," said Babcock.

"Okay. My worst fault. What do you want to know."

Sinescu sipped his coffee. His hands were still trembling. "That mask you're wearing," he started.

"Not for discussion. No comment, no comment. Sorry about that, don't mean to be rude; a personal matter. Ask me something—" Without warning, he stood up, blaring, "Get that damn thing out of here!" Sam's wife's cup smashed, coffee brown across the table. A fawn-colored puppy was sitting in the middle of the carpet, cocking its head, bright-eyed, tongue out.

The table tipped, Sam's wife struggled up behind it. Her face was pink, dripping with tears. She scooped up the puppy without pausing and ran out. "I better go with her," Sam said, getting up.

"Go on; and, Sam, take a holiday. Drive her into Winnemucca, see a movie."

"Yeah, guess I will." He disappeared behind the bookshelf wall.

The tall figure sat down again, moving like a man; it leaned back in the same posture, arms on the arms of the chair. It was still. The hands gripping the wood were shapely and perfect but unreal: there was something wrong about the fingernails. The brown, well-combed hair above the mask was a wig; the ears were wax. Sinescu nervously fumbled his surgical mask up over his mouth and nose. "Might as well get along," he said, and stood up.

"That's right, I want to take you over to Engineering and R and D," said Babcock. "Jim, I'll be back in a little while. Want to talk to you."

"Sure," said the motionless figure.

Babcock had had a shower, but sweat was soaking through the armpits of his shirt again. The silent elevator, the green carpet, a little blurred. The air cool, stale. Seven years, blood and money, five hundred good men. Psych section, Cosmetic, Engineering, R and D, Medical, Immunology, Supply, Serology, Administration. The glass doors. Sam's apartment empty, gone to Winnemucca with Irma. Psych. Good men, but were they the best? Three of the best had turned it down. Buried in the files. *Not like an ordinary amputation, this man has had everything cut off.*

The tall figure had not moved. Babcock sat down. The silver mask looked back at him.

"Jim, let's level with each other."

"Bad, huh."

"Sure it's bad. I left him in his room with a bottle. I'll see him again before he leaves, but God knows what he'll say in Washington. Listen, do me a favor, take that thing off."

"Sure." The hand rose, plucked at the edge of the silver mask, lifted it away. Under it, the tan-pink face, sculptured nose and lips, eyebrows, eyelashes, not handsome but good-looking, normal-looking. Only the eyes wrong; pupils too big. And the lips that did not open or move when it spoke. "I can take anything off. What does that prove."

"Jim. Cosmetic spent eight and a half months on that model and the first thing you do is slap a mask over it. We've asked you what's wrong, offered to make any changes you want."

"No comment."

"You talked about phasing out the project. Did you think you were kidding?"

A pause. "Not kidding."

"All right, then open up, Jim, tell me; I have to know. They won't shut the project down; they'll keep you alive but that's all. There are seven hundred on the volunteer list, including two U.S. senators. Suppose one of them gets pulled out of an auto wreck tomorrow. We can't wait till then to decide; we've got to know now. Whether to let the next one die or put him into a TP body like yours. So talk to me."

"Suppose I tell you something but it isn't the truth."

"Why would you lie?"

"Why do you lie to a cancer patient."

"I don't get it. Come on, Jim."

"Okay, try this. Do I look like a man to you."

"Sure."

"Bull. Look at this face." Calm and perfect. Beyond the fake irises, a wink of metal. "Suppose we had all the other problems solved and I could go into Winnemucca tomorrow; can you see me walking down the street, going into a bar, taking a taxi."

"Is that all it is?" Babcock drew a deep breath. "Jim, sure there's a difference, but for Christ's sake, it's like any other prosthesis—people get used to it. Like that arm of Sam's. You see it, but after a while you forget it, you don't notice."

"Bull. You pretend not to notice. Because it would embarrass the cripple."

Babcock looked down at his clasped hands. "Sorry for yourself?"

"Don't give me that," the voice blared. The tall figure was standing. The hands slowly came up, the fists clenched. "I'm in this thing, I've been in it for two years. I'm in it when I go to sleep, and when I wake up, I'm still in it."

Babcock looked up at him. "What do you want, facial mobility? Give us twenty years, maybe ten, we'll lick it."

"No. No."

"Then what?"

"I want you to close down Cosmetic."

"But that's—"

"Just listen. The first model looked like a tailor's dummy, so you spent eight months and came up with this one, and it looks like a corpse. The whole idea was to make me look like a man, the first model pretty good, the second model better, until you've got something that can smoke cigars and joke with women and go bowling and nobody will know the difference. You can't do it, and if you could, what for?"

"I don't— Let me think about this. What do you mean, a metal—"

"Metal, sure, but what difference does that make. I'm talking about shape. Function. Wait a minute." The tall figure strode across the room, unlocked a cabinet, came back with rolled sheets of paper. "Look at this."

The drawing showed an oblong metal box on four jointed legs. From one end protruded a tiny mushroom-shaped head on a jointed stem and a cluster of arms ending in probes, drills, grapples. "For moon prospecting."

"Too many limbs," said Babcock after a moment. "How would you—"

"With the facial nerves. Plenty of them left over. Or here." Another drawing. "A module plugged into the control system of a spaceship. That's where I belong, in space. Sterile environment, low grav, I can go where a man can't go and do what a man can't do. I can be an asset, not a goddamn billion-dollar liability."

Babcock rubbed his eyes. "Why didn't you say anything before?"

"You were all hipped on prosthetics. You would have told me to tend my knitting."

Babcock's hands were shaking as he rolled up the drawings. "Well, by God, this just may do it. It just might." He stood up and turned toward the door. "Keep your—" He cleared his throat. "I mean, hang tight, Jim."

"I'll do that."

When he was alone, he put on his mask again and stood motionless a moment, eye shutters closed. Inside, he was running clean and cool; he could feel the faint reassuring hum of pumps, click of valves and relays. They had given him that: cleaned out all the offal, replaced it with machinery that did not bleed, ooze or suppurate. He thought of the lie he had told Babcock. *Why do you lie to a cancer patient?* But they would never get it, never understand.

He sat down at the drafting table, clipped a sheet of paper to it and with a pencil began to sketch a rendering of the moon-prospector design. When he had blocked in the prospector itself, he began to draw the background of craters. His pencil moved more slowly and stopped; he put it down with a click.

No more adrenal glands to pump adrenaline into his blood, so he could not feel fright or rage. They had released him from all that—love, hate, the whole sloppy mess—but they had forgotten there was still one emotion he could feel.

Sinescu, with the black bristles of his beard sprouting through his oily skin. A whitehead ripe in the crease beside his nostril.

Moon landscape, clean and cold. He picked up the pencil again.

Babcock, with his broad pink nose shining with grease, crusts of white matter in the corners of his eyes. Food mortar between his teeth.

Sam's wife, with raspberry-colored paste on her mouth. Face smeared with tears, a bright bubble in one nostril. And the damn dog, shiny nose, wet eyes . . .

He turned. The dog was there, sitting on the carpet, wet red tongue out—*left the door open again*—dripping, wagged its tail twice, then started to get up. He reached for the metal T square, leaned back, swinging it like an ax, and the dog yelped once as metal sheared bone, one eye spouting red, writhing on its back, dark stain of piss across the carpet, and he hit it again, hit it again.

The body lay twisted on the carpet, fouled with blood, ragged black lips drawn back from teeth. He wiped off the T square with a paper towel, then scrubbed it in the sink with soap and steel wool, dried it and hung it up. He got a sheet of drafting paper, laid it on the floor, rolled the body over onto it without spilling any blood on the carpet. He lifted the body in the paper, carried it out onto the patio, then onto the unroofed section, opening the doors with his shoulder. He looked over the wall. Two stories down, concrete roof, vents sticking out of it, nobody watching. He held the dog out, let it slide off the paper, twisting as it fell. It struck one of the vents, bounced, a red smear. He carried the paper back inside, poured the blood down the drain, then put the paper into the incinerator chute.

Splashes of blood were on the carpet, the feet of the drafting table, the cabinet, his trouser legs. He sponged them all up with paper towels and warm water. He took off his clothing, examined it minutely, scrubbed it in the sink, then put it in the washer. He washed the sink, rubbed himself down with disinfectant and dressed again. He walked through into Sam's silent apartment, closing the glass door behind him. Past the potted philodendron, overstuffed furniture, red-and-yellow painting on the wall, out onto the roof, leaving the door ajar. Then back through the patio, closing doors.

Too bad. How about some goldfish.

He sat down at the drafting table. He was running clean and cool. The dream this morning came back to his mind, the last one, as he was struggling up out of sleep: *slithery kidneys burst gray lungs blood and hair ropes of guts covered with yellow fat oozing and sliding and oh god the stink like the breath of an outhouse no sound nowhere he was putting a yellow stream down the slide of the dunghole and*

He began to ink in the drawing, first with a fine steel pen, then with a nylon brush. *his heel slid and he was falling could not stop himself falling into slimy bulging softness higher than his chin, higher and he could not move paralyzed and he tried to scream tried to scream tried to scream*

The prospector was climbing a crater slope with its handling members retracted and its head tilted up. Behind it the distant ringwall and the horizon, the black sky, the pinpoint stars. And he was there, and it was not far enough, not yet, for the earth hung overhead like a rotten fruit, blue with mold, crawling, wrinkling, purulent and alive.

AFTERWORD

Theme, if such a thing exists, is the spirit of a story, its ghost, which can be separated from the story only at the cost of the patient's life. What I think is much more interesting and useful is the idea of a story as *mechanism*. What

is the story supposed to accomplish? What means are used?
Do they work? Etc.

"Masks" was the result of a deliberate effort to make a
story about what I call here a TP or "total prosthesis"—a
complete artificial body. I wanted to do this because it was
topical, in the sense that there had been a lot of discussion
of this kind of thing and a good deal of R and D on
sophisticated artificial limbs. The subject was one which had
a deep attraction for me; I had written about it in two early
stories called "Ask Me Anything" and "Four in One," and
again in a collaboration with James Blish, "Tiger Ride."
And, finally, I wanted to do it because it seemed to me that
most treatments of the subject in science fiction had been
romantic failures, and that to do it realistically would be an
achievement.

I read and thought about prosthetic problems until I was
sure I knew how my protagonist's artificial body would be
built and maintained. I realized that it would take a govern-
ment-funded effort comparable to the Manhattan Project, so
I couldn't put it in the corner of a lab somewhere: the
background of the story grew out of this. The other charac-
ters were those who had to be there.

Glimpses of scenes and action came to me spontane-
ously: the first of these was the one which gave the story its
title—the silvery mask worn by the protagonist. As I got
deeper into the story, I became more and more convinced
that the psychic effect of losing the whole body and having
it replaced by a prosthetic system had been too casually
shrugged off by previous writers, even C. L. Moore in her
beautiful "No Woman Born."

The protagonist of my story is the ultimate eunuch: as
another character remarks, "This man has had everything
cut off." Such a catastrophic loss can be compensated for
only by a massive mental tilt. The man in the story has lost
the physiological basis of every human emotion, with one
exception. He has no heart to accelerate its beat, no gonads,

no sweat glands, no endocrines except the pineal: he can't feel love, fear, hate, affection. But he can and must accept his own clean smooth functioning as the norm. When he looks at the sweaty, oozing meat that other people are made of, his one possible emotion is disgust, brought to an intensity we cannot imagine.

Given this, and the fact that the man is intelligent, I saw that the conflict of the story must turn on his effort to conceal the truth about himself, because if it became known the project would be terminated and his life shortened. My problem in writing the story was to hold this back as a revelation, and at the same time to build the story logically, without leaving out anything essential.

The story is a mechanism designed to draw the reader in, provoke his curiosity and interest, involve him in the argument, and give him a series of emotional experiences culminating (I hope) in a double view of the protagonist, from inside and outside, which will squeeze out of him a drop of sympathy and horror.

—*Damon Knight*

Fortitude

Kurt Vonnegut, Jr.

This story describes by implication political tyranny in personal terms. The cyborg in question has no self-regulating qualities. All freedom has been forfeited; responses to the environment are highly controlled, and doctors are the ruling gods of life. The heroine's wants are completely supplied; every possible measure for her physical and mental health is being taken. She need suspend only her freedom of choice, a small loss for the remarkable gains she has made.

THE TIME: *The present.* THE PLACE: *Upstate New York, a large room filled with pulsing, writhing, panting machines that perform the functions of various organs of the human body—heart, lungs, liver, and so on. Color-coded pipes and wires swoop upward from the machines to converge and pass through a hole in the ceiling. To one side is a fantastically complicated master control console.*

DR. ELBERT LITTLE, *a kindly, attractive young general practitioner, is being shown around by the creator and boss of the operation,* DR. NORBERT FRANKENSTEIN. FRANKEN- STEIN *is sixty-five, a crass medical genius. Seated at the console, wearing headphones and watching meters and flashing lights, is* DR. TOM SWIFT, FRANKENSTEIN's *enthusiastic first assistant.*

LITTLE: Oh, my God—oh, my God—

FRANKENSTEIN: Yeah. Those are her kidneys over there. That's her liver, of course. There you got her pancreas.

LITTLE: Amazing. Dr. Frankenstein, after seeing this, I wonder if I've even been *practicing* medicine, if I've ever even *been* to medical school. (*Pointing*) That's her *heart?*

FRANKENSTEIN: That's a Westinghouse heart. They make a damn good heart, if you ever need one. They make a kidney I wouldn't touch with a ten-foot pole.

LITTLE: That heart is probably worth more than the whole township where I practice.

FRANKENSTEIN: That pancreas is worth your whole state. Vermont?

LITTLE: Vermont.

FRANKENSTEIN: What we paid for the pancreas—yeah,

we could have bought Vermont for that. Nobody'd ever made a pancreas before, and we had to have one in ten days or lose the patient. So we told all the big organ manufacturers, "Okay, you guys got to have a crash program for a pancreas. Put every man you got on the job. We don't care what it costs, as long as we get a pancreas by next Tuesday."

LITTLE: And they succeeded.

FRANKENSTEIN: The patient's still alive, isn't she? Believe me, those are some expensive sweetbreads.

LITTLE: But the patient could afford them.

FRANKENSTEIN: You don't live like this on Blue Cross.

LITTLE: And how many operations has she had? In how many years?

FRANKENSTEIN: I gave her her first major operation thirty-six years ago. She's had seventy-eight operations since then.

LITTLE: And how old is she?

FRANKENSTEIN: One hundred.

LITTLE: What *guts* that woman must have!

FRANKENSTEIN: You're looking at 'em.

LITTLE: I mean—what *courage!* What *fortitude!*

FRANKENSTEIN: We knock her out, you know. We don't operate without anesthetics.

LITTLE: Even so . . .

FRANKENSTEIN *taps* SWIFT *on the shoulder.* SWIFT *frees an ear from the headphones, divides his attention between the visitors and the console.*

FRANKENSTEIN: Dr. Tom Swift, this is Dr. Elbert Little. Tom here is my first assistant.

SWIFT: Howdy-doody.

FRANKENSTEIN: Dr. Little has a practice up in Vermont. He happened to be in the neighborhood. He asked for a tour.

LITTLE: What do you hear in the headphones?

SWIFT: Anything that's going on in the patient's room. (*He offers the headphones*) Be my guest.

LITTLE (*listening to headphones*): Nothing.

SWIFT: She's having her hair brushed now. The beautician's up there. She's always quiet when her hair's being brushed. (*He takes the headphones back*)

FRANKENSTEIN (*to* SWIFT): We should *congratulate* our young visitor here.

SWIFT: What for?

LITTLE: Good question. What for?

FRANKENSTEIN: Oh, I know about the great honor that has come your way.

LITTLE: I'm not sure *I* do.

FRANKENSTEIN: You are *the* Dr. Little, aren't you, who was named the Family Doctor of the Year by the *Ladies' Home Journal* last month?

LITTLE: Yes, that's right. I don't know how in the hell they decided. And I'm even more flabbergasted that a man of *your* caliber would know about it.

FRANKENSTEIN: I read the *Ladies' Home Journal* from cover to cover every month.

LITTLE: You *do?*

FRANKENSTEIN: I only got one patient, Mrs. Lovejoy. And Mrs. Lovejoy reads the *Ladies' Home Journal*, so *I* read it, too. That's what we talk about—what's in the *Ladies' Home Journal*. We read all about you last month. Mrs. Lovejoy kept saying, "Oh, what a nice young man he must be. So *understanding.*"

LITTLE: Um.

FRANKENSTEIN: Now here you are in the flesh. I bet she wrote you a letter.

LITTLE: Yes, she did.

FRANKENSTEIN: She writes thousands of letters a year, gets thousands of letters back. Some pen pal she is.

LITTLE: Is she—uh—generally *cheerful* most of the time?

FRANKENSTEIN: If she isn't, that's our fault down here. If she gets unhappy, that means something down *here* isn't working right. She was blue about a month ago. Turned out it was a bum transistor in the console. (*He reaches over* SWIFT's *shoulder, changes a setting on the console. The machinery subtly adjusts to the new setting.*) There—she'll be all depressed for a couple of minutes now. (*He changes the setting again*) There. Now, pretty quick, she'll be happier than she was before. She'll sing like a bird.

LITTLE *conceals his horror imperfectly.* CUT TO *patient's room, which is full of flowers and candy boxes and books. The patient is* SYLVIA LOVEJOY, *a billionaire's widow.* SYLVIA *is no longer anything but a head connected to pipes and wires coming up through the floor, but this is not immediately apparent. The first shot of her is a* CLOSE-UP, *with* GLORIA, *a gorgeous beautician, standing behind her.* SYLVIA *is a heartbreakingly good-looking old lady, once a famous beauty. She is crying now.*

SYLVIA: Gloria—

GLORIA: Ma'am?

SYLVIA: Wipe these tears away before somebody comes in and sees them.

GLORIA (*wanting to cry herself*): Yes, ma'am. (*She wipes the tears away with Kleenex, studies the results*) There. There.

SYLVIA: I don't know what came over me. Suddenly I was so sad I couldn't stand it.

GLORIA: Everybody has to cry *sometimes*.

SYLVIA: It's passing now. Can you tell I've been crying?

GLORIA: No. No. (*She is unable to control her own tears any more. She goes to a window so* SYLVIA *can't see her cry.* CAMERA BACKS AWAY *to reveal the tidy, clinical abomination of the head and wires and pipes. The head is on a tripod. There is a black box with winking colored lights hanging under the head, where the chest would normally be. Mechanical arms come out of the box where arms would normally be. There is a table within easy reach of the arms. On it are a pen and paper, a partially solved jigsaw puzzle and a bulky knitting bag. Sticking out of the bag are needles and a sweater in progress. Hanging over* SYLVIA'S *head is a microphone on a boom.*)

SYLVIA (*sighing*): Oh, what a *foolish* old woman you

must think I am. (GLORIA *shakes her head in denial, is unable to reply*) Gloria? Are you still there?

GLORIA: Yes.

SYLVIA: Is anything the matter?

GLORIA: No.

SYLVIA: You're *such* a good friend, Gloria. I want you to know I feel that with all my heart.

GLORIA: I like you, too.

SYLVIA: If you ever have any problems I can help you with, I hope you'll ask me.

GLORIA: I will, I *will*.

HOWARD DERBY, *the hospital mail clerk, dances in with an armload of letters. He is a merry old fool.*

DERBY: Mailman! Mailman!

SYLVIA (*brightening*): Mailman! God *bless* the mailman!

DERBY: How's the patient today?

SYLVIA: Very sad a moment ago. But now that I see you, I want to sing like a bird.

DERBY: Fifty-three letters today. There's even one from Leningrad.

SYLVIA: There's a blind woman in Leningrad. Poor soul, *poor* soul.

DERBY (*making a fan of the mail, reading postmarks*): West Virginia, Honolulu, Brisbane, Australia—

SYLVIA *selects an envelope at random.*

SYLVIA: Wheeling, West Virginia. Now, who do I know in Wheeling? (*She opens the envelope expertly with her mechanical hands, reads*) "Dear Mrs. Lovejoy: You don't know me, but I just read about you in the *Reader's Digest*, and I'm sitting here with tears streaming down my cheeks." *Reader's Digest*? My goodness—that article was printed fourteen years ago! And she just *read* it?

DERBY: Old *Reader's Digests* go on and on. I've got one at home I'll bet is ten years old. I still read it every time I need a little inspiration.

SYLVIA (*reading on*): "I am never going to complain

about anything that ever happens to me ever again. I thought I was as unfortunate as a person can get when my husband shot his girlfriend six months ago and then blew his own brains out. He left me with seven children and with eight payments still to go on a Buick Roadmaster with three flat tires and a busted transmission. After reading about you, though, I sit here and count my blessings." Isn't that a nice letter?

DERBY: Sure is.

SYLVIA: There's a P.S.: "Get well real soon, you *hear?*" (*She puts the letter on the table*) There isn't a letter from Vermont, is there?

DERBY: Vermont?

SYLVIA: Last month, when I had that low spell, I wrote what I'm afraid was a very stupid, self-centered, self-pitying letter to a young doctor I read about in the *Ladies' Home Journal.* I'm so ashamed. I live in fear and trembling of what he's going to say back to me—if he answers at all.

GLORIA: What could he say? What could he *possibly* say?

SYLVIA: He could tell me about the *real* suffering going on out there in the world, about people who don't know where the next meal is coming from, about people so poor they've never *been* to a doctor in their whole *lives.* And to think of all the help I've had—all the tender, loving care, all the latest wonders science has to offer.

CUT TO *corridor outside* SYLVIA's *room. There is a sign on the door saying,* ALWAYS ENTER SMILING! FRANKENSTEIN *and* LITTLE *are about to enter.*

LITTLE: She's in *there?*

FRANKENSTEIN: Every part of her that isn't downstairs.

LITTLE: And everybody obeys this sign, I'm sure.

FRANKENSTEIN: Part of the therapy. We treat the *whole* patient here.

GLORIA *comes from the room, closes the door tightly, then bursts into noisy tears.*

FRANKENSTEIN (*to* GLORIA, *disgusted*): Oh, for crying out loud. And what is this?

GLORIA: Let her *die*, Dr. Frankenstein. For the love of God, let her *die!*

LITTLE: This is her *nurse*?

FRANKENSTEIN: She hasn't got brains enough to be a nurse. She is a lousy beautician. A hundred bucks a week she makes—just to take care of one woman's face and hair. (*To* GLORIA) You blew it, honeybunch. You're through.

GLORIA: What?

FRANKENSTEIN: Pick up your check and scram.

GLORIA: I'm her closest friend.

FRANKENSTEIN: Drop her a line.

GLORIA: I'm her *only* friend.

FRANKENSTEIN: Some friend! You just asked me to knock her off.

GLORIA: In the name of mercy, yes, I did.

FRANKENSTEIN: You're that sure there's a heaven, eh? You want to send her right up there so she can get her wings and harp.

GLORIA: I know there's a hell. I've seen it. It's in there, and you're its great inventor.

FRANKENSTEIN: (*stung, letting a moment pass before replying*): Christ, the things people say sometimes.

GLORIA: It's time somebody who loves her spoke up.

FRANKENSTEIN: Love.

GLORIA: You wouldn't know what it was.

FRANKENSTEIN: Love. (*More to himself than to her*) Do I have a wife? No. Do I have a mistress? No. I have loved only two women in my life—my mother and that woman in there. I wasn't able to save my mother from death. I had just graduated from medical school and my mother was dying of cancer of the everything. "Okay, wise guy," I said to myself, "you're such a hot-shot doctor from Heidelberg, now, let's see you save your mother from death." And everybody told me there wasn't anything I could do for her, and I said, "I don't give a damn. I'm gonna do something anyway." And they finally decided I was nuts and they put me in a crazyhouse for a little while. When I got out, she was dead—the way all the wise men said she had to be. What those wise men didn't know was all the wonderful things machinery could do—and neither did I, but I was gonna find out. So I went to the Massachusetts Institute of Technology and I studied mechanical engineering and electrical engineering and chemical engineering for six long years. I lived in an attic. I ate two-day-old bread and the kind of cheese they put in mousetraps. When I got out of MIT, I said to myself, "Okay, boy—it's just barely possible now that you're the only guy on earth with the proper education to practice twentieth century medicine." I went to work for the Curley Clinic in Boston. They brought in this woman who was beautiful on the outside and a mess on the inside. She was the image of my mother. She was the widow of a man who had left her five hundred million dollars. She didn't have any relatives. The wise men said again, "This lady's gotta die." And I said to them, "Shut up and listen. I'm gonna tell you what we're gonna do."

Silence.

LITTLE: That's—that's quite a story.

FRANKENSTEIN: It's a story about *love*. (*To* GLORIA) That love story started years and years before you were born, you great lover, you. And it's still going on.

GLORIA: Last month, she asked me to bring her a pistol so she could shoot herself.

FRANKENSTEIN: You think I don't know that? (*Jerking a thumb at* LITTLE) Last month, she wrote him a letter and said, "Bring me some cyanide, doctor, if you're a doctor with any heart at all."

LITTLE (*startled*): You *knew* that. You—you read her mail?

FRANKENSTEIN: So we'll know what she's *really* feeling. She might try to fool us sometime—just *pretend* to be happy. I told you about that bum transistor last month. We maybe wouldn't have known anything was wrong if we hadn't read her mail and listened to what she was saying to lame-brains like this one here. (*Feeling challenged*) Look— you go in there all by yourself. Stay as long as you want, ask her anything. Then you come back out and tell me the truth: Is that a happy woman in there, or is that a woman in hell?

LITTLE (*hesitating*): I—

FRANKENSTEIN: Go on in! I got some more things to say to this young lady—to Miss Mercy Killing of the Year. I'd like to show her a body that's been in a casket for a couple of years sometime—let her see how pretty death is, this thing she wants for her friend.

LITTLE *gropes for something to say, finally mimes his wish to be fair to everyone. He enters the patient's room.* CUT TO *room.* SYLVIA *is alone, faced away from the door.*

SYLVIA: Who's that?

LITTLE: A friend—somebody you wrote a letter to.

SYLVIA: That could be anybody. Can I see you, please? (LITTLE *obliges. She looks him over with growing affection.*) Dr. Little—family doctor from Vermont.

LITTLE (*bowing slightly*): Mrs. Lovejoy—how are you today?

SYLVIA: Did you bring me cyanide?

LITTLE: No.

SYLVIA: I wouldn't take it today. It's such a lovely day. I wouldn't want to miss it, or tomorrow, either. Did you come on a snow-white horse?

LITTLE: In a blue Oldsmobile.

SYLVIA: What about your patients, who love and need you so?

LITTLE: Another doctor is covering for me. I'm taking a week off.

SYLVIA: Not on my account.

LITTLE: No.

SYLVIA: Because I'm fine. You can see what wonderful hands I'm in.

LITTLE: Yes.

SYLVIA: One thing I don't need is another doctor.

LITTLE: Right.

Pause.

SYLVIA: I do wish I had somebody to talk to about death, though. You've seen a lot of it, I suppose.

LITTLE: Some.

SYLVIA: And it was a blessing for some of them—when they died?

LITTLE: I've heard that said.

SYLVIA: But you don't say so yourself.

LITTLE: It's not a professional thing for a doctor to say, Mrs. Lovejoy.

SYLVIA: Why have other people said that certain deaths have been a blessing?

LITTLE: Because of the pain the patient was in, because he couldn't be cured at any price—at any price within his means. Or because the patient was a vegetable, had lost his mind and couldn't get it back.

SYLVIA: At any price.

LITTLE: As far as I know, it is not now possible to beg, borrow or steal an artificial mind for someone who's lost one. If I asked Dr. Frankenstein about it, he might tell me that it's the coming thing.

Pause.

SYLVIA: It *is* the coming thing.

LITTLE: He's told you so?

SYLVIA: I asked him yesterday what would happen if my brain started to go. He was serene. He said I wasn't to worry my pretty little head about that. "We'll cross that bridge when we come to it," he told me. (*Pause*) Oh, God, the bridges I've crossed!

CUT TO *room full of organs, as before.* SWIFT *is at the console.* FRANKENSTEIN *and* LITTLE *enter.*

FRANKENSTEIN: You've made the grand tour and now here you are back at the beginning.

LITTLE: And I still have to say what I said at the beginning: "My God—oh, my God."

FRANKENSTEIN: It's gonna be a little tough going back to the aspirin-and-laxative trade after this, eh?

LITTLE: Yes. (*Pause*) What's the cheapest thing here?

FRANKENSTEIN: The simplest thing. It's the goddamn pump.

LITTLE: What does a heart go for these days?

FRANKENSTEIN: Sixty thousand dollars. There are cheaper ones and more expensive ones. The cheap ones are junk. The expensive ones are jewelry.

LITTLE: And how many are sold a year now?

FRANKENSTEIN: Six hundred, give or take a few.

LITTLE: Give one, that's life. Take one, that's death.

FRANKENSTEIN: If the trouble is the heart. It's lucky if you have trouble that cheap. (*To* SWIFT) Hey, Tom—put her to sleep so he can see how the day ends around here.

SWIFT: It's twenty minutes ahead of time.

FRANKENSTEIN: What's the difference? We put her to sleep for twenty minutes extra, she still wakes up tomorrow feeling like a million bucks, unless we got another bum transistor.

LITTLE: Why don't you have a television camera aimed at her, so you can watch her on a screen?

FRANKENSTEIN: She didn't want one.

LITTLE: She gets what she wants?

FRANKENSTEIN: She got *that*. What the hell do we have to watch her face for? We can look at the meters down here and find out more about her than she can know about herself. (*To* SWIFT) Put her to sleep, Tom.

SWIFT (*to* LITTLE): It's just like slowing down a car or banking a furnace.

LITTLE: Um.

FRANKENSTEIN: Tom, too, has degrees in both engineering and medicine.

LITTLE: Are you tired at the end of a day, Tom?

swift: It's a good kind of tiredness—as though I'd
flown a big jet from New York to Honolulu, or something
like that. (*Taking hold of a lever*) And now we'll bring Mrs.
Lovejoy in for a happy landing. (*He pulls the lever gradually
and the machinery slows down*) There.

frankenstein: Beautiful.

little: She's asleep?

frankenstein: Like a baby.

swift: All I have to do now is wait for the night man to
come on.

little: Has anybody ever taken her a suicide weapon?

frankenstein: No. We wouldn't worry about it if they
did. The arms are designed so she can't possibly point a gun
at herself or get poison to her lips, no matter how she tries.
That was Tom's stroke of genius.

little: Congratulations.

Alarm bell rings. Light flashes.

frankenstein: Who could that be? (*To* little) Somebody just went into her room. We better check! (*To*
swift) Lock the door up there, Tom—so whoever it is, we
got 'em. (swift *pushes a button that locks door upstairs. To*
little) You come with me.

cut to *patient's room.* sylvia *is asleep, snoring gently.*
gloria *has just sneaked in. She looks around furtively, takes
a revolver from her purse, makes sure it's loaded, then hides
it in* sylvia's *knitting bag. She is barely finished when*
frankenstein *and* little *enter breathlessly,* frankenstein
opening the door with a key.

frankenstein: What's this?

gloria: I left my watch up here. (*Pointing to watch*)
I've got it now.

frankenstein: Thought I told you never to come into
this building again.

gloria: I won't.

frankenstein (*to* little): You keep her right there.
I'm gonna check things over. Maybe there's been a little
huggery buggery. (*To* gloria) How would you like to be in

court for attempted murder, eh? (*Into microphone*) Tom? Can you hear me?

SWIFT (*voice from squawk box on wall*): I hear you.

FRANKENSTEIN: Wake her up again. I gotta give her a check.

SWIFT: Cock-a-doodle-doo.

Machinery can be heard speeding up below. SYLVIA *opens her eyes, sweetly dazed.*

SYLVIA (*to* FRANKENSTEIN): Good morning, Norbert.

FRANKENSTEIN: How do you feel?

SYLVIA: The way I always feel when I wake up—fine—vaguely at sea. Gloria! Good morning!

GLORIA: Good morning.

SYLVIA: Dr. Little! You're staying another day?

FRANKENSTEIN: It isn't morning. We'll put you back to sleep in a minute.

SYLVIA: I'm sick again?

FRANKENSTEIN: I don't think so.

SYLVIA: I'm going to have to have another operation?

FRANKENSTEIN: Calm down, calm down. (*He takes an ophthalmoscope from his pocket*)

SYLVIA: How can I be calm when I think about another operation?

FRANKENSTEIN (*into microphone*): Tom—give her some tranquilizers.

SWIFT (*squawk box*): Coming up.

SYLVIA: What else do I have to lose? My ears? My hair?

FRANKENSTEIN: You'll be calm in a minute.

SYLVIA: My eyes ? My eyes, Norbert—are they going next?

FRANKENSTEIN (*to* GLORIA): Oh, boy, baby doll—will you look what you've done? (*Into microphone*) Where the hell are those tranquilizers?

SWIFT: Should be taking effect just about now.

SYLVIA: Oh, well. It doesn't matter. (*As* FRANKENSTEIN *examines her eyes*) It *is* my eyes, isn't it?

FRANKENSTEIN: It isn't your anything.

SYLVIA: Easy come, easy go.

FRANKENSTEIN: You're healthy as a horse.

SYLVIA: I'm sure somebody manufactures excellent eyes.

FRANKENSTEIN: RCA makes a damn good eye, but we aren't gonna buy one for a while yet. (*He backs away, satisfied*) Everything's all right up here. (*To* GLORIA) Lucky for you.

SYLVIA: I love it when friends of mine are lucky.

SWIFT: Put her to sleep again?

FRANKENSTEIN: Not yet. I want to check a couple of things down there.

SWIFT: Roger and out.

CUT TO LITTLE, GLORIA *and* FRANKENSTEIN *entering the machinery room minutes later.* SWIFT *is at the console.*

SWIFT: Night man's late.

FRANKENSTEIN: He's got troubles at home. You want a good piece of advice, boy? Don't ever get married. (*He scrutinizes meter after meter*)

GLORIA (*appalled by her surroundings*): My God—oh, my God—

LITTLE: You've never seen this before?

GLORIA: No.

FRANKENSTEIN: She was the great hair specialist. We took off everything else—everything but the hair. (*The reading on a meter puzzles him*) What's this? (*He socks the meter, which then gives him the proper reading*) That's more like it.

GLORIA (*emptily*): Science.

FRANKENSTEIN: What did you think it was like down here?

GLORIA: I was afraid to think. Now I can see why.

FRANKENSTEIN: You got any scientific background at all—any way of appreciating even slightly what you're seeing here?

GLORIA: I flunked earth science twice in high school.

FRANKENSTEIN: What do they teach in beauty college?

GLORIA: Dumb things for dumb people. How to paint a face. How to curl or uncurl hair. How to cut hair. How to dye hair. Fingernails. Toenails in the summertime.

FRANKENSTEIN: I suppose you're gonna crack off about this place after you get out of here—gonna tell people all the crazy stuff that goes on.

GLORIA: Maybe.

FRANKENSTEIN: Just remember this: You haven't got the brains or the education to talk about any aspect of our operation. Right?

GLORIA: Maybe.

FRANKENSTEIN: What *will* you say to the outside world?

GLORIA: Nothing very complicated—just that . . .

FRANKENSTEIN: Yes?

GLORIA: That you have the head of a dead woman connected to a lot of machinery, and you play with it all day long, and you aren't married or anything, and that's all you do.

FREEZE SCENE *as a still photograph.* FADE TO *black.* FADE IN *same still. Figures begin to move.*

FRANKENSTEIN (*aghast*): How can you call her dead? She reads the *Ladies' Home Journal!* She talks! She knits! She writes letters to pen pals all over the world!

GLORIA: She's like some horrible fortunetelling machine in a penny arcade.

FRANKENSTEIN: I thought you loved her.

GLORIA: Every so often, I see a tiny little spark of what she used to be. I love that spark. Most people say they love her for her courage. What's that courage worth, when it comes from down here? You could turn a few faucets and switches down here and she'd be volunteering to fly a rocket ship to the moon. But no matter what you do down here, that little spark goes on thinking, "For the love of God—somebody get me out of here!"

FRANKENSTEIN (*glancing at the console*): Dr. Swift—is that microphone open?

SWIFT: Yeah. (*Snapping his fingers*) I'm sorry.

FRANKENSTEIN: Leave it open. (*To* GLORIA) She's heard every word you've said. How does that make you feel?

GLORIA: She can hear me now?

FRANKENSTEIN: Run off at the mouth some more. You're saving me a lot of trouble. Now I won't have to explain to her what sort of friend you really were and why I gave you the old heave-ho.

GLORIA (*drawing nearer to the microphone*): Mrs. Lovejoy?

SWIFT (*reporting what he has heard on the headphones*): She says, "What is it, dear?"

GLORIA: There's a loaded revolver in your knitting bag, Mrs. Lovejoy—in case you don't want to live any more.

FRANKENSTEIN (*not in the least worried about the pistol but filled with contempt and disgust for* GLORIA): You total imbecile. Where did you get a pistol?

GLORIA: From a mail-order house in Chicago. They had an ad in *Real True Romances*.

FRANKENSTEIN: They sell guns to crazy broads.

GLORIA: I could have had a bazooka if I'd wanted one. Fourteen-ninety-eight.

FRANKENSTEIN: I am going to get that pistol now and it is going to be exhibit A at your trial. (*He leaves*).

LITTLE (*to* SWIFT): Shouldn't you put the patient to sleep?

SWIFT: There's no way she can hurt herself.

GLORIA (*to* LITTLE): What does he mean?

LITTLE: Her arms are fixed so she can't point a gun at herself.

GLORIA (*sickened*): They even thought of that.

CUT TO SYLVIA'S *room.* FRANKENSTEIN *is entering.* SYLVIA *is holding the pistol thoughtfully.*

FRANKENSTEIN: Nice playthings you have.

SYLVIA: You mustn't get mad at Gloria, Norbert. I asked her for this. I begged her for this.

FRANKENSTEIN: Last month.

SYLVIA: Yes.

FRANKENSTEIN: But everything is better now.

SYLVIA: Everything but the spark.

FRANKENSTEIN: Spark?

SYLVIA: The spark that Gloria says she loves—the tiny spark of what I used to be. As happy as I am right now, that spark is begging me to take this gun and put it out.

FRANKENSTEIN: And what is your reply?

SYLVIA: I am going to do it, Norbert. This is goodbye. (*She tries every which way to aim the gun at herself, fails and fails, while* FRANKENSTEIN *stands calmly by*) That's no accident, is it?

FRANKENSTEIN: We very much don't want you to hurt yourself. We love you, too.

SYLVIA: And how much longer must I live like this? I've never dared ask before.

FRANKENSTEIN: I would have to pull a figure out of a hat.

SYLVIA: Maybe you'd better not. (*Pause*) Did you pull one out of a hat?

FRANKENSTEIN: At least five hundred years.

Silence.

SYLVIA: So I will still be alive—long after you are gone?

FRANKENSTEIN: Now is the time, my dear Sylvia, to tell you something I have wanted to tell you for years. Every organ downstairs has the capacity to take care of two human beings instead of one. And the plumbing and wiring have been designed so that a second human being can be hooked up in two shakes of a lamb's tail. (*Silence*) Do you understand what I am saying to you, Sylvia? (*Silence. Passionately*) Sylvia! I will be that second human being! Talk about marriage! Talk about great love stories from the past! Your kidney will be my kidney! Your liver will be my liver! Your heart will be my heart! Your ups will be my ups and your downs will be my downs! We will live in such perfect harmony, Sylvia, that the gods themselves will tear out their hair in envy!

SYLVIA: This is what you want?

FRANKENSTEIN: More than anything in this world.

SYLVIA: Well, then—here it is, Norbert. (*She empties the revolver into him*)

CUT TO *same room almost a half hour later. A second tripod has been set up, with* FRANKENSTEIN'S *head on top.* FRANKENSTEIN *is asleep and so is* SYLVIA. SWIFT, *with* LITTLE *standing by, is feverishly making a final connection to the machinery below. There are pipe wrenches and a blowtorch and other plumber's and electrician's tools lying around.*

SWIFT: That's gotta be it. (*He straightens up, looks around*) That's gotta be it.

LITTLE (*consulting watch*): Twenty-eight minutes since the first shot was fired.

SWIFT: Thank God you were around.

LITTLE: What you really needed was a plumber.

SWIFT (*into microphone*): Charley, we're all set up here. You all set down there?

CHARLEY (*squawk box*): All set.

SWIFT: Give 'em plenty of martinis.

GLORIA *appears numbly in doorway.*

CHARLEY: They've got 'em. They'll be higher than kites.

SWIFT: Better give 'em a touch of LSD, too.

CHARLEY: Coming up.

SWIFT: Hold it! I forgot the phonograph. (*To* LITTLE) Dr. Frankenstein said that if this ever happened, he wanted a certain record playing when he came to. He said it was in with the other records—in a plain white jacket. (*To* GLORIA) See if you can find it.

GLORIA *goes to phonograph, finds the record.*

GLORIA: This it?

SWIFT: Put it on.

GLORIA: Which side?

SWIFT: I don't know.

GLORIA: There's tape over one side.

SWIFT: The side *without* tape. (GLORIA *puts record on. Into microphone*) Stand by to wake up the patients.

CHARLEY: Standing by.

*Record begins to play. It is a Jeanette MacDonald–
Nelson Eddy duet, "Ah, Sweet Mystery of Life."*

SWIFT: (*into microphone*): Wake 'em up!

FRANKENSTEIN *and* SYLVIA *wake up, filled with formless
pleasure. They dreamily appreciate the music, eventually
catch sight of each other, perceive each other as old and
beloved friends.*

SYLVIA: Hi, there.

FRANKENSTEIN: Hello.

SYLVIA: How do you feel?

FRANKENSTEIN: Fine. Just fine.

No Woman Born

C. L. Moore

This story was decades ahead of its time when it was first published in 1944. It shows us an extraordinary person, a woman who is also a dancer, and how neither physical or technical obstacles nor the discouragement of her male friends can stop her from pursuing her extraordinary destiny as a dancer. Unlike the cyborg in Blish's story and in Knight's, Deirdre is a great success in her new guise.

She had been the loveliest creature whose image ever moved along the airways. John Harris, who was once her manager, remembered doggedly how beautiful she had been as he rose in the silent elevator toward the room where Deirdre sat waiting for him.

Since the theater fire that had destroyed her a year ago, he had never been quite able to let himself remember her beauty clearly, except when some old poster, half in tatters, flaunted her face at him, or a maudlin memorial program flashed her image unexpectedly across the television screen. But now he had to remember.

The elevator came to a sighing stop and the door slid open. John Harris hesitated. He knew in his mind that he had to go on, but his reluctant muscles almost refused him. He was thinking helplessly, as he had not allowed himself to think until this moment, of the fabulous grace that had poured through her wonderful dancer's body, remembering her soft and husky voice with the little burr in it that had fascinated the audiences of the whole world.

There had never been anyone so beautiful.

In times before her, other actresses had been lovely and adulated, but never before Deirdre's day had the entire world been able to take one woman so wholly to its heart. So few outside the capitals had ever seen Bernhardt or the fabulous Jersey Lily. And the beauties of the movie screen had had to limit their audiences to those who could reach the theaters. But Deirdre's image had once moved glowingly across the television screens of every home in the civilized world. And in many outside the bounds of civilization. Her

soft, husky songs had sounded in the depths of jungles, her
lovely, languorous body had woven its patterns of rhythm in
desert tents and polar huts. The whole world knew every
smooth motion of her body and every cadence of her voice,
and the way a subtle radiance had seemed to go on behind
her features when she smiled.

And the whole world had mourned her when she died in
the theater fire.

Harris could not quite think of her as other than dead,
though he knew what sat waiting him in the room ahead.
He kept remembering the old words James Stephens wrote
long ago for another Deirdre, also lovely and beloved and
unforgotten after two thousand years.

> *The time comes when our hearts sink utterly,*
> *When we remember Deirdre and her tale,*
> *And that her lips are dust . . .*
> *There has been again no woman born*
> *Who was so beautiful; not one so beautiful*
> *Of all the women born—*

That wasn't quite true, of course—there had been one.
Or maybe, after all, this Deirdre who died only a year ago
had not been beautiful in the sense of perfection. He
thought the other one might not have been either, for there
are always women with perfection of feature in the world,
and they are not the ones that legend remembers. It was the
light within, shining through her charming, imperfect features, that had made this Deirdre's face so lovely. No one
else he had ever seen had anything like the magic of the lost
Deirdre.

> *Let all men go apart and mourn together—*
> *No man can ever love her. Not a man*
> *Can dream to be her lover. . . . No man say—*
> *What could one say to her? There are no words*
> *That one could say to her.*

No, no words at all. And it was going to be impossible to go through with this. Harris knew it overwhelmingly just as his finger touched the buzzer. But the door opened almost instantly, and then it was too late.

Maltzer stood just inside, peering out through his heavy spectacles. You could see how tensely he had been waiting. Harris was a little shocked to see that the man was trembling. It was hard to think of the confident and imperturbable Maltzer, whom he had known briefly a year ago, as shaken like this. He wondered if Diedre herself were as tremulous with sheer nerves—but it was not time yet to let himself think of that.

"Come in, come in," Maltzer said irritably. There was no reason for irritation. The year's work, so much of it in secrecy and solitude, must have tried him physically and mentally to the very breaking point.

"She all right?" Harris asked inanely, stepping inside.

"Oh yes . . . yes, *she's* all right." Maltzer bit his thumbnail and glanced over his shoulder at an inner door, where Harris guessed she would be waiting.

"No," Maltzer said, as he took an involuntary step toward it. "We'd better have a talk first. Come over and sit down. Drink?"

Harris nodded, and watched Maltzer's hands tremble as he tilted the decanter. The man was clearly on the very verge of collapse, and Harris felt a sudden cold uncertainty open up in him in the one place where until now he had been oddly confident.

"She *is* all right?" he demanded, taking the glass.

"Oh yes, she's perfect. She's so confident it scares me." Maltzer gulped his drink and poured another before he sat down.

"What's wrong, then?"

"Nothing, I guess. Or . . . well, I don't know. I'm not sure any more. I've worked toward this meeting for nearly a year, but now—well, I'm not sure it's time yet. I'm just not sure."

He stared at Harris, his eyes large and indistinguishable behind the lenses. He was a thin, wire-taut man with all the bone and sinew showing plainly beneath the dark skin of his face. Thinner, now, than he had been a year ago when Harris saw him last.

"I've been too close to her," he said now. "I have no perspective any more. All I can see is my own work. And I'm just not sure that's ready yet for you or anyone to see."

"She thinks so?"

"I never saw a woman so confident." Maltzer drank, the glass clicking on his teeth. He looked up suddenly through the distorting lenses. "Of course a failure now would mean—well, absolute collapse," he said.

Harris nodded. He was thinking of the year of incredibly painstaking work that lay behind this meeting, the immense fund of knowledge, of infinite patience, the secret collaboration of artists, sculptors, designers, scientists, and the genius of Maltzer governing them all as an orchestra conductor governs his players.

He was thinking too, with a certain unreasoning jealousy, of the strange, cold, passionless intimacy between Maltzer and Deirdre in that year, a closer intimacy than any two humans can ever have shared before. In a sense the Deirdre whom he saw in a few minutes would *be* Maltzer, just as he thought he detected in Maltzer now and then small mannerisms of inflection and motion that had been Deirdre's own. There had been between them a sort of unimaginable marriage stranger than anything that could ever have taken place before.

"—so many complications," Maltzer was saying in his worried voice with its faintest possible echo of Deirdre's lovely, cadenced rhythm. (The sweet, soft huskiness he would never hear again.) "There was shock, of course. Terrible shock. And a great fear of fire. We had to conquer that before we could take the first steps. But we did it. When you go in you'll probably find her sitting before the fire." He caught the startled question in Harris' eyes and smiled. "No, she can't feel the warmth now, of course. But she likes to watch the flames. She's mastered any abnormal fear of them quite beautifully."

"She can—" Harris hesitated. "Her eyesight's normal now?"

"Perfect," Maltzer said. "Perfect vision was fairly simple to provide. After all, that sort of thing has already been worked out, in other connections. I might even say her vision's a little better than perfect, from our own standpoint." He shook his head irritably. "I'm not worried about the mechanics of the thing. Luckily they got to her before the brain was touched at all. Shock was the only danger to her sensory centers, and we took care of all that first of all, as soon as communication could be established. Even so, it needed great courage on her part. Great courage." He was silent for a moment, staring into his empty glass.

"Harris," he said suddenly, without looking up, "have I made a mistake? Should we have let her die?"

Harris shook his head helplessly. It was an unanswerable question. It had tormented the whole world for a year now. There had been hundreds of answers and thousands of words written on the subject. Has anyone the right to preserve a brain alive when its body is destroyed? Even if a new body can be provided, necessarily so very unlike the old?

"It's not that she's—ugly—now," Maltzer went on hurriedly, as if afraid of an answer. "Metal isn't ugly. And Deirdre . . . well, you'll see. I tell you, I can't see myself. I know the whole mechanism so well—it's just mechanics to me. Maybe she's—grotesque, I don't know. Often I've wished I hadn't been on the spot, with all my ideas, just when the fire broke out. Or that it could have been anyone but Deirdre. She was so beautiful—Still, if it had been someone else I think the whole thing might have failed completely. It takes more than just an uninjured brain. It takes strength and courage beyond common, and—well, something more. Something—unquenchable. Deirdre has it. She's still Deirdre. In a way she's still beautiful. But I'm not sure anybody but myself could see that. And you know what she plans?"

"No—what?"

"She's going back on the air-screen."

Harris looked at him in stunned disbelief.

"She *is* still beautiful," Maltzer told him fiercely. "She's got courage, and a serenity that amazes me. And she isn't in the least worried or resentful about what's happened. Or afraid what the verdict of the public will be. But I am, Harris. I'm terrified."

They looked at each other for a moment more, neither speaking. Then Maltzer shrugged and stood up.

"She's in there," he said, gesturing with his glass.

Harris turned without a word, not giving himself time to hesitate. He crossed toward the inner door.

The room was full of a soft, clear, indirect light that climaxed in the fire crackling on a white tiled hearth. Harris paused inside the door, his heart beating thickly. He did not see her for a moment. It was a perfectly commonplace room, bright, light, with pleasant furniture, and flowers on the tables. Their perfume was sweet on the clear air. He did not see Deirdre.

Then a chair by the fire creaked as she shifted her weight in it. The high back hid her, but she spoke. And for one dreadful moment it was the voice of an automaton that sounded in the room, metallic, without inflection.

"Hel-lo—" said the voice. Then she laughed and tried again. And it was the old, familiar, sweet huskiness he had not hoped to hear again as long as he lived.

In spite of himself he said, "Deirdre!" and her image rose before him as if she herself had risen unchanged from the chair, tall, golden, swaying a little with her wonderful dancer's poise, the lovely, imperfect features lighted by the glow that made them beautiful. It was the cruelest thing his memory could have done to him. And yet the voice—after that one lapse, the voice was perfect.

"Come and look at me, John," she said.

He crossed the floor slowly, forcing himself to move. That instant's flash of vivid recollection had nearly wrecked his hard-won poise. He tried to keep his mind perfectly blank as he came at last to the verge of seeing what no one but Maltzer had so far seen or known about in its entirety. No one at all had known what shape would be forged to clothe the most beautiful woman on Earth, now that her beauty was gone.

He had envisioned many shapes. Great, lurching robot forms, cylindrical, with hinged arms and legs. A glass case with the brain floating in it and appendages to serve its needs. Grotesque visions, like nightmares come nearly true. And each more inadequate than the last, for what metal shape could possibly do more than house ungraciously the mind and brain that had once enchanted a whole world?

Then he came around the wing of the chair, and saw her.

The human brain is often too complicated a mechanism to function perfectly. Harris' brain was called upon to perform a very elaborate series of shifting impressions. First, incongruously, he remembered a curious inhuman figure he had once glimpsed leaning over the fence rail outside a farmhouse. For an instant the shape had stood up integrated, ungainly, impossibly human, before the glancing eye resolved it into an arrangement of brooms and buckets. What the eye had found only roughly humanoid, the suggestible brain had accepted fully formed. It was thus now, with Deirdre.

The first impression that his eyes and mind took from sight of her was shocked and incredulous, for his brain said to him unbelievingly, *"This is Deirdre! She hasn't changed at all!"*

Then the shift of perspective took over, and even more shockingly, eye and brain said, "No, not Deirdre—not human. Nothing but metal coils. Not Deirdre at all—" And that was the worst. It was like walking from a dream of someone beloved and lost, and facing anew, after that heart-breaking reassurance of sleep, the inflexible fact that nothing can bring the lost to life again. Deirdre was gone, and this was only machinery heaped in a flowered chair.

Then the machinery moved, exquisitely, smoothly, with a grace as familiar as the swaying poise he remembered. The sweet, husky voice of Deirdre said,

"It's me, John darling. It really is, you know."

And it was.

That was the third metamorphosis, and the final one. Illusion steadied and became factual, real. It was Deirdre.

He sat down bonelessly. He had no muscles. He looked at her speechless and unthinking, letting his senses take in the sight of her without trying to rationalize what he saw.

She was golden still. They had kept that much of her, the first impression of warmth and color which had once belonged to her sleek hair and the apricot tints of her skin. But they had had the good sense to go no farther. They had not tried to make a wax image of the lost Deirdre. (*No woman born who was so beautiful—Not one so beautiful, of all the women born—*)

And so she had no face. She had only a smooth, delicately modeled ovoid for her head, with a . . . a sort of crescent-shaped mask across the frontal area where her eyes would have been if she had needed eyes. A narrow, curved quarter-moon, with the horns turned upward. It was filled in with something translucent, like cloudy crystal, and tinted the aquamarine of the eyes Deirdre used to have. Through that, then, she saw the world. Through that she looked without eyes, and behind it, as behind the eyes of a human—she was.

Except for that, she had no features. And it had been wise of those who designed her, he realized now. Subconsciously he had been dreading some clumsy attempt at human features that might creak like a marionette's in parodies of animation. The eyes, perhaps, had had to open in the same place upon her head, and at the same distance apart, to make easy for her an adjustment to the stereoscopic vision she used to have. But he was glad they had not given her two eye-shaped openings with glass marbles inside them. The mask was better.

(Oddly enough, he did not once think of the naked brain that must lie inside the metal. The mask was symbol enough for the woman within. It was enigmatic; you did not know if her gaze was on you searchingly, or wholly withdrawn. And it had no variations of brilliance such as once had played across the incomparable mobility of Deirdre's face. But eyes, even human eyes, are as a matter of fact enigmatic enough. They have no expression except what the lids impart; they take all animation from the features. We automatically watch the eyes of the friend we speak with, but if he happens to be lying down so that he speaks across his shoulder and his face is upside-down to us, quite as automatically we watch the mouth. The gaze keeps shifting nervously between mouth and eyes in their reversed order, for it is the position in the face, not the feature itself, which we are accustomed to accept as the seat of the soul. Deirdre's mask was in that proper place; it was easy to accept it as a mask over eyes.)

She had, Harris realized as the first shock quieted, a very beautifully shaped head—a bare, golden skull. She turned it a little, gracefully upon her neck of metal, and he saw that the artist who shaped it had given her the most delicate suggestion of cheekbones, narrowing in the blankness below the mask to the hint of a human face. Not too much. Just enough so that when the head turned you saw by its modeling that it had moved, lending perspective and foreshortening to the expressionless golden helmet. Light did not slip uninterrupted as if over the surface of a golden egg. Brancusi himself had never made anything more simple or more subtle than the modeling of Deirdre's head.

But all expression, of course, was gone. All expression had gone up in the smoke of the theater fire, with the lovely, mobile, radiant features which had meant Deirdre.

As for her body, he could not see its shape. A garment

hid her. But they had made no incongruous attempt to give
her back the clothing that once had made her famous. Even
the softness of cloth would have called the mind too sharply
to the remembrance that no human body lay beneath the
folds, nor does metal need the incongruity of cloth for its
protection. Yet without garments, he realized, she would
have looked oddly naked, since her new body was humanoid,
not angular machinery.

The designer had solved his paradox by giving her a robe
of very fine metal mesh. It hung from the gentle slope of her
shoulders in straight, pliant folds like a longer Grecian
chlamys, flexible, yet with weight enough of its own not to
cling too revealingly to whatever metal shape lay beneath.

The arms they had given her were left bare, and the feet
and ankles. And Maltzer had performed his greatest miracle
in the limbs of the new Deirdre. It was a mechanical miracle
basically, but the eye appreciated first that he had also
showed supreme artistry and understanding.

Her arms were pale shining gold, tapered smoothly,
without modeling, and flexible their whole length in diminishing metal bracelets fitting one inside the other clear down
to the slim, round wrists. The hands were more nearly
human than any other feature about her, though they, too,
were fitted together in delicate, small sections that slid upon
one another with the flexibility almost of flesh. The fingers'
bases were solider than human, and the fingers themselves
tapered to longer tips.

Her feet, too, beneath the tapering broader rings of the
metal ankles, had been constructed upon the model of human feet. Their finely tooled sliding segments gave her an
arch and a heel and a flexible forward section formed almost
like the *sollerets* of medieval armor.

She looked, indeed, very much like a creature in armor,
with her delicately plated limbs and her featureless head like
a helmet with a visor of glass, and her robe of chain-mail.
But no knight in armor ever moved as Deirdre moved, or

wore his armor upon a body of such inhumanly fine proportions. Only a knight from another world, or a knight of Oberon's court, might have shared that delicate likeness.

Briefly he had been surprised at the smallness and exquisite proportions of her. He had been expecting the ponderous mass of such robots as he had seen, wholly automatons. And then he realized that for them, much of the space had to be devoted to the inadequate mechanical brains that guided them about their duties. Deirdre's brain still preserved and proved the craftsmanship of an artisan far defter than man. Only the body was of metal, and it did not seem complex, though he had not yet been told how it was motivated.

Harris had no idea how long he sat staring at the figure in the cushioned chair. She was still lovely—indeed, she was still Deirdre—and as he looked he let the careful schooling of his face relax. There was no need to hide his thoughts from her.

She stirred upon the cushions, the long, flexible arms moving with a litheness that was not quite human. The motion disturbed him as the body itself had not, and in spite of himself his face froze a little. He had the feeling that from behind the crescent mask she was watching him very closely.

Slowly she rose.

The motion was very smooth. Also it was serpentine, as if the body beneath the coat of mail were made in the same interlocking sections as her limbs. He had expected and feared mechanical rigidity; nothing had prepared him for this more than human suppleness.

She stood quietly, letting the heavy mailed folds of her garment settle about her. They fell together with a faint ringing sound, like small bells far off, and hung beautifully in pale golden, sculptured folds. He had risen automatically as she did. Now he faced her, staring. He had never seen her stand perfectly still, and she was not doing it now. She swayed just a bit, vitality burning inextinguishably in her brain as once it had burned in her body, and stolid immobility was as impossible to her as it had always been. The golden garment caught points of light from the fire and glimmered at him with tiny reflections as she moved.

Then she put her featureless helmeted head a little to one side, and he heard her laughter as familiar in its small, throaty, intimate sound as he had ever heard it from her living throat. And every gesture, every attitude, every flowing of motion into motion was so utterly Deirdre that the overwhelming illusion swept his mind again and this was the flesh-and-blood woman as clearly as if he saw her standing there whole once more, like Phoenix from the fire.

"Well, John," she said in the soft, husky, amused voice he remembered perfectly. "Well, John, is it I?" She knew it was. Perfect assurance sounded in the voice. "The shock will wear off, you know. It'll be easier and easier as time goes on. I'm quite used to myself now. See?"

She turned away from him and crossed the room smoothly, with the old, poised, dancer's glide, to the mirror that paneled one side of the room. And before it, as he had so often seen her preen before, he watched her preening now, running flexible metallic hands down the folds of her metal garment, turning to admire herself over one metal shoulder, making the mailed folds tinkle and sway as she struck an arabesque position before the glass.

His knees let him down into the chair she had vacated. Mingled shock and relief loosened all his muscles in him, and she was more poised and confident than he.

"It's a miracle," he said with conviction. "It's you. But I don't see how—" He had meant, "—how, without face or body—" but clearly he could not finish that sentence.

She finished it for him in her own mind, and answered without self-consciousness. "It's motion, mostly," she said, still admiring her own suppleness in the mirror. "See?" And very lightly on her springy, armored feet she flashed through an enchaînement of brilliant steps, swinging round with a pirouette to face him. "That was what Maltzer and I worked out between us, after I began to get myself under control again." Her voice was somber for a moment, remembering a dark time in the past. Then she went on, "It wasn't easy, of course, but it was fascinating. You'll never guess how fascinating, John! We knew we couldn't work out anything like a facsimile of the way I used to look, so we had to find some other basis to build on. And motion is the other basis of recognition, after actual physical likeness."

She moved lightly across the carpet toward the window and stood looking down, her featureless face averted a little and the light shining across the delicately hinted curves of the cheekbones.

"Luckily," she said, her voice amused, "I never was beautiful. It was—well, vivacity, I suppose, and muscular coordination. Years and years of training, and all of it engraved here"—she struck her golden helmet a light, ringing blow with golden knuckles—"in the habit patterns grooved into my brain. So this body . . . did he tell you? . . . works entirely through the brain. Electromagnetic currents flowing along from ring to ring, like this." She rippled a boneless arm at him with a motion like flowing water. "Nothing holds me together—nothing!—except muscles of magnetic currents. And if I'd been somebody else—somebody who moved differently, why the flexible rings would have moved differently too, guided by the impulse from another brain. I'm not conscious of doing anything I haven't always done. The same impulses that used to go out to my muscles go out now to—this." And she made a shuddering, serpentine motion of both arms at him, like a Cambodian dancer, and then laughed wholeheartedly, the sound of it ringing through the room with such full-throated merriment that he could not help seeing again the familiar face crinkled with pleasure, the white teeth shining. "It's all perfectly subconscious now," she told him. "It took lots of practice at first, of course, but now even my signature looks just as it always did—the co-ordination is duplicated that delicately." She rippled her arms at him again and chuckled.

"But the voice, too," Harris protested inadequately. "It's *your* voice, Deirdre."

"The voice isn't only a matter of throat construction and breath control, my darling Johnnie! At least, so Professor Maltzer assured me a year ago, and I certainly haven't any reason to doubt him!" She laughed again. She was laughing a little too much, with a touch of the bright, hysteric overexcitement he remembered so well. But if any woman ever had reason for mild hysteria, surely Deirdre had it now.

The laughter rippled and ended, and she went on, her voice eager. "He says voice control is almost wholly a matter of hearing what you produce, once you've got adequate mechanism, of course. That's why deaf people, with the same vocal chords as ever, let their voices change completely and lose all inflection when they've been deaf long enough. And luckily, you see, I'm not deaf!"

She swung around to him, the folds of her robe twinkling and ringing, and rippled up and up a clear, true scale to a lovely high note, and then cascaded down again like water over a falls. But she left him no time for applause. "Perfectly simple, you see. All it took was a little matter of genius from the professor to get it worked out for me! He started with a new variation of the old Vodor you must remember hearing about, years ago. Originally, of course, the thing was ponderous. You know how it worked—speech broken down to a few basic sounds and built up again in combinations produced from a keyboard. I think originally the sounds were a sort of *ktch* and a *shooshing* noise, but we've got it all worked to a flexibility and range quite as good as human now. All I do is—well, mentally play on the keyboard of my . . . my sound-unit, I suppose it's called. It's much more complicated than that, of course, but I've learned to do it unconsciously. And I regulate it by ear, quite automatically now. If you were—*here*—instead of me, and you'd had the same practice, your own voice would be coming out of the same keyboard and diaphragm instead of mine. It's all a matter of the brain patterns that operated the body and now operate the machinery. They send out very strong impulses that are stepped up as much as necessary somewhere or other in here—" Her hands waved vaguely over the mesh-robed body.

She was silent a moment, looking out the window. Then she turned away and crossed the floor to the fire, sinking again into the flowered chair. Her helmet-skull turned its mask to face him and he could feel a quiet scrutiny behind the aquamarine of its gaze.

"It's—odd," she said, "being here in this . . . this . . . instead of a body. But not as odd or as alien as you might think. I've thought about it a lot—I've had plenty of time to think—and I've begun to realize what a tremendous force the human ego really is. I'm not sure I want to suggest it has any mystical power it can impress on mechanical things, but it does seem to have a power of some sort. It does instill its own force into inanimate objects, and they take on a personality of their own. People do impress their personalities on the houses they live in, you know. I've noticed that often. Even empty rooms. And it happens with other things too, especially, I think, with inanimate things that men depend on for their lives. Ships, for instance—they always have personalities of their own.

"And planes—in wars you always hear of planes crippled too badly to fly, but struggling back anyhow with their crews. Even guns acquire a sort of ego. Ships and guns and planes are 'she' to the men who operate them and depend on them for their lives. It's as if machinery with complicated moving parts almost simulates life, and does acquire from the men who used it—well, not exactly life, of course—but a personality. I don't know what. Maybe it absorbs some of the actual electrical impulses their brains throw off, especially in times of stress.

"Well, after awhile I began to accept the idea that this new body of mine could behave at least as responsively as a ship or a plane. Quite apart from the fact that my own brain controls its 'muscles.' I believe there's an affinity between men and the machines they make. They make them out of their own brains, really, a sort of mental conception and gestation, and the result responds to the minds that created them, and to all human minds that understand and manipulate them."

She stirred uneasily and smoothed a flexible hand along her mesh-robed metal thigh. "So this is myself," she said. "Metal—but me. And it grows more and more myself the longer I live in it. It's my house and the machine my life depends on, but much more intimately in each case than any real house or machine ever was before to any other human. And you know, I wonder if in time I'll forget what flesh felt like—my own flesh, when I touched it like this— and the metal against the metal will be so much the same I'll never even notice?"

Harris did not try to answer her. He sat without moving, watching her expressionless face. In a moment she went on.

"I'll tell you the best thing, John," she said, her voice softening to the old intimacy he remembered so well that he could see superimposed upon the blank skull the warm, intent look that belonged with the voice. "I'm not going to live forever. It may not sound like a—best thing—but it is, John. You know, for a while that was the worst of all, after I knew I was—after I woke up again. The thought of living on and on in a body that wasn't mine, seeing everyone I knew grow old and die, and not being able to stop—

"But Maltzer says my brain will probably wear out quite normally—except, of course, that I won't have to worry about looking old!—and when it gets tired and stops, the body I'm in won't be any longer. The magnetic muscles that hold it into my own shape and motions will let go when the brain lets go, and there'll be nothing but a . . . a pile of disconnected rings. If they ever assemble it again, it won't be me." She hesitated. "I like that, John," she said, and he felt from behind the mask a searching of his face.

He knew and understood that somber satisfaction. He could not put it into words; neither of them wanted to do that. But he understood. It was the conviction of mortality, in spite of her immortal body. She was not cut off from the rest of her race in the essence of their humanity, for though she wore a body of steel and they perishable flesh, yet she must perish too, and the same fears and faiths still united her to mortals and humans, though she wore the body of Oberon's inhuman knight. Even in her death she must be unique—dissolution in a shower of tinkling and clashing rings, he thought, and almost envied her the finality and beauty of that particular death—but afterward, oneness with humanity in however much or little awaited them all. So she could feel that this exile in metal was only temporary, in spite of everything.

(And providing, of course, that the mind inside the metal did not veer from its inherited humanity as the years went by. A dweller in a house may impress his personality upon the walls, but subtly the walls too, may impress their own shape upon the ego of the man. Neither of them thought of that, at the time.)

Deirdre sat a moment longer in silence. Then the mood vanished and she rose again, spinning so that the robe belled out ringing about her ankles. She rippled another scale up and down, faultlessly and with the same familiar sweetness of tone that had made her famous.

"So I'm going right back on the stage, John," she said serenely. "I can still sing. I can still dance. I'm still myself in everything that matters, and I can't imagine doing anything else for the rest of my life."

He could not answer without stammering a little. "Do you think . . . will they accept you, Deirdre? After all—"

"They'll accept me," she said in that confident voice. "Oh, they'll come to see a freak at first, of course, but they'll stay to watch—Deirdre. And come back again and again just as they always did. You'll see, my dear."

But hearing her sureness, suddenly Harris himself was unsure. Maltzer had not been, either. She was so regally confident, and disappointment would be so deadly a blow at all that remained of her—

She was so delicate a being now, really. Nothing but a glowing and radiant mind poised in metal, dominating it, bending the steel to the illusion of her lost loveliness with a sheer self-confidence that gleamed through the metal body. But the brain sat delicately on its poise of reason. She had been through intolerable stresses already, perhaps more terrible depths of despair and self-knowledge than any human brain had yet endured before her, for—since Lazarus himself—who had come back from the dead?

But if the world did not accept her as beautiful, what then? If they laughed, or pitied her, or came only to watch a jointed freak performing as if on strings where the loveliness of Deirdre had once enchanted them, what then? And he could not be perfectly sure they would not. He had known her too well in the flesh to see her objectively even now, in metal. Every inflection of her voice called up the vivid memory of the face that had flashed its evanescent beauty in some look to match the tone. She was Deirdre to Harris simply because she had been so intimately familiar in every poise and attitude, through so many years. But people who knew her only slightly, or saw her for the first time in metal—what would they see?

A marionette? Or the real grace and loveliness shining through?

He had no possible way of knowing. He saw her too clearly as she had been to see her now at all, except so linked with the past that she was not wholly metal. And he knew what Maltzer feared, for Maltzer's psychic blindness toward her lay at the other extreme. He had never known Deirdre except as a machine, and he could not see her objectively any more than Harris could. To Maltzer she was pure metal, a robot his own hands and brain had devised, mysteriously animated by the mind of Deirdre, to be sure, but to all outward seeming a thing of metal solely. He had worked so long over each intricate part of her body, he knew so well how every jointure in it was put together, that he could not see the whole. He had studied many film records of her, of course, as she used to be, in order to gauge the accuracy of his facsimile, but this thing he had made was a copy only. He was too close to Deirdre to see her. And Harris, in a way, was too far. The indomitable Deirdre herself shone so vividly through the metal that his mind kept superimposing one upon the other.

How would an audience react to her? Where in the scale between these two extremes would their verdict fall?

For Deirdre, there was only one possible answer.

"I'm not worried," Deirdre said serenely, and spread her golden hands to the fire to watch lights dancing in reflection upon their shining surfaces. "I'm still myself. I've always had . . . well, power over my audiences. Any good performer knows when he's got it. Mine isn't gone. I can still give them what I always gave, only now with greater variations and more depths than I'd ever have done before. Why, look—" She gave a little wriggle of excitement.

"You know the arabesque principle—getting the longest possible distance from fingertip to toetip with a long, slow curve through the whole length? And the brace of the other leg and arm giving contrast? Well, look at me. I don't work on hinges now. I can make every motion a long curve if I want to. My body's different enough now to work out a whole new school of dancing. Of course there'll be things I used to do that I won't attempt now—no more dancing *sur les pointes*, for instance—but the new things will more than balance the loss. I've been practicing. Do you know I can turn a hundred *fouettés* now without a flaw? And I think I could go right on and turn a thousand, if I wanted."

She made the firelight flash on her hands, and her robe rang musically as she moved her shoulders a little. "I've already worked out one new dance for myself," she said. "God knows I'm no choreographer, but I did want to experiment first. Later, you know, really creative men like Massanchine or Fokhileff may want to do something entirely new for me—a whole new sequence of movements based on a new technique. And music—that could be quite different, too. Oh, there's no end to the possibilities! Even my voice has more range and power. Luckily I'm not an actress—it would be silly to try to play Camille or Juliet with a cast of ordinary people. Not that I couldn't, you know." She turned her head to stare at Harris through the mask of glass. "I honestly think I could. But it isn't necessary. There's too much else. Oh, I'm not worried!"

"Maltzer's worried," Harris reminded her.

She swung away from the fire, her metal robe ringing, and into her voice came the old note of distress that went with a furrowing of her forehead and a sidewise tilt of the head. The head went sidewise as it had always done, and he could see the furrowed brow almost as clearly as if flesh still clothed her.

"I know. And I'm worried about him, John. He's worked so awfully hard over me. This is the doldrums now, the letdown period, I suppose. I know what's on his mind. He's afraid I'll look just the same to the world as I look to him. Tooled metal. He's in a position no one ever quite achieved before, isn't he? Rather like God." Her voice rippled a little with amusement. "I suppose to God we must look like a collection of cells and corpuscles ourselves. But Maltzer lacks a god's detached viewpoint."

"He can't see you as I do, anyhow." Harris was choosing his words with difficulty. "I wonder, though—would it help him any if you postponed your debut awhile? You've been with him too closely, I think. You don't quite realize how near a breakdown he is. I was shocked when I saw him just now."

The golden head shook. "No. He's close to a breaking point, maybe, but I think the only cure's action. He wants me to retire and stay out of sight, John. Always. He's afraid for anyone to see me except a few old friends who remember me as I was. People he can trust to be—kind." She laughed. It was very strange to hear that ripple of mirth from the blank, unfeatured skull. Harris was seized with sudden panic at the thought of what reaction it might evoke in an audience of strangers. As if he had spoken the fear aloud, her voice denied it. "I don't need kindness. And it's no kindness to Maltzer to hide me under a bushel. He *has* worked too hard, I know. He's driven himself to a breaking point. But it'll be a complete negation of all he's worked for if I hide myself now. You don't know what a tremendous lot of genius and artistry went into me, John. The whole idea from the start was to re-create what I'd lost so that it could be proved that beauty and talent need not be sacrificed by the destruction of parts or all the body.

"It wasn't only for me that we meant to prove that. There'll be others who suffer injuries that once might have ruined them. This was to end all suffering like that forever. It was Maltzer's gift to the whole race as well as to me. He's really a humanitarian, John, like most great men. He'd never have given up a year of his life to this work if it had been for any one individual alone. He was seeing thousands of others beyond me as he worked. And I won't let him ruin all he's achieved because he's afraid to prove it now he's got it. The whole wonderful achievement will be worthless if I don't take the final step. I think his breakdown, in the end, would be worse and more final if I never tried than if I tried and failed."

Harris sat in silence. There was no answer he could make to that. He hoped the little twinge of shamefaced jealousy he suddenly felt did not show, as he was reminded anew of the intimacy closer than marriage which had of necessity bound these two together. And he knew that any reaction of his would in its way be almost as prejudiced as Maltzer's, for a reason at once the same and entirely opposite. Except that he himself came fresh to the problem, while Maltzer's view-

point was colored by a year of overwork and physical and
mental exhaustion.

"What are you going to do?" he asked.

She was standing before the fire when he spoke, swaying
just a little so that highlights danced all along her golden
body. Now she turned with a serpentine grace and sank into
the cushioned chair beside her. It came to him suddenly
that she was much more than humanly graceful—quite as
much as he had once feared she would be less than human.

"I've already arranged for a performance," she told him,
her voice a little shaken with a familiar mixture of excitement and defiance.

Harris sat up with a start. "How? Where? There hasn't
been any publicity at all yet, has there? I didn't know—"

"Now, now, Johnnie," her amused voice soothed him.
"You'll be handling everything just as usual once I get
started back to work—that is, if you still want to. But this
I've arranged for myself. It's going to be a surprise. I . . . I
felt it had to be a surprise." She wriggled a little among the
cushions. "Audience psychology is something I've always felt
rather than known, and I do feel this is the way it ought to
be done. There's no precedent. Nothing like this ever happened before. I'll have to go by my own intuition."

"You mean it's to be a complete surprise?"

"I think it must be. I don't want the audience coming in
with preconceived ideas. I want them to see me exactly as I
am now *first*, before they know who or what they're seeing.
They must realize I can still give as good a performance as
ever before they remember and compare it with my past
performances. I don't want them to come ready to pity my
handicaps—I haven't got any!—or full of morbid curiosity.
So I'm going on the air after the regular eight-o'clock tele-
cast of the feature from Teleo City. I'm just going to do one
specialty in the usual vaude program. It's all been arranged.
They'll build up to it, of course, as the highlight of the
evening, but they aren't to say who I am until the end of the

performance—if the audience hasn't recognized me already, by then."

"Audience?"

"Of course. Surely you haven't forgotten they still play to a theater audience at Teleo City? That's why I want to make my debut there. I've always played better when there were people in the studio, so I could gauge reactions. I think most performers do. Anyhow, it's all arranged."

"Does Maltzer know?"

She wriggled uncomfortably. "Not yet."

"But he'll have to give his permission too, won't he? I mean—"

"Now look, John! That's another idea you and Maltzer will have to get out of your minds. I don't belong to him. In a way he's just been my doctor through a long illness, but I'm free to discharge him whenever I choose. If there were ever any legal disagreement, I suppose he'd be entitled to quite a lot of money for the work he's done on my new body—for the body itself, really, since it's his own machine, in one sense. But he doesn't own it, or me. I'm not sure just how the question would be decided by the courts—there again, we've got a problem without precedent. The body may be his work, but the brain that makes it something more than a collection of metal rings is *me,* and he couldn't restrain me against my will even if he wanted to. Not legally, and not—" She hesitated oddly and looked away. For the first time Harris was aware of something beneath the surface of her mind which was quite strange to him.

"Well, anyhow," she went on, "that question won't come up. Maltzer and I have been much too close in the past year to clash over anything as essential as this. He knows in his heart that I'm right, and he won't try to restrain me. His work won't be completed until I do what I was built to do. And I intend to do it."

That strange little quiver of something—something un-Deirdre—which had so briefly trembled beneath the surface of familiarity stuck in Harris' mind as something he must recall and examine later. Now he said only,

"All right. I suppose I agree with you. How soon are you going to do it?"

She turned her head so that even the glass mask through which she looked out at the world was foreshortened away from him, and the golden helmet with its hint of sculptured cheekbone was entirely enigmatic.

"Tonight," she said.

Maltzer's thin hand shook so badly that he could not turn the dial. He tried twice and then laughed nervously and shrugged at Harris.

"You get her," he said.

Harris glanced at his watch. "It isn't time yet. She won't be on for half an hour."

Maltzer made a gesture of violent impatience. "Get it, get it!"

Harris shrugged a little in turn and twisted the dial. On the tilted screen above them shadows and sound blurred together and then clarified into a somber medieval hall, vast, vaulted, people in bright costume moving like pygmies through its dimness. Since the play concerned Mary of Scotland, the actors were dressed in something approximating Elizabethan garb, but as every era tends to translate costume into terms of the current fashions, the women's hair was dressed in a style that would have startled Elizabeth, and their footgear was entirely anachronistic.

The hall dissolved and a face swam up into soft focus upon the screen. The dark, lush beauty of the actress who was playing the Stuart queen glowed at them in velvety perfection from the clouds of her pearl-strewn hair. Maltzer groaned.

"She's competing with *that*," he said hollowly.

"You think she can't?"

Maltzer slapped the chair arms with angry palms. Then

the quivering of his fingers seemed suddenly to strike him, and he muttered to himself, "Look at 'em! I'm not even fit to handle a hammer and saw." But the mutter was an aside. "Of course she can't compete," he cried irritably. "She hasn't any sex. She isn't female any more. She doesn't know that yet, but she'll learn."

Harris stared at him, feeling a little stunned. Somehow the thought had not occurred to him before at all, so vividly had the illusion of the old Deirdre hung about the new one.

"She's an abstraction now," Maltzer went on, drumming his palms upon the chair in quick, nervous rhythms. "I don't know what it'll do to her, but there'll be change. Remember Abelard? She's lost everything that made her essentially what the public wanted, and she's going to find it out the hard way. After that—" He grimaced savagely and was silent.

"She hasn't lost everything," Harris defended. "She can dance and sing as well as ever, maybe better. She still has grace and charm and—"

"Yes, but where did the grace and charm come from? Not out of the habit patterns in her brain. No, out of human contacts, out of all the things that stimulate sensitive minds to creativeness. And she's lost three of her five senses. Everything she can't see and hear is gone. One of the strongest stimuli to a woman of her type was the knowledge of sex competition. You know how she sparkled when a man came into the room? All that's gone, and it was an essential. You know how liquor stimulated her? She's lost that. She couldn't taste food or drink even if she needed it. Perfume, flowers, all the odors we respond to mean nothing to her now. She can't feel anything with tactual delicacy any more. She used to surround herself with luxuries—she drew her stimuli from them—and that's all gone too. She's withdrawn from all physical contacts."

He squinted at the screen, not seeing it, his face drawn into lines like the lines of a skull. All flesh seemed to have dissolved off his bones in the past year, and Harris thought almost jealously that even in that way he seemed to be drawing nearer Deirdre in her fleshlessness with every passing week.

"Sight," Maltzer said, "is the most highly civilized of the senses. It was the last to come. The other senses tie us in closely with the very roots of life; I think we perceive with them more keenly than we know. The things we realize through taste and smell and feeling stimulate directly, without a detour through the centers of conscious thought. You know how often a taste or odor will recall a memory to you so subtly you don't know exactly what caused it? We need those primitive senses to tie us in with nature and the race. Through those ties Deirdre drew her vitality without realizing it. Sight is a cold, intellectual thing compared with the other senses. But it's all she has to draw on now. She isn't a human being any more, and I think what humanity is left in her will drain out little by little and never be replaced. Abelard, in a way, was a prototype. But Deirdre's loss is complete."

"She isn't human," Harris agreed slowly. "But she isn't pure robot either. She's something somewhere between the two, and I think it's a mistake to try to guess just where, or what the outcome will be."

"I don't have to guess," Maltzer said in a grim voice. "I know. I wish I'd let her die. I've done something to her a thousand times worse than the fire ever could. I should have let her die in it."

"Wait," said Harris. "Wait and see. I think you're wrong."

On the television screen Mary of Scotland climbed the scaffold to her doom, the gown of traditional scarlet clinging warmly to supple young curves as anachronistic in their way as the slippers beneath the gown, for—as everyone but playwrights knows—Mary was well into middle age before she died. Gracefully this latter-day Mary bent her head, sweeping the long hair aside, kneeling to the block.

Maltzer watched stonily, seeing another woman entirely.

"I shouldn't have let her," he was muttering. "I shouldn't have let her do it."

"So you really think you'd have stopped her if you could?" Harris asked quietly. And the other man after a moment's pause shook his head jerkily.

"No, I suppose not. I keep thinking if I worked and waited a little longer maybe I could make it easier for her, but—no, I suppose not. She's got to face them sooner or later, being herself." He stood up abruptly, shoving back his chair. "If she only weren't so . . . so frail. She doesn't realize how delicately poised her very sanity is. We gave her what we could—the artists and the designers and I, all gave our very best—but she's so pitifully handicapped even with all we could do. She'll always be an abstraction and a . . . a freak, cut off from the world by handicaps worse in their way than anything any human being ever suffered before. Sooner or later she'll realize it. And then—" He began to pace up and down with quick, uneven steps, striking his hands together. His face was twitching with a little *tic* that drew up one eye to a squint and released it again at irregular intervals. Harris could see how very near collapse the man was.

"Can you imagine what it's like?" Maltzer demanded fiercely. "Penned into a mechanical body like that, shut out from all human contacts except what leaks in by way of sight and sound? To know you aren't human any longer? She's been through shocks enough already. When that shock fully hits her—"

"Shut up," said Harris roughly. "You won't do her any good if you break down yourself. Look—the vaude's starting."

Great golden curtains had swept together over the unhappy Queen of Scotland and were parting again now, all sorrow and frustration wiped away once more as cleanly as

the passing centuries had already expunged them. Now a
line of tiny dancers under the tremendous arch of the stage
kicked and pranced with the precision of little mechanical
dolls too small and perfect to be real. Vision rushed down
upon them and swept along the row, face after stiffly smiling face racketing by like fence pickets. Then the sight rose
into the rafters and looked down upon them from a great
height, the grotesquely foreshortened figures still prancing
in perfect rhythm even from this inhuman angle.

There was applause from an invisible audience. Then
someone came out and did a dance with lighted torches that
streamed long, weaving ribbons of fire among clouds of what
looked like cotton wool but was most probably asbestos.
Then a company in gorgeous pseudo-period costumes pos-
tured its way through the new singing ballet form of dance,
roughly following a plot which had been announced as *Les
Sylphides*, but had little in common with it. Afterward the
precision dancers came on again, solemn and charming as
performing dolls.

Maltzer began to show signs of dangerous tension as act
succeeded act. Deirdre's was to be the last, of course. It
seemed very long indeed before a face in close-up blotted out
the stage, and a master of ceremonies with features like an
amiable marionette's announced a very special number as
the finale. His voice was almost cracking with excitement—
perhaps he, too, had not been told until a moment before
what lay in store for the audience.

Neither of the listening men heard what it was he said,
but both were conscious of a certain indefinable excitement
rising among the audience, murmurs and rustlings and a
mounting anticipation as if time had run backward here and
knowledge of the great surprise had already broken upon
them.

Then the golden curtains appeared again. They quivered
and swept apart on long upward arcs, and between them the
stage was full of a shimmering golden haze. It was, Harris
realized in a moment, simply a series of gauze curtains, but

the effect was one of strange and wonderful anticipation, as if something very splendid must be hidden in the haze. The world might have looked like this on the first morning of creation, before heaven and earth took form in the mind of God. It was a singularly fortunate choice of stage set in its symbolism, though Harris wondered how much necessity had figured in its selection, for there could not have been much time to prepare an elaborate set.

The audience sat perfectly silent, and the air was tense. This was no ordinary pause before an act. No one had been told, surely, and yet they seemed to guess—

The shimmering haze trembled and began to thin, veil by veil. Beyond was darkness, and what looked like a row of shining pillars set in a balustrade that began gradually to take shape as the haze drew back in shining folds. Now they could see that the balustrade curved up from left and right to the head of a sweep of stairs. Stage and stairs were carpeted in black velvet; black velvet draperies hung just ajar behind the balcony, with a glimpse of dark sky beyond them trembling with dim synthetic stars.

The last curtain of golden gauze withdrew. The stage was empty. Or it seemed empty. But even through the aerial distances between this screen and the place it mirrored, Harris thought that the audience was not waiting for the performer to come on from the wings. There was no rustling, no coughing, no sense of impatience. A presence upon the stage was in command from the first drawing of the curtains; it filled the theater with its calm domination. It gauged its timing, holding the audience as a conductor with lifted baton gathers and holds the eyes of his orchestra.

For a moment everything was motionless upon the stage. Then, at the head of the stairs, where the two curves of the pillared balustrade swept together, a figure stirred.

Until that moment she had seemed another shining column in the row. Now she swayed deliberately, light catching and winking and running molten along her limbs and her robe of metal mesh. She swayed just enough to show that she was there. Then, with every eye upon her, she stood quietly to let them look their fill. The screen did not swoop to a close-up upon her. Her enigma remained inviolate and the television watchers saw her no more clearly than the audience in the theater.

Many must have thought her at first some wonderfully animate robot, hung perhaps from wires invisible against the velvet, for certainly she was no woman dressed in metal—her proportions were too thin and fine for that. And perhaps the impression of robotism was what she meant to convey at first. She stood quiet, swaying just a little, a masked and inscrutable figure, faceless, very slender in her robe that hung in folds as pure as a Grecian chlamys, though she did not look Grecian at all. In the visored golden helmet and the robe of mail that odd likeness to knighthood was there again, with its implications of medieval richness behind the simple lines. Except that in her exquisite slimness she called to mind no human figure in armor, not even the comparative delicacy of a St. Joan. It was the chivalry and delicacy of some other world implicit in her outlines.

A breath of surprise had rippled over the audience when she moved. Now they were tensely silent again, waiting. And the tension, the anticipation, was far deeper than the surface importance of the scene could ever have evoked. Even those who thought her a manikin seemed to feel the forerunning of greater revelations.

Now she swayed and came slowly down the steps, moving with a suppleness just a little better than human. The swaying strengthened. By the time she reached the stage floor she was dancing. But it was no dance that any human creature could ever have performed. The long, slow, languorous rhythms of her body would have been impossible to a figure hinged at its joints as human figures hinge. (Harris remembered incredulously that he had feared once to find her jointed like a mechanical robot. But it was humanity that seemed, by contrast, jointed and mechanical now.)

The languor and the rhythm of her patterns looked im-

promptu, as all good dances should, but Harris knew what
hours of composition and rehearsal must lie behind it, what
laborious graving into her brain of strange new pathways,
the first to replace the old ones and govern the mastery of
metal limbs.

To and fro over the velvet carpet, against the velvet
background, she wove the intricacies of her serpentine
dance, leisurely and yet with such hypnotic effect that the
air seemed full of looping rhythms, as if her long, tapering
limbs had left their own replicas hanging upon the air and
fading only slowly as she moved away. In her mind, Harris
knew, the stage was a whole, a background to be filled in
completely with the measured patterns of her dance, and she
seemed almost to project that completed pattern to her
audience so that they saw her everywhere at once, her
golden rhythms fading upon the air long after she had gone.

Now there was music, looping and hanging in echoes
after her like the shining festoons she wove with her body.
But it was no orchestral music. She was humming, deep and
sweet and wordlessly, as she glided her easy, intricate path
about the stage. And the volume of the music was amazing.
It seemed to fill the theater, and it was not amplified by
hidden loudspeakers. You could tell that. Somehow, until
you heard the music she made, you had never realized before
the subtle distortions that amplification puts into music.
This was utterly pure and true as perhaps no ear in all her
audience had ever heard music before.

While she danced the audience did not seem to breathe.
Perhaps they were beginning already to suspect who and
what it was that moved before them without any fanfare of
the publicity they had been half-expecting for weeks now.
And yet, without the publicity, it was not easy to believe the
dancer they watched was not some cunningly motivated
manikin swinging on unseen wires about the stage.

Nothing she had done yet had been human. The dance
was no dance a human being could have performed. The
music she hummed came from a throat without vocal

chords. But now the long, slow rhythms were drawing to their close, the pattern tightening in to a finale. And she ended as inhumanly as she had danced, willing them not to interrupt her with applause, dominating them now as she had always done. For her implication here was that a machine might have performed the dance, and a machine expects no applause. If they thought unseen operators had put her through those wonderful paces, they would wait for the operators to appear for their bows. But the audience was obedient. It sat silently, waiting for what came next. But its silence was tense and breathless.

The dance ended as it had begun. Slowly, almost carelessly, she swung up the velvet stairs, moving with rhythms as perfect as her music. But when she reached the head of the stairs she turned to face her audience, and for a moment stood motionless, like a creature of metal, without volition, the hands of the operator slack upon its strings.

Then, startlingly, she laughed.

It was lovely laughter, low and sweet and full-throated. She threw her head back and let her body sway and her shoulders shake, and the laughter, like the music, filled the theater, gaining volume from the great hollow of the roof and sounding in the ears of every listener, not loud, but as intimately as if each sat alone with the woman who laughed.

And she was a woman now. Humanity had dropped over her like a tangible garment. No one who had ever heard that laughter before could mistake it here. But before the reality of who she was had quite time to dawn upon her listeners she let the laughter deepen into music, as no human voice could have done. She was humming a familiar refrain close in the ear of every hearer. And the humming in turn swung into words. She sang in her clear, light, lovely voice:

"The yellow rose of Eden, is blooming in my heart—"

It was Deirdre's song. She had sung it first upon the airways a month before the theater fire that had consumed her. It was a commonplace little melody, simple enough to take first place in the fancy of a nation that had always liked its songs simple. But it had a certain sincerity too, and no taint of the vulgarity of tune and rhythm that foredooms so many popular songs to oblivion after their novelty fades.

No one else was ever able to sing it quite as Deirdre did. It had been identified with her so closely that though for a while after her accident singers tried to make it a memorial for her, they failed so conspicuously to give it her unmistakable flair that the song died from their sheer inability to sing it. No one ever hummed the tune without thinking of her and the pleasant, nostalgic sadness of something lovely and lost.

But it was not a sad song now. If anyone had doubted whose brain and ego motivated this shining metal suppleness, they could doubt no longer. For the voice was Deirdre, and the song. And the lovely, poised grace of her mannerisms that made up recognition as certainly as sight of a familiar face.

She had not finished the first line of her song before the audience knew her.

And they did not let her finish. The accolade of their interruption was a tribute more eloquent than polite waiting could ever have been. First a breath of incredulity rippled over the theater, and a long, sighing gasp that reminded Harris irrelevantly as he listened to the gasp which still goes up from matinee audiences at the first glimpse of the fabulous Valentino, so many generations dead. But this gasp did not sigh itself away and vanish. Tremendous tension lay behind it, and the rising tide of excitement rippled up in little murmurs and spatterings of applause that ran together into one overwhelming roar. It shook the theater. The television screen trembled and blurred a little to the volume of that transmitted applause.

Silenced before it, Deirdre stood gesturing on the stage, bowing and bowing as the noise rolled up about her, shaking perceptibly with the triumph of her own emotion.

Harris had an intolerable feeling that she was smiling

radiantly and that the tears were pouring down her cheeks. He even thought, just as Maltzer leaned forward to switch off the screen, that she was blowing kisses over the audience in the timehonored gesture of the grateful actress, her golden arms shining as she scattered kisses abroad from the featureless helmet, the face that had no mouth.

"Well?" Harris said, not without triumph.

Maltzer shook his head jerkily, the glasses unsteady on his nose so that the blurred eyes behind them seemed to shift.

"Of course they applauded, you fool," he said in a savage voice. "I might have known they would under this setup. It doesn't prove anything. Oh, she was smart to surprise them—I admit that. But they were applauding themselves as much as her. Excitement, gratitude for letting them in on a historic performance, mass hysteria—_you_ know. It's from now on the test will come, and this hasn't helped any to prepare her for it. Morbid curiosity when the news gets out—people laughing when she forgets she isn't human. And they will, you know. There are always those who will. And the novelty wearing off. The slow draining away of humanity for lack of contact with any human stimuli any more—"

Harris remembered suddenly and reluctantly the moment that afternoon which he had shunted aside mentally, to consider later. The sense of something unfamiliar beneath the surface of Deirdre's speech. Was Maltzer right? Was the drainage already at work? Or was there something deeper than this obvious answer to the question? Certainly she had been through experiences too terrible for ordinary people to comprehend. Scars might still remain. Or, with her body, had she put on a strange, metallic something of the mind, that spoke to no sense which human minds could answer?

For a few minutes neither of them spoke. Then Maltzer

rose abruptly and stood looking down at Harris with an abstract scowl.

"I wish you'd go now," he said.

Harris glanced up at him, startled. Maltzer began to pace again, his steps quick and uneven. Over his shoulder he said,

"I've made up my mind, Harris. I've got to put a stop to this."

Harris rose. "Listen," he said. "Tell me one thing. What makes you so certain you're right? Can you deny that most of it's speculation—hearsay evidence? Remember, I talked to Deirdre, and she was just as sure as you are in the opposite direction. Have you any real reason for what you think?"

Maltzer took his glasses off and rubbed his nose carefully, taking a long time about it. He seemed reluctant to answer. But when he did, at last, there was a confidence in his voice Harris had not expected.

"I have a reason," he said. "But you won't believe it. Nobody would."

"Try me."

Maltzer shook his head. "Nobody *could* believe it. No two people were ever in quite the same relationship before as Deirdre and I have been. I helped her come back out of complete—oblivion. I knew her before she had voice or hearing. She was only a frantic mind when I first made contact with her, half insane with all that had happened and fear of what would happen next. In a very literal sense she was reborn out of that condition, and I had to guide her through every step of the way. I came to know her thoughts before she thought them. And once you've been that close to another mind, you don't lose the contact easily." He put the glasses back on and looked blurrily at Harris through the heavy lenses. "Deirdre is worried," he said. "I know it. You won't believe me, but I can—well, sense it. I tell you, I've been too close to her very mind itself to make any mistake. You don't see it, maybe. Maybe even she doesn't know it yet. But the worry's there. When I'm with her, I feel it. And I don't want it to come any nearer the surface of her mind than it's come already. I'm going to put a stop to this before it's too late."

Harris had no comment for that. It was too entirely outside his own experience. He said nothing for a moment. Then he asked simply, "How?"

"I'm not sure yet. I've got to decide before she comes back. And I want to see her alone."

"I think you're wrong," Harris told him quietly. "I think you're imagining things. I don't think you *can* stop her."

Maltzer gave him a slanted glance. "I can stop her," he said, in a curious voice. He went on quickly, "She has enough already—she's nearly human. She can live normally as other people live, without going back on the screen. Maybe this taste of it will be enough. I've got to convince her it is. If she retires now, she'll never guess how cruel her own audiences could be, and maybe that deep sense of—distress, uneasiness, whatever it is—won't come to the surface. It mustn't. She's too fragile to stand that." He slapped his hands together sharply. "I've got to stop her. For her own sake I've got to do it!" He swung round again to face Harris. "Will you go now?"

Never in his life had Harris wanted less to leave a place. Briefly he thought of saying simply, "No I won't." But he had to admit in his own mind that Maltzer was at least partly right. This was a matter between Deirdre and her creator, the culmination, perhaps, of that year's long intimacy so like marriage that this final trial for supremacy was a need he recognized.

He would not, he thought, forbid the showdown if he could. Perhaps the whole year had been building up to this one moment between them in which one or the other must prove himself victor. Neither was very stable just now, after the long strain of the year past. It might very well be that the mental salvation of one or both hinged upon the outcome of the clash. But because each was so strongly motivated not by selfish concern but by solicitude for the other in this strange combat, Harris knew he must leave them to settle the thing alone.

He was in the street and hailing a taxi before the full significance of something Maltzer had said came to him. "*I can stop her,*" he had declared, with an odd inflection in his voice.

Suddenly Harris felt cold. Maltzer had made her—of course he could stop her if he chose. Was there some key in that supple golden body that could immobilize it at its maker's will? Could she be imprisoned in the cage of her own body? No body before in all history, he thought, could have been designed more truly to be a prison for its mind than Deirdre's, if Maltzer chose to turn the key that locked her in. There must be many ways to do it. He could simply withhold whatever source of nourishment kept her brain alive, if that were the way he chose.

But Harris could not believe he would do it. The man wasn't insane. He would not defeat his own purpose. His determination rose from his solicitude for Deirdre; he would not even in the last extremity try to save her by imprisoning her in the jail of her own skull.

For a moment Harris hesitated on the curb, almost turning back. But what could he do? Even granting that Maltzer would resort to such tactics, self-defeating in their very nature, how could any man on earth prevent him if he did it subtly enough? But he never would. Harris knew he never would. He got into his cab slowly, frowning. He would see them both tomorrow.

He did not. Harris was swamped with excited calls about yesterday's performance, but the message he was awaiting did not come. The day went by very slowly. Toward evening he surrendered and called Maltzer's apartment.

It was Deirdre's face that answered, and for once he saw no remembered features superimposed upon the blankness

of her helmet. Masked and faceless, she looked at him in-
scrutably.

"Is everything all right?" he asked, a little uncomfortable.

"Yes, of course," she said, and her voice was a bit metallic for the first time, as if she were thinking so deeply of
some other matter that she did not trouble to pitch it properly. "I had a long talk with Maltzer last night, if that's
what you mean. You know what he wants. But nothing's
been decided yet."

Harris felt oddly rebuffed by the sudden realization of
the metal of her. It was impossible to read anything from
face or voice. Each had its mask.

"What are you going to do?" he asked.

"Exactly as I'd planned," she told him, without inflection.

Harris floundered a little. Then, with an effort at practi-
cality, he said, "Do you want me to go to work on booking,
then?"

She shook the delicately modeled skull. "Not yet. You
saw the reviews today, of course. They—*did* like me." It was
an understatement, and for the first time a note of warmth
sounded in her voice. But the preoccupation was still there,
too. "I'd already planned to make them wait awhile after my
first performance," she went on. "A couple of weeks, anyhow. You remember that little farm of mine in Jersey, John?
I'm going over today. I won't see anyone except the servants
there. Not even Maltzer. Not even you. I've got a lot to
think about. Maltzer has agreed to let everything go until
we've both thought things over. He's taking a rest, too. I'll
see you the moment I get back, John. Is that all right?"

She blanked out almost before he had time to nod and
while the beginning of a stammered argument was still on
his lips. He sat there staring at the screen.

The two weeks that went by before Maltzer called him
again were the longest Harris had ever spent. He thought of
many things in the interval. He believed he could sense in

that last talk with Deirdre something of the inner unrest that Maltzer had spoken of—more an abstraction than a distress, but some thought had occupied her mind which she would not—or was it that she could not?—share even with her closest confidants. He even wondered whether, if her mind was as delicately poised as Maltzer feared, one would ever know whether or not it had slipped. There was so little evidence one way or the other in the unchanging outward form of her.

Most of all he wondered what two weeks in a new environment would do to her untried body and newly patterned brain. If Maltzer were right, then there might be some perceptible—drainage—by the time they met again. He tried not to think of that.

Maltzer televised him on the morning set for her return. He looked very bad. The rest must have been no rest at all. His face was almost a skull now, and the blurred eyes behind their lenses burned. But he seemed curiously at peace, in spite of his appearance. Harris thought he had reached some decision, but whatever it was had not stopped his hands from shaking or the nervous *tic* that drew his face sidewise into a grimace at intervals.

"Come over," he said briefly, without preamble. "She'll be here in half an hour." And he blanked out without waiting for an answer.

When Harris arrived, he was standing by the window looking down and steadying his trembling hands on the sill.

"I can't stop her," he said in a monotone, and again without preamble. Harris had the impression that for two weeks his thoughts must have run over and over the same track, until any spoken word was simply a vocal interlude in the circling of his mind. "I couldn't do it. I even tried threats, but she knew I didn't mean them. There's only one way out, Harris." He glanced up briefly, hollow-eyed behind the lenses. "Never mind. I'll tell you later."

"Did you explain everything to her that you did to me?"

"Nearly all. I even taxed her with that . . . that sense of distress I *know* she feels. She denied it. She was lying. We both knew. It was worse after the performance than before. When I saw her that night, I tell you I *knew*—she senses something wrong, but she won't admit it." He shrugged. "Well—"

Faintly in the silence they heard the humming of the elevator descending from the helicopter platform on the roof. Both men turned to the door.

She had not changed at all. Foolishly, Harris was a little surprised. Then he caught himself and remembered that she would never change—never, until she died. He himself might grow white-haired and senile; she would move before him then as she moved now, supple, golden, enigmatic.

Still, he thought she caught her breath a little when she saw Maltzer and the depths of his swift degeneration. She had no breath to catch, but her voice was shaken as she greeted them.

"I'm glad you're both here," she said, a slight hesitation in her speech. "It's a wonderful day outside. Jersey was glorious. I'd forgotten how lovely it is in summer. Was the sanitarium any good, Maltzer?"

He jerked his head irritably and did not answer. She went on talking in a light voice, skimming the surface, saying nothing important.

This time Harris saw her as he supposed her audiences would, eventually, when the surprise had worn off and the image of the living Deirdre faded from memory. She was all metal now, the Deirdre they would know from today on. And she was not less lovely. She was not even less human— yet. Her motion was a miracle of flexible grace, a pouring of suppleness along every limb. (From now on, Harris realized suddenly, it was her body and not her face that would have mobility to express emotion; she must act with her limbs and her lithe, robed torso.)

But there was something wrong. Harris sensed it almost tangibly in her inflections, her elusiveness, the way she fenced with words. This was what Maltzer had meant, this was what Harris himself had felt just before she left for the country. Only now it was strong—certain. Between them and the old Deirdre whose voice still spoke to them a veil of—detachment—had been drawn. Behind it she was in distress. Somehow, somewhere, she had made some discovery that affected her profoundly. And Harris was terribly afraid that he knew what the discovery must be. Maltzer was right.

He was still leaning against the window, staring out unseeingly over the vast panorama of New York, webbed with traffic bridges, winking with sunlit glass, its vertiginous distances plunging downward into the blue shadows of Earth-level. He said now, breaking into the light-voiced chatter, "Are you all right, Deirdre?"

She laughed. It was lovely laughter. She moved lithely across the room, sunlight glinting on her musical mailed robe, and stooped to a cigarette box on a table. Her fingers were deft.

"Have one?" she said, and carried the box to Maltzer. He let her put the brown cylinder between his lips and hold a light to it, but he did not seem to be noticing what he did. She replaced the box and then crossed to a mirror on the far wall and began experimenting with a series of gliding ripples that wove patterns of pale gold in the glass. "Of course I'm all right," she said.

"You're lying."

Deirdre did not turn. She was watching him in the mirror, but the ripple of her motion went on slowly, languorously, undisturbed.

"No," she told them both.

Maltzer drew deeply on his cigarette. Then with a hard pull he unsealed the window and tossed the smoking stub far out over the gulfs below. He said,

"You can't deceive me, Deirdre." His voice, suddenly, was quite calm. "I created you, my dear. I know. I've sensed that uneasiness in you growing and growing for a long while now. It's much stronger today than it was two weeks ago. Something happened to you in the country. I don't know what it was, but you've changed. Will you admit to yourself what it is, Deirdre? Have you realized yet that you must not go back on the screen?"

"Why, no," said Deirdre, still not looking at him except obliquely, in the glass. Her gestures were slower now, weaving lazy patterns in the air. "No, I haven't changed my mind."

She was all metal—outwardly. She was taking unfair advantage of her own metal-hood. She had withdrawn far within, behind the mask of her voice and her facelessness. Even her body, whose involuntary motions might have betrayed what she was feeling, in the only way she could be subject to betrayal now, she was putting through ritual motions that disguised it completely. As long as these looping, weaving patterns occupied her, no one had any way of guessing even from her motion what went on in the hidden brain inside her helmet.

Harris was struck suddenly and for the first time with the completeness of her withdrawal. When he had seen her last in this apartment she had been wholly Deirdre, not masked at all, overflowing the metal with the warmth and ardor of the woman he had known so well. Since then— since the performance on the stage—he had not seen the familiar Deirdre again. Passionately he wondered why. Had she begun to suspect even in her moment of triumph what a fickle master an audience could be? Had she caught, perhaps, the sound of whispers and laughter among some small portion of her watchers, though the great majority praised her?

Or was Maltzer right? Perhaps Harris' first interview with her had been the last bright burning of the lost Deirdre, animated by excitement and the pleasure of meeting after so long a time, animation summoned up in a last strong effort to convince him. Now she was gone, but whether in self-protection against the possible cruelties of human beings, or whether in withdrawal to metal-hood, he could not guess. Humanity might be draining out of her fast, and the brassy taint of metal permeating the brain it housed.

Maltzer laid his trembling hand on the edge of the opened window and looked out. He said in a deepened voice, the querulous note gone for the first time:

"I've made a terrible mistake, Deirdre. I've done you irreparable harm." He paused a moment, but Deirdre said nothing. Harris dared not speak. In a moment Maltzer went on. "I've made you vulnerable, and given you no weapons to fight your enemies with. And the human race is your enemy, my dear, whether you admit it now or later. I think you know that. I think it's why you're so silent. I think you must have suspected it on the stage two weeks ago, and verified it in Jersey while you were gone. They're going to hate you, after a while, because you are still beautiful, and they're going to persecute you because you are different—and help-less. Once the novelty wears off, my dear, your audience will be simply a mob."

He was not looking at her. He had bent forward a little, looking out the window and down. His hair stirred in the wind that blew very strongly up this high, and whined thinly around the open edge of the glass.

"I meant what I did for you," he said, "to be for every-one who meets with accidents that might have ruined them. I should have known my gift would mean worse ruin than any mutilation could be. I know now that there's only one legitimate way a human being can create life. When he tries another way, as I did, he has a lesson to learn. Remember the lesson of the student Frankenstein? He learned, too. In a way, he was lucky—the way he learned. He didn't have to watch what happened afterward. Maybe he wouldn't have had the courage—I know I haven't."

Harris found himself standing without remembering that he rose. He knew suddenly what was about to happen. He understood Maltzer's air of resolution, his new, unnatu-ral calm. He knew, even, why Maltzer had asked him here today, so that Deirdre might not be left alone. For he remembered that Frankenstein, too, had paid with his life for the unlawful creation of life.

Maltzer was leaning head and shoulders from the window now, looking down with almost hypnotized fascination. His voice came back to them remotely in the breeze, as if a barrier already lay between them.

Deirdre had not moved. Her expressionless mask, in the mirror, watched him calmly. She *must* have understood. Yet she gave no sign, except that the weaving of her arms had almost stopped now, she moved so slowly. Like a dance seen in a nightmare, under water.

It was impossible, of course, for her to express any emotion. The fact that her face showed none now should not, in fairness, be held against her. But she watched so wholly without feeling— Neither of them moved toward the window. A false step, now, might send him over. They were quiet, listening to his voice.

"We who bring life into the world unlawfully," said Maltzer, almost thoughtfully, "must make room for it by withdrawing our own. That seems to be an inflexible rule. It works automatically. The thing we create makes living unbearable. No, it's nothing you can help, my dear. I've asked you to do something I created you incapable of doing. I made you to perform a function, and I've been asking you to forego the one thing you were made to do. I believe that if you do it, it will destroy you, but the whole guilt is mine, not yours. I'm not even asking you to give up the screen, any more. I know you can't, and live. But I can't live and watch you. I put all my skill and all my love in one final masterpiece, and I can't bear to watch it destroyed. I can't live and watch you do only what I made you to do, and ruin yourself because you must do it.

"But before I go, I have to make sure you understand." He leaned a little farther, looking down, and his voice grew more remote as the glass came between them. He was saying almost unbearable things now, but very distantly, in a cool, passionless tone filtered through wind and glass, and with the distant humming of the city mingled with it, so that the words were curiously robbed of poignancy. "I can be a coward," he said, "and escape the consequences of what I've done, but I can't go and leave you—not understanding. It would be even worse than the thought of your failure, to think of you bewildered and confused when the mob turns on you. What I'm telling you, my dear, won't be any real news—I think you sense it already, though you may not admit it to yourself. We've been too close to lie to each other, Deirdre—I know when you aren't telling the truth. I know the distress that's been growing in your mind. You are not wholly human, my dear. I think you know that. In so many ways, in spite of all I could do, you must always be less than human. You've lost the senses of perception that kept you in touch with humanity. Sight and hearing are all that remain, and sight, as I've said before, was the last and coldest of the senses to develop. And you're so delicately poised on a sort of thin edge of reason. You're only a clear, glowing mind animating a metal body, like a candle flame in a glass. And as precariously vulnerable to the wind."

He paused. "Try not to let them ruin you completely," he said after a while. "When they turn against you, when they find out you're more helpless than they—I wish I could have made you stronger, Deirdre. But I couldn't. I had too much skill for your good and mine, but not quite enough skill for that."

He was silent again, briefly, looking down. He was balanced precariously now, more than halfway over the sill and supported only by one hand on the glass. Harris watched with an agonized uncertainty, not sure whether a sudden leap might catch him in time or send him over. Deirdre was still weaving her golden patterns, slowly and unchangingly, watching the mirror and its reflection, her face and masked eyes enigmatic.

"I wish one thing, though," Maltzer said in his remote voice. "I wish—before I finish—that you'd tell me the truth, Deirdre. I'd be happier if I were sure I'd—reached you. Do you understand what I've said? Do you believe me? Because if you don't, then I know you're lost beyond all hope. If you'll admit your own doubt—and I know you do doubt—I can think there may be a chance for you after all. Were you lying to me, Deirdre? Do you know how . . . how wrong I've made you?"

There was silence. Then very softly, a breath of sound, Deirdre answered. The voice seemed to hang in midair, because she had no lips to move and localize it for the imagination.

"Will you listen, Maltzer?" she asked.

"I'll wait," he said. "Go on. Yes or no?"

Slowly she let her arms drop to her sides. Very smoothly and quietly she turned from the mirror and faced him. She swayed a little, making her metal robe ring.

"I'll answer you," she said. "But I don't think I'll answer that. Not with yes or no, anyhow. I'm going to walk a little, Maltzer. I have something to tell you, and I can't talk standing still. Will you let me move about without—going over?"

He nodded distantly. "You can't interfere from that distance," he said. "But keep the distance. What do you want to say?"

She began to pace a little way up and down her end of the room, moving with liquid ease. The table with the cigarette box was in her way, and she pushed it aside carefully, watching Maltzer and making no swift motions to startle him.

"I'm not—well, subhuman," she said, a faint note of indignation in her voice. "I'll prove it in a minute, but I want to say something else first. You must promise to wait and listen. There's a flaw in your argument, and I resent it. I'm not a Frankenstein monster made out of dead flesh. I'm myself—alive. You didn't create my life, you only preserved it. I'm not a robot, with compulsions built into me that I have to obey. I'm free-willed and independent, and, Maltzer —I'm human."

Harris had relaxed a little. She knew what she was doing. He had no idea what she planned, but he was willing to wait now. She was not the indifferent automaton he had thought. He watched her come to the table again in a lap of her pacing, and stoop over it, her eyeless mask turned to Maltzer to make sure a variation of her movement did not startle him.

"I'm human," she repeated, her voice humming faintly and very sweetly. "Do you think I'm not?" she asked, straightening and facing them both. And then suddenly, almost overwhelmingly, the warmth and the old ardent charm were radiant all around her. She was robot no longer, enigmatic no longer. Harris could see as clearly as in their first meeting the remembered flesh still gracious and beautiful as her voice evoked his memory. She stood swaying a little, as she had always swayed, her head on one side, and she was chuckling at them both. It was such a soft and lovely sound, so warmly familiar.

"Of course I'm myself," she told them, and as the words sounded in their ears neither of them could doubt it. There was hypnosis in her voice. She turned away and began to pace again, and so powerful was the human personality which she had called up about her that it beat out at them in deep pulses, as if her body were a furnace to send out those comforting waves of warmth. "I have handicaps, I know," she said. "But my audiences will never know. I won't let them know. I think you'll believe me, both of you, when I say I could play Juliet just as I am now, with a cast of ordinary people, and make the world accept it. Do you think I could, John? Maltzer, don't you believe I could?"

She paused at the far end of her pacing path and turned to face them, and they both stared at her without speaking. To Harris she was the Deirdre he had always known, pale gold, exquisitely graceful in remembered postures, the inner radiance of her shining through metal as brilliantly as it had ever shone through flesh. He did not wonder, now, if it were real. Later he would think again that it might be only a disguise, something like a garment she had put off with her lost body, to wear again only when she chose. Now the spell of her compelling charm was too strong for wonder. He watched, convinced for the moment that she was all she seemed to be. She could play Juliet if she said she could. She could sway a whole audience as easily as she swayed him. Indeed, there was something about her just now more convincingly human than anything he had noticed before. He realized that in a split second of awareness before he saw what it was.

She was looking at Maltzer. He, too, watched, spellbound in spite of himself, not dissenting. She glanced from one to the other. Then she put back her head and laughter came welling and choking from her in a great, full-throated tide. She shook in the strength of it. Harris could almost see her round throat pulsing with the sweet low-pitched waves of laughter that were shaking her. Honest mirth, with a little derision in it.

Then she lifted one arm and tossed her cigarette into the empty fireplace.

Harris choked, and his mind went blank for one moment of blind denial. He had not sat here watching a robot smoke and accepting it as normal. He could not! And yet he had. That had been the final touch of conviction which swayed his hypnotized mind into accepting her humanity. And she had done it so deftly, so naturally, wearing her radiant humanity with such rightness, that his watching mind had not even questioned what she did.

He glanced at Maltzer. The man was still halfway over the window ledge, but through the opening of the window he, too, was staring in stupefied disbelief and Harris knew they had shared the same delusion.

Deirdre was still shaking a little with laughter. "Well,"

she demanded, the rich chuckling making her voice quiver, "am I all robot, after all?"

Harris opened his mouth to speak, but he did not utter a word. This was not his show. The byplay lay wholly between Deirdre and Maltzer; he must not interfere. He turned his head to the window and waited.

And Maltzer for a moment seemed shaken in his conviction.

"You . . . you *are* an actress," he admitted slowly. "But I . . . I'm not convinced I'm wrong. I think—" He paused. The querulous note was in his voice again, and he seemed racked once more by the old doubts and dismay. Then Harris saw him stiffen. He saw the resolution come back, and understood why it had come. Maltzer had gone too far already upon the cold and lonely path he had chosen to turn back, even for stronger evidence than this. He had reached his conclusions only after mental turmoil too terrible to face again. Safety and peace lay in the course he had steeled himself to follow. He was too tired, too exhausted by months of conflict, to retrace his path and begin all over. Harris could see him groping for a way out, and in a moment he saw him find it.

"That was a trick," he said hollowly. "Maybe you could play it on a larger audience, too. Maybe you have more tricks to use. I might be wrong. But, Deirdre"—his voice grew urgent—"you haven't answered the one thing I've got to know. You can't answer it. You *do* feel—dismay. You've learned your own inadequacy, however well you can hide it from us—even from us. I *know*. Can you deny that, Deirdre?"

She was not laughing now. She let her arms fall, and the flexible golden body seemed to droop a little all over, as if the brain that a moment before had been sending out strong, sure waves of confidence had slackened its power, and the intangible muscles of her limbs slackened with it. Some of the glowing humanity began to fade. It receded within her and was gone, as if the fire in the furnace of her body were sinking and cooling.

"Maltzer," she said uncertainly, "I can't answer that—yet. I can't—"

And then, while they waited in anxiety for her to finish the sentence, she *blazed*. She ceased to be a figure in stasis —she *blazed*.

It was something no eyes could watch and translate into terms the brain could follow; her motion was too swift. Maltzer in the window was a whole long room-length away. He had thought himself safe at such a distance, knowing no normal human being could reach him before he moved. But Deirdre was neither normal nor human.

In the same instant she stood drooping by the mirror she was simultaneously at Maltzer's side. Her motion negated time and destroyed space. And as a glowing cigarette tip in the dark describes closed circles before the eyes when the holder moves it swiftly, so Deirdre blazed in one continuous flash of golden motion across the room.

But curiously, she was not blurred. Harris, watching, felt his mind go blank again, but less in surprise than because no normal eyes and brain could perceive what it was he looked at.

(In that moment of intolerable suspense his complex human brain paused suddenly, annihilating time in its own way, and withdrew to a cool corner of its own to analyze in a flashing second what it was he had just seen. The brain could do it timelessly; words are slow. But he knew he had watched a sort of tesseract of human motion, a parable of fourth-dimensional activity. A one-dimensional point, moved through space, creates a two-dimensional line, which in motion creates a three-dimensional cube. Theoretically the cube, in motion, would produce a fourth-dimensional figure. No human creature had ever seen a figure of three dimensions moved through space and time before—until this moment. She had not blurred; every motion she made was distinct, but not like moving figures on a strip of film. Not like anything that those who use our language had ever seen before, or created words to express. The mind saw, but without perceiving. Neither words nor thoughts could resolve what happened into terms for human brains. And perhaps she had not actually and literally moved through the fourth dimension. Perhaps—since Harris was able to see her—it had been almost and not quite that unimaginable thing. But it was close enough.)

While to the slow mind's eye she was still standing at the far end of the room, she was already at Maltzer's side, her long, flexible fingers gentle but very firm upon his arms. She waited—

The room shimmered. There was sudden violent heat beating upon Harris' face. Then the air steadied again and Deirdre was saying softly, in a mournful whisper:

"I'm sorry—I had to do it. I'm sorry—I didn't mean you to know—"

Time caught up with Harris. He saw it overtake Maltzer too, saw the man jerk convulsively away from the grasping hands, in a ludicrously futile effort to forestall what had already happened. Even thought was slow, compared with Deirdre's swiftness.

The sharp outward jerk was strong. It was strong enough to break the grasp of human hands and catapult Maltzer out and down into the swimming gulfs of New York. The mind leaped ahead to a logical conclusion and saw him twisting and turning and diminishing with dreadful rapidity to a tiny point of darkness that dropped away through sunlight toward the shadows near the earth. The mind even conjured up a shrill, thin cry that plummeted away with the falling body and hung behind it in the shaken air.

But the mind was reckoning on human factors.

Very gently and smoothly Deirdre lifted Maltzer from the window sill and with effortless ease carried him well back into the safety of the room. She set him down before a sofa and her golden fingers unwrapped themselves from his arms slowly, so that he could regain control of his own body before she released him.

He sank to the sofa without a word. Nobody spoke for an unmeasurable length of time. Harris could not. Deirdre waited patiently. It was Maltzer who regained speech first, and it came back on the old track, as if his mind had not yet relinquished the rut it had worn so deep.

"All right," he said breathlessly. "All right, you can stop me this time. But I know, you see. I know! You can't hide your feeling from me, Deirdre. I know the trouble you feel. And next time—next time I won't wait to talk!"

Deirdre made the sound of a sigh. She had no lungs to expel the breath she was imitating, but it was hard to realize that. It was hard to understand why she was not panting heavily from the terrible exertion of the past minutes; the mind knew why, but could not accept the reason. She was still too human.

"You still don't see," she said. "Think, Maltzer, think!"

There was a hassock beside the sofa. She sank upon it gracefully, clasping her robed knees. Her head tilted back to watch Maltzer's face. She saw only stunned stupidity on it now; he had passed through too much emotional storm to think at all.

"All right," she told him. "Listen—I'll admit it. You're right. I *am* unhappy. I do know what you said was true— but not for the reason you think. Humanity and I are far apart, and drawing farther. The gap will be hard to bridge. Do you hear me, Maltzer?"

Harris saw the tremendous effort that went into Maltzer's wakening. He saw the man pull his mind back into focus and sit up on the sofa with weary stiffness.

"You . . . you do admit it, then?" he asked in a bewildered voice.

Deirdre shook her head sharply.

"Do you still think of me as delicate?" she demanded. "Do you know I carried you here at arm's length halfway across the room? Do you realize you weigh *nothing* to me? I could"—she glanced around the room and gestured with sudden, rather appalling violence—"tear this building down," she said quietly. "I could tear my way through these walls, I think. I've found no limit yet to the strength I can put forth if I try." She held up her golden hands and looked at them. "The metal would break, perhaps," she said reflectively, "but then, I have no feeling—"

Maltzer gasped, "*Deirdre*—"

She looked up with what must have been a smile. It sounded clearly in her voice. "Oh, I won't. I wouldn't have to do it with my hands, if I wanted. Look—listen!"

She put her head back and a deep, vibrating hum gathered and grew in what one still thought of as her throat. It deepened swiftly and the ears began to ring. It was deeper, and the furniture vibrated. The walls began almost imperceptibly to shake. The room was full and bursting with a sound that shook every atom upon its neighbor with a terrible, disrupting force.

The sound ceased. The humming died. Then Deirdre laughed and made another and quite differently pitched sound. It seemed to reach out like an arm in one straight direction—toward the window. The opened panel shook. Deirdre intensified her hum, and slowly, with imperceptible jolts that merged into smoothness, the window jarred itself shut.

"You see?" Deirdre said. "You see?"

But still Maltzer could only stare. Harris was staring too, his mind beginning slowly to accept what she implied. Both were too stunned to leap ahead to any conclusions yet.

Deirdre rose impatiently and began to pace again, in a ringing of metal robe and a twinkling of reflected lights. She was pantherlike in her suppleness. They could see the power behind that lithe motion now; they no longer thought of her as helpless, but they were far still from grasping the truth.

"You were wrong about me, Maltzer," she said with an effort at patience in her voice. "But you were right too, in a way you didn't guess. I'm not afraid of humanity. I haven't anything to fear from them. Why"—her voice took on a tinge of contempt—"already I've set a fashion in women's clothing. By next week you won't see a woman on the street without a mask like mine, and every dress that isn't cut like a chlamys will be out of style. I'm not afraid of humanity! I won't lose touch with them unless I want to. I've learned a lot—I've learned too much already."

Her voice faded for a moment, and Harris had a quick and appalling vision of her experimenting in the solitude of her farm, testing the range of her voice, testing her eyesight—could she see microscopically and telescopically?—and was her hearing as abnormally flexible as her voice?

"You were afraid I had lost feeling and scent and taste," she went on, still pacing with that powerful, tigerish tread. "Hearing and sight would not be enough, you think? But why do you think sight is the last of the senses? It may be the latest, Maltzer—Harris—*but why do you think it's the last?*"

She may not have whispered that. Perhaps it was only their hearing that made it seem thin and distant, as the brain contracted and would not let the thought come through in its stunning entirety.

"No," Deirdre said, "I haven't lost contact with the human race. I never will, unless I want to. It's too easy . . . too easy."

She was watching her shining feet as she paced, and her masked face was averted. Sorrow sounded in her soft voice now.

"I didn't mean to let you know," she said. "I never would have, if this hadn't happened. But I couldn't let you go believing you'd failed. You made a perfect machine, Maltzer. More perfect than you knew."

"But, Deirdre—" breathed Maltzer, his eyes fascinated and still incredulous upon her, "but, Deirdre, if we did succeed—what's wrong? I can feel it now—I've felt it all along. You're so unhappy—you still are. Why, Deirdre?"

She lifted her head and looked at him, eyelessly, but with a piercing stare.

"Why are you so sure of that?" she asked gently.

"You think I could be mistaken, knowing you as I do? But I'm not Frankenstein . . . you say my creation's flawless. Then what—"

"Could you ever duplicate this body?" she asked.

Maltzer glanced down at his shaking hands. "I don't know. I doubt it. I—"

"Could anyone else?"

He was silent. Deirdre answered for him. "I don't believe anyone could. I think I was an accident. A sort of mutation halfway between flesh and metal. Something accidental and . . . and unnatural, turning off on a wrong course of evolution that never reaches a dead end. Another brain in a body like this might die or go mad, as you thought I would. The synapses are too delicate. You were— call it lucky—with me. From what I know now, I don't think a . . . a baroque like me could happen again." She paused a moment. "What you did was kindle the fire for the Phoenix, in a way. And the Phoenix rises perfect and renewed from its own ashes. Do you remember why it had to reproduce itself that way?"

Maltzer shook his head.

"I'll tell you," she said. "It was because there was only one Phoenix. Only one in the whole world."

They looked at each other in silence. Then Deirdre shrugged a little.

"He always came out of the fire perfect, of course. I'm not weak, Maltzer. You needn't let that thought bother you any more. I'm not vulnerable and helpless. I'm not subhuman." She laughed dryly. "I suppose," she said, "that I'm— superhuman."

"But—not happy."

"I'm afraid. It isn't unhappiness, Maltzer—it's fear. I don't want to draw so far away from the human race. I wish I needn't. That's why I'm going back on the stage—to keep in touch with them while I can. But I wish there could be others like me. I'm . . . I'm lonely, Maltzer."

Silence again. Then Maltzer said, in a voice as distant as when he had spoken to them through glass, over gulfs as deep as oblivion: "Then I am Frankenstein, after all."

"Perhaps you are," Deirdre said very softly. "I don't know. Perhaps you are."

She turned away and moved smoothly, powerfully, down the room to the window. Now that Harris knew, he could almost hear the sheer power purring along her limbs as she walked. She leaned the golden forehead against the glass—it clinked faintly, with a musical sound—and looked down into the depths Maltzer had hung above. Her voice was reflective as she looked into those dizzy spaces which had offered oblivion to her creator.

"There's one limit I can think of," she said, almost inaudibly. "Only one. My brain will wear out in another forty years or so. Between now and then I'll learn . . . I'll change . . . I'll know more than I can guess today. I'll change—That's frightening. I don't like to think about that." She laid a curved golden hand on the latch and pushed the window open a little, very easily. Wind whined around its edge. "I could put a stop to it now, if I wanted," she said. "If I wanted. But I can't, really. There's so much still untried. My brain's human, and no human brain could leave such possibilities untested. I wonder, though . . . I do wonder—"

Her voice was soft and familiar in Harris' ears, the voice Deirdre had spoken and sung with, sweetly enough to enchant a world. But as preoccupation came over her a certain flatness crept into the sound. When she was not listening to her own voice, it did not keep quite to the pitch of trueness. It sounded as if she spoke in a room of brass, and echoes from the walls resounded in the tones that spoke there.

"I wonder," she repeated, the distant taint of metal already in her voice.

Camouflage

Henry Kuttner

Henry Kuttner and C. L. Moore were a famous writing team in science fiction until Kuttner's sudden death in 1958. Yet each was well known and very successful individually. The positive outlook toward cyborgs in both of their stories in this volume makes for an interesting comparison with the views of other writers.

Talman was sweating by the time he reached 16 Knobhill Road. He had to force himself to touch the annunciator plate. There was a low whirring as photoelectrics checked and okayed his fingerprints; then the door opened and Talman walked into the dim hallway. He glanced behind him to where, beyond the hills, the spaceport's lights made a pulsating, wan nimbus.

Then he went on, down a ramp, into a comfortably furnished room where a fat, gray-haired man was sitting in an easy chair, fingering a highball glass. Tension was in Talman's voice as he said, "Hello, Brown. Everything all right?"

A grin stretched Brown's sagging cheeks. "Sure," he said. "Why not? The police weren't after you, were they?"

Talman sat down and began mixing himself a drink from the server nearby. His thin, sensitive face was shadowed.

"You can't argue with your glands. Space does that to me anyway. All the way from Venus I kept expecting somebody to walk up to me and say, 'You're wanted for questioning.' "

"Nobody did."

"I didn't know what I'd find here."

"The police didn't expect us to head for Earth," Brown said, rumpling his gray hair with a shapeless paw. "And that was your idea."

"Yeah. Consulting psychologist to—"

"—to criminals. Want to step out?"

"No," Talman said frankly, "not with the profits we've got in sight already. This thing's big."

Brown grinned. "Sure it is. Nobody ever organized crime before, in just this way. There wasn't any crime worth a row of pins until we started."

"Where are we now, though? On the run."

"Fern's found a foolproof hideout."

"Where?"

"In the Asteroid Belt. We need one thing, though."

"What's that?"

"An atomic power plant."

Talman looked startled. But he saw that Brown wasn't kidding. After a moment, he put down his glass and scowled.

"I'd say it's impossible. A power plant's too big."

"Yeah," Brown said, "except that this one's going by space to Callisto."

"Hijacking? We haven't enough men—"

"The ship's under Transplant-control."

Talman cocked his head to one side. "Uh. That's out of my line—"

"There'll be a skeleton crew, of course. But we'll take care of them—and take their places. Then it'll simply be a matter of unhitching the Transplant and rigging up manuals. It isn't out of your line at all. Fern and Cunningham can do the technical stuff, but we've got to find out first just how dangerous a Transplant can be."

"I'm no engineer."

Brown went on, ignoring the comment. "The Transplant who's handling this Callisto shipment used to be Bart Quentin. You knew him, didn't you?"

Talman, startled, nodded. "Sure. Years ago. Before—"

"You're in the clear, as far as the police are concerned. Go to see Quentin. Pump him. Find out . . . Cunningham will tell you what to find out. After that, we can go ahead. I hope."

"I don't know. I'm not—"

Brown's brows came down. *"We've got to find a hide-*

out! That's absolutely vital right now. Otherwise, we might as well walk into the nearest police station and hold out our hands for cuffs. We've been clever, but now—we've *got* to hide. Fast!"

"Well . . . I get that. But do you know what a Transplant really is?"

"A free brain. One that can use artificial gadgets."

"Technically, yeah. Ever seen a Transplant working a power-digger? Or a Venusian sea-dredge? Enormously complicated controls it'd normally take a dozen men to handle?"

"Implying a Transplant's a superman?"

"No," Talman said slowly, "I don't mean that. But I've got an idea it'd be safer to tangle with a dozen men than with one Transplant."

"Well," Brown said, "go up to Quebec and see Quentin. He's there now, I found out. Talk to Cunningham first. We'll work out the details. What we've got to know are Quentin's powers and his vulnerable points. And whether or not he's telepathic. You're an old friend of Quentin, and you're a psychologist, so you're the guy for the job."

"Yeah."

"We've got to get that power plant. *We've got to hide, now!*"

Talman thought that Brown had probably planned this from the beginning. The fat man was shrewd enough; he'd been sufficiently clever to realize that ordinary criminals would stand no chance in a highly technical, carefully specialized world. Police forces could call on the sciences to aid them. Communication was excellent and fast, even between the planets. There were gadgets—The only chance of bringing off a successful crime was to do it fast and then make an almost instantaneous get-away.

But the crime had to be planned. When competing against an organized social unit, as any crook does, it's wise to create a similar unit. A blackjack has no chance against a rifle. A strong-arm bandit was doomed to quick failure, for a similar reason. The traces he left would be analyzed; chemistry, psychology, and criminology would track him down; he'd be made to confess. Made to, without any third-degree methods. So—

So Cunningham was an electronics engineer. Fern was an astrophysicist. Talman himself was a psychologist. Big, blond Dalquist was a hunter, by choice and profession, beautifully integrated and tremendously fast with a gun. Cotton was a mathematician—and Brown himself was the coordinator. For three months the combination had worked successfully on Venus. Then, inevitably, the net closed, and the unit filtered back to Earth, ready to take the next step in the long-range plan. What it was Talman hadn't known till now. But he could readily see its logical necessity.

In the vast wilderness of the Asteroid Belt they could hide forever, if necessary, emerging to pull off a coup whenever opportunity offered. Safe, they could build up an underground criminal organization, with a spy-system flung broadcast among the planets—yes, it was the inevitable way. Just the same, he felt hesitant about matching wits with Bart Quentin. The man wasn't—human—any more—

He was worried on the way to Quebec. Cosmopolitan though he was, he couldn't help anticipating tension, embarrassment, when he saw Quent. To pretend to ignore that— accident—would be too obvious. Still—He remembered that, seven years ago, Quentin had possessed a fine, muscular physique, and had been proud of his skill as a dancer. As for Linda, he wondered what had happened on that score. She couldn't still be Mrs. Bart Quentin, under the circumstances. Or could she?

He watched the St. Lawrence, a dull silver bar, below the plane as it slanted down. Robot pilots—a narrow beam.

Only during violent storms did standard pilots take over. In space it was a different matter. And there were other jobs, enormously complicated, that only human brains could handle. A very special type of brain, at that.

A brain like Quentin's.

Talman rubbed his narrow jaw and smiled wanly, trying to locate the source of his worry. Then he had the answer. Did Quent, in this new incarnation, possess more than five senses? Could he detect reactions a normal man could not appreciate? If so, Van Talman was definitely sunk.

He glanced at his seatmate, Dan Summers of Wyoming Engineers, through whom he had made the contact with Quentin. Summers, a blond young man with sun-wrinkles around his eyes, grinned casually.

"Nervous?"

"Could be that," Talman said. "I was wondering how much he'll have changed."

"Results are different in every case."

The plane, beam-controlled, slid down the slopes of sunset air toward the port. Quebec's lighted towers made an irregular backdrop.

"They do change, then?"

"I suppose, psychically, they've got to. You're a psychologist, Mr. Talman. How'd you feel, if—"

"There might be compensations."

Summers laughed. "That's an understatement. Compensations . . . why, immortality's only one such . . . compensation!"

"You consider that a blessing?" Talman asked.

"Yes, I do. He'll remain at the peak of his powers for God knows how long. There'll be no deterioration. Fatigue poisons are automatically eliminated by irradiation. Brain cells can't replace themselves, of course, the way . . . say . . . muscular tissue can; but Quent's brain can't be injured, in its specially built case. Arteriosclerosis isn't any problem, with the plasmic solution we use—no calcium's deposited on the artery walls. The physical condition of his brain is automatically and perfectly controlled. The only ailments Quent can ever get are mental."

"Claustrophobia? No. You say he's got eye lenses. There'd be an automatic feeling of extension."

Summers said, "If you notice any change—outside of the perfectly normal one of mental growth in seven years— I'll be interested. With me—well, I grew up with the Transplants. I'm no more conscious of their mechanical, interchangeable bodies than a physician would think of a friend as a bundle of nerves and veins. It's the reasoning faculty that counts, and that hasn't altered."

Talman said thoughtfully, "You're a sort of physician, to the Transplants, anyway. A layman might get another sort of reaction. Especially if he were used to seeing . . . a face."

"I'm never conscious of that lack."

"Is Quent?"

Summers hesitated. "No," he said finally, "I'm sure he isn't. He's beautifully adjusted. The reconditioning to Transplant life takes about a year. After that it's all velvet."

"I've seen Transplants working, on Venus, from a distance. But there aren't many spotted away from Earth."

"We haven't enough trained technicians. It takes literally half a lifetime to train a man to handle Transplantation. A man has to be a qualified electronic engineer before he even starts." Summers laughed. "The insurance companies cover a lot of the initial expense, though."

Talman was puzzled. "How's that?"

"They underwrite. Occupational risk, immortality. Working in atomic research is dangerous, my friend!"

They emerged from the plane into the cool night air. Talman said, as they walked toward a waiting car, "We grew up together, Quentin and I. But his accident happened two years after I left Earth, and I never saw him since."

"As a Transplant? Uh-huh. Well, it's an unfortunate name. Some jackass tagged the label on, whereas propaganda experts should have worked it out. Unfortunately it stuck. Eventually we hope to popularize the—Transplants. Not yet. We're only starting. We've only two hundred and thirty of·them so far, the successful ones."

"Many failures?"

"Not now. In the early days—It's *complicated*. From the first trephining to the final energizing and reconditioning, it's the most nerve-racking, brain-straining, difficult technical task the human mind's ever worked out. Reconciling a colloid mechanism with an electronic hookup—but the result's worth it."

"Technologically. I wonder about the human values."

"Psychologically? We–ell . . . Quentin will tell you about that angle. And technologically you don't know the half of it. No colloid machine, like the brain, has ever been developed—till now. And this isn't purely mechanical. It's merely a miracle, the synthesis of intelligent living tissue with delicate, responsive machinery."

"But handicapped by the limitation of the machine—and the brain."

"You'll see. Here we are. We're dining with Quent—"

Talman stared. "*Dining?*"

"Yeah." Summers' eyes showed quizzical amusement. "No, he doesn't eat steel shavings. In fact—"

The shock of meeting Linda again took Talman by surprise. He had not expected to see her. Not now, under these altered conditions. But she hadn't changed much; she was still the same warm, friendly woman he remembered, a little older now, yet very lovely and very gracious. She had always had charm. She was slim and tall, her head crowned by a bizarre coiffure of honey-amber coils, her brown eyes without the strain Talman might have expected.

He took her hands. "Don't say it," he said. "I know how long it's been."

"We won't count the years, Van." She laughed up at him. "We'll pick up right where we left off. With a drink, eh?"

"I could use one," Summers said, "but I've got to report back to headquarters. I'll just see Quent for a minute. Where is he?"

"In there." Linda nodded toward a door and turned back to Talman. "So you've been on Venus? You look bleached enough. Tell me how it's been."

"All right." He took the shaker from her hands and swirled the Martinis carefully. He felt embarrassment. Linda lifted an eyebrow.

"Yes, we're still married, Bart and I. You're surprised."

"A little."

"He's still Bart," she said quietly. "He may not look it, but he's the man I married, all right. So you can relax, Van."

He poured the Martinis. Without looking at her, he said, "As long as you're satisfied—"

"I know what you're thinking. That it'd be like having a machine for a husband. At first . . . well, I got over that feeling. We both did, after a while. There was constraint; I suppose you'll feel it when you see him. Only that isn't important, really. He's—Bart." She pushed a third glass toward Talman, and he looked at it in surprise.

"Not—"

She nodded.

The three of them dined together. Talman watched the two-foot-by-two cylinder resting on the table opposite him and tried to read personality and intelligence into the double lenses. He couldn't help imagining Linda as a priestess, serving some sort of alien god-image, and the concept was disturbing. Now Linda was forking chilled, sauce-daubed shrimps into the metallic compartment and spooning them out when the amplifier signaled.

Talman had expected a flat, toneless voice, but the sonovox gave depth and timbre whenever Quentin spoke.

"Those shrimps are perfectly usable, Van. It's only habit that makes us throw chow out after I've had it in my food-box. I taste the stuff, all right—but I haven't any salivary juices."

"You—taste 'em."

Quentin laughed a little. "Look, Van. Don't try to pretend this seems natural to you. You'll have to get used to it."

"It took me a long time," Linda said. "But after a while I found myself thinking it was just the sort of silly thing Bart always used to do. Remember the time you put on that suit of armor for the Chicago board meeting?"

"Well, I made my point," Quentin said. "I forget what it was now, but—we were talking about taste. I can taste these shrimps, Van. Certain nuances are lacking, yeah. Very delicate sensations are lost on me. But there's more to it than sweet and sour, salt and bitter. Machines could taste years ago."

"There's no digestion—"

"And there's no pylorospasm. What I lose in refinements of taste I make up for in freedom from gastrointestinal disorders."

"You don't burp any more, either," Linda said. "Thank God."

"I can talk with my mouth full, too," Quentin said. "But I'm not the super-machine-bodied-brain you're subconsciously thinking I am, chum. I don't spit death rays."

Talman grinned uneasily. "Was I thinking that?"

"I'll bet you were. But—" The timbre of the voice changed. "I'm not super. I'm plenty human, inside, and don't think I don't miss the old days sometimes. Lying on the beach and feeling the sun on my skin, little things like that. Dancing in rhythm to music, and—"

"Darling," Linda said.

The voice changed again. "Yeah. It's the small, trivial factors that make up a complete life. But I've got substitutes now—parallel factors. Reactions quite impossible to describe, because they're . . . let's say . . . electronic vibrations instead of the familiar neural ones. I *do* have senses, but through mechanical organs. When impulses reach my brain, they're automatically translated into familiar symbols. Or—" He hesitated. "Not so much now, though."

Linda laid a bit of planked fish in the food-compartment. "Delusions of grandeur, eh?"

"Delusions of alteration—but no delusion, my love. You see, Van, when I first turned into a Transplant, I had no standard of comparison except the arbitrary one I already knew. That was suited to a human body—only. When, later, I felt an impulse from a digger gadget, I'd automatically feel as if I had my foot on a car accelerator. Now those old symbols are fading. I . . . feel . . . more directly now, without translating the impulses into the old-time images."

"That would be faster," Talman said.

"It is. I don't have to think of the value of pi when I get a pi signal. I don't have to break down the equation. I'm beginning to sense what the equation means."

"Synthesis with a machine?"

"Yet I'm no robot. It doesn't affect the identity, the personal essence of Bart Quentin." There was a brief silence, and Talman saw Linda look sharply toward the cylinder. Then Quentin continued in the same tone. "I get a tremendous bang out of solving problems. I always did. And now it's not just on paper. I carry out the whole task myself, from conception to finish. I dope out the application, and . . . Van, I *am* the machine!"

"Machine?" Talman said.

"Ever noticed, when you're driving or piloting, how you identify yourself with the machine? It's an extension of you. I go one step farther. And it's satisfying. Suppose you could carry empathy to the limit and *be* one of your patients while you were solving his problem? It's an—ecstasy."

Talman watched Linda pour sauterne into a separate chamber. "Do you ever get drunk any more?" he asked.

Linda gurgled. "Not on liquor—but Bart gets high, all right!"

"How?"

"Figure it out," Quentin said, a little smugly.

"Alcohol's absorbed into the bloodstream, thence reaching the brain—the equivalent of intravenous shots, maybe?"

"I'd rather put cobra venom in my circulatory system," the Transplant said. "My metabolic balance is too delicate, too perfectly organized, too upset by introducing foreign substances. No, I use electrical stimulus—an induced high-frequency current that gets me high as a kite."

Talman stared. "And that's a substitute?"

"It is. Smoking and drinking are irritants, Van. So's thinking, for that matter! When I feel the psychic need for a binge, I've a gadget that provides stimulating irritation—and I'll bet you'd get more of a bang out of it than you would out of a quart of mescal."

"He quotes Housman," Linda said. "And does animal imitations. With his tonal control, Bart's a wonder." She stood up. "If you'll excuse me for a bit, I've got some K.P. Automatic as the kitchen is, there are still buttons to push."

"Can I help?" Talman offered.

"Thanks, no. Stay here with Bart. Want me to hitch up your arms, darling?"

"Nope," Quentin said. "Van can take care of my liquid diet. Step it up, Linda—Summers said I've got to get back on the job soon."

"The ship's ready?"

"Almost."

Linda paused in the doorway, biting her lips. "I'll never get used to your handling a spaceship all by yourself. Especially that thing."

"It may be jury-rigged, but it'll get to Callisto."

"Well . . . there's a skeleton crew, isn't there?"

"There is," Quentin said, "but it isn't needed. The insurance companies demand an emergency crew. Summers did a good job, rigging the ship in six weeks."

"With chewing gum and paper clips," Linda remarked. "I only hope it holds." She went out as Quentin laughed softly. There was a silence. Then, as never before, Talman felt that his companion was . . . was . . . had changed. For he felt Quentin gazing at him, and—Quentin wasn't there.

"Brandy, Van," the voice said. "Pour a little in my box."

Talman started to obey, but Quentin checked him. "Not out of the bottle. It's been a long time since I mixed rum and coke in my mouth. Use the inhaler. That's it. Now. Have a drink yourself and tell me how you feel."

"About—?"

"Don't you know?"

Talman went to the window and stood looking down at the reflected fluorescent shining in the St. Lawrence. "Seven years, Quent. It's hard to get used to you in this—form."

"I haven't lost anything."

"Not even Linda," Talman said. "You're lucky."

Quentin said steadily, "She stuck with me. The accident, five years ago, wrecked me. I was fooling around with atomic research, and there were chances that had to be taken. I was mangled, butchered, in the explosion. Don't think Linda and I hadn't planned in advance. We knew the occupational risk."

"And yet you——"

"We figured the marriage could last, even if—But afterward I almost insisted on a divorce. She convinced me we could still make a go of it. And we have."

Talman nodded. "I'd say so."

"That . . . kept . . . me going, for quite a while," Quentin said softly. "You know how I felt about Linda. It's always been just about a perfect equation. Even though the factors have changed, we've adjusted." Suddenly Quentin's laugh made the psychologist swing around. "I'm no monster, Van. Try and get over that idea!"

"I never thought that," Talman protested. "You're—"

"What?"

Silence again. Quentin grunted.

"In five years I've learned to notice how people react to me. Give me some more brandy. I still imagine I taste it with my palate. Odd how associations hang on."

Talman poured liquor from the inhaler. "So you figure you haven't changed, except physically."

"And you figure me as a raw brain in a metal cylinder. Not as the guy you used to get drunk with on Third Avenue. Oh, I've changed—sure. But it's a normal change. There's nothing innately alien about limbs that are metal extensions. It's one step beyond driving a car. If I were the sort of supergadget you subconsciously think I am, I'd be an utter introvert and spend my time working out cosmic equations." Quentin used a vulgar expletive. "And if I did that, I'd go nuts. Because I'm no superman. I'm an ordinary guy, a good physicist, and I've had to adjust to a new body. Which, of course, has its handicaps."

"What, for example?"

"The senses. Or the lack of them. I helped develop a lot of compensatory apparatus. I read escapist fiction, I get drunk by electrical irritation, I taste even if I can't eat. I watch teleshows. I try to get the equivalent of all the purely human sensory pleasures I can. It makes a balance that's very necessary."

"It would be. Does it work, though?"

"Look. I've got eyes that are delicately sensitive to shades and gradations of color. I've got arm attachments that can be refined down until they can handle microscopic apparatus. I can draw pictures—and, under a pseudonym, I'm a pretty popular cartoonist. I do that as a sideline. My real job is still physics. And it's still a good job. You know

the feeling of pure pleasure you get when you've worked out
a problem, in geometry or electronics or psychology—or
anything? Now I work out questions infinitely more complicated, requiring split-second reaction as well as calculation.
Like handling a spaceship. More brandy. It's volatile stuff in
a hot room."

"You're still Bart Quentin," Talman said, "but I feel
surer of that when I keep my eyes shut. Handling a spaceship—"

"I've lost nothing human," Quentin insisted. "The emotional basics haven't changed. It . . . isn't really pleasant
to have you come in and look at me with plain horror, but I
can understand the reason. We've been friends for a long
time, Van. You may forget that before I do."

Sweat was suddenly cold on Talman's stomach. But despite Quentin's words, he felt certain by now that he had
part of the answer for which he had come to Quebec. The
Transplant had no abnormal powers—there were no telepathic functions.

There were more questions to be asked, of course.

He poured more brandy and smiled at the dully-shining
cylinder across the table. He could hear Linda singing softly
from the kitchen.

The spaceship had no name, for two reasons. One was
that she would make only a single trip, to Callisto; the other
was odder. She was not, essentially, a ship with a cargo. She
was a cargo with a ship.

Atomic power plants are not ordinary dynamos that can
be dismantled and crated on a freight car. They are tremendously big, powerful, bulky, and behemothic. It takes two
years to complete an atomic setup, and even after that the
initial energizing must take place on Earth, at the enormous
standards control plant that covers seven counties of Pennsylvania. The Department of Weights, Measures, and Power
has a chunk of metal in a thermostatically-controlled glass

case in Washington; it's the standard meter. Similarly, in Pennsylvania, there is, under fantastic precautionary conditions, the one key atomic-disrupter in the Solar System.

There was only one requirement for fuel; it was best to filter it through a wire screen with, approximately, a one-inch gauge. And that was an arbitrary matter, for convenience in setting up a standard of fuels. For the rest, atomic power ate anything.

Few people played with atomic power; the stuff's violent. The research engineers worked on a stagger system. Even so, only the immortality insurance—the Transplantidae—kept neuroses from developing into psychoses.

The Callisto-bound power plant was too big to be loaded on the largest ship of any commercial line, but it had to get to Callisto. So the technicians built a ship around the power plant. It was not exactly jury-rigged, but it was definitely unstandardized. It occasionally, in matters of design, departed wildly from the norm. The special requirements were met deftly, often unorthodoxly, as they came up. Since the complete control would be in the hands of the Transplant Quentin, only casual accommodations were provided for the comfort of the small emergency crew. They weren't intended to wander through the entire ship unless a breakdown made it necessary, and a breakdown was nearly impossible. In fact, the vessel was practically a living entity. But not quite.

The Transplant had extensions—tools—throughout various sections of the great craft. Yet they were specialized to deal with the job in hand. There were no sensory attachments, except auditory and ocular. Quentin was, for the nonce, simply a super spaceship drive control. The brain cylinder was carried into the craft by Summers, who inserted it—somewhere!—plugged it in, and that finished the construction job.

* * *

At 2400 the mobile power plant took off for Callisto.

A third of the way to the Martian orbit, six spacesuited men came into an enormous chamber that was a technician's nightmare.

From a wall amplifier, Quentin's voice said, "What are you doing here, Van?"

"Okay," Brown said. "This is it. We'll work fast now. Cunningham, locate the connection. Dalquist, keep your gun ready."

"What'll I look for?" the big blond man asked.

Brown glanced at Talman. "You're certain there's no mobility?"

"I'm certain," Talman said, his eyes moving. He felt naked exposed to Quentin's gaze, and didn't like it.

Cunningham, gaunt, wrinkled and scowling, said, "The only mobility's in the drive itself. I was sure of that before Talman double-checked. When a Transplant's plugged in for one job, it's limited to the tools it needs for that job."

"Well, don't waste time talking. Break the circuit."

Cunningham stared through his vision plate. "Wait a minute. This isn't standardized equipment. It's experimental . . . casual. I've got to trace a few . . . um."

Talman was surreptitiously trying to spot the Transplant's eye lenses, and failing. From somewhere in that maze of tubes, coils, wires, grids and engineering hash, he knew, Quentin was looking at him. From several places, undoubtedly—there'd be overall vision, with eyes spotted strategically around the room.

And it was a big room, this central control chamber. The light was misty yellow. It was like some strange, unearthly cathedral in its empty, towering height, a hugeness that dwarfed the six men. Bare grids, abnormally large, hummed and sparked; great vacuum tubes flamed eerily. Around the walls above their heads ran a metal platform, twenty feet up, a metal guard rail casually precautionary. It was reached by two ladders, on opposite walls of the room. Overhead hung a celestial globe, and the dim throbbing of tremendous power murmured in the chlorinated atmosphere.

The amplifier said, "What is this, piracy?"

Brown said casually, "Call it that. And relax. You won't be harmed. We may even send you back to Earth, when we can figure out a safe way to do it."

Cunningham was investigating lucite mesh, taking care to touch nothing. Quentin said, "This cargo isn't worth hijacking. It isn't radium I'm carrying, you know."

"I need a power plant," Brown remarked curtly.

"How did you get aboard?"

Brown lifted a hand to mop sweat from his face, and then, grimacing, refrained. "Find anything yet, Cunningham?"

"Give me time. I'm only an electronics man. This setup's screwy. Fern, give me a hand here."

Talman's discomfort was growing. He realized that Quentin, after the first surprised comment, had ignored him. Some indefinable compulsion made him tilt back his head and say Quentin's name.

"Yeah," Quentin said. "Well? So you're in with this gang?"

"Yes."

"And you were pumping me, up in Quebec. To make sure I was harmless."

Talman made his voice expressionless. "We had to be certain."

"I see. How'd you get aboard? The radar automatically dodges approaching masses. You couldn't have brought your own ship alongside in space."

"We didn't. We got rid of the emergency crew and took their suits."

"Got rid of them?"

Talman moved his eyes toward Brown. "What else could we do? We can't afford half measures in a gamble as big as this. Later on, they'd have been a danger to us, after our plans started moving. Nobody's going to know anything about it except us. And you." Again Talman looked at Brown. "I think, Quent, you'd better throw in with us."

The amplifier ignored whatever implied threat lay in the suggestion.

"What do you want the power plant for?"

"We've got an asteroid picked out," Talman said, tilting his head back to search the great crowded hollow of the ship, swimming a little in the haze of its poisonous atmosphere. He half expected Brown to cut him short, but the fat man didn't speak. It was, he thought, curiously difficult to talk persuasively to someone whose location you didn't know. "The only trouble is, it's airless. With the plant, we can manufacture our own air. It'd be a miracle if anybody ever found us in the Asteroid Belt."

"And then what? Piracy?"

Talman did not answer. The voicebox said thoughtfully, "It might make a good racket, at that. For a while, anyhow. Long enough to clean up quite a lot. Nobody will expect anything like it. Yeah, you might get away with the idea."

"Well," Talman said, "if you think that, what's the next logical step?"

"Not what you think. I wouldn't play along with you. Not for moral reasons, especially, but for motives of self-preservation. I'd be useless to you. Only in a highly intricate, widespread civilization is there any need for Transplants. I'd be excess baggage."

"If I gave you my word——"

"You're not the big shot," Quentin told him. Talman instinctively sent another questioning look at Brown. And from the voicebox on the wall came a curious sound like a smothered laugh.

"All right," Talman said, shrugging. "Naturally you won't decide in our favor right away. Think it over. Remember you're not Bart Quentin any more—you've got certain mechanical handicaps. While we haven't got too much time, we can spare a little—say ten minutes—while Cun-

ningham looks things over. Then . . . well, we aren't playing for marbles, Quent." His lips thinned. "If you'll throw
in with us and guide the ship under our orders, we can
afford to let you live. But you've got to make up your mind
fast. Cunningham is going to trace you down and take over
the controls. After that——"

"What makes you so sure I can be traced down?" Quentin asked calmly. "I know just how much my life would be
worth once I'd landed you where you want to go. You don't
need me. You couldn't give me the right maintenance even
if you wanted to. No, I'd simply join the crewmen you've
disposed of. I'll give you an ultimatum of my own."

"You'll—what?"

"Keep quiet and don't monkey with anything, and I'll
land in an isolated part of Callisto and let you all escape,"
Quentin said. "If you don't, God help you."

For the first time Brown showed he had been conscious
of that distant voice. He turned to Talman.

"Bluff?"

Talman nodded slowly. "Must be. He's harmless."

"Bluff," Cunningham said, without looking up from his
task.

"No," the amplifier told him quietly, "I'm not bluffing.
And be careful with that board. It's part of the atomic
hookup. If you fool with the wrong connections, you're apt
to blast us all out of space."

Cunningham jerked back from the maze of wires snak-
ing out of the bakelite before him. Fern, some distance
away, turned a swarthy face to watch. "Easy," he said.
"We've got to be sure what we're doing."

"Shut up," Cunningham grunted. "I *do* know. Maybe
that's what the Transplant's afraid of. I'll be plenty careful
to stay clear of atomic connections, but——" He paused to
study the tangled wires. "No. This isn't atomic—I think.
Not the control leads, anyway. Suppose I break this connection——" His gloved hand came up with a rubber-sheathed
cutter.

The voicebox said, "Cunningham—don't." Cunningham poised the cutter. The amplifier sighed.

"You first, then. Here it is!"

Talman felt the transparent faceplate slap painfully against his nose. The immense room bucked dizzily as he went reeling forward, unable to check himself. All around him he saw grotesque spacesuited figures reeling and stumbling. Brown lost his balance and fell heavily.

Cunningham had been slammed forward into the wires as the ship abruptly decelerated. Now he hung like a trapped fly in the tangle, his limbs, his head, his whole body jerking and twitching with spasmodic violence. The devil's dance increased in fury.

"Get him out of there!" Dalquist yelled.

"Hold it!" Fern shouted. "I'll cut the power——" But he didn't know how. Talman, dry-throated, watched Cunningham's body sprawling, arching, shaking in spastic agony. Bones cracked suddenly.

Cunningham jerked more limply now, his head flopping grotesquely.

"Get him down," Brown snapped, but Fern shook his head.

"Cunningham's dead. And that hookup's dangerous."

"How? Dead?"

Under his thin mustache Fern's lips parted in a humorless smile. "A guy in an epileptic fit can break his own neck."

"Yeah," Dalquist said, obviously shaken. "His neck's broken, all right. Look at the way his head goes."

"Put a twenty-cycle alternating current through yourself and you'd go into convulsions too," Fern advised.

"We can't just leave him there!"

"We can," Brown said, scowling. "Stay away from the walls, all of you." He glared at Talman. "Why didn't you——"

"Sure, I know. But Cunningham should have had sense enough to stay away from bare wires."

"Few wires are insulated around here," the fat man growled. "You said the Transplant was harmless."

"I said he had no mobility. And that he wasn't a telepath." Talman realized that his voice sounded defensive.

Fern said, "A signal's supposed to sound whenever the ship accelerates or decelerates. It didn't go off that time. The Transplant must have cut it out himself, so we wouldn't be warned."

They looked up into that humming, vast, yellow emptiness. Claustrophobia gripped Talman. The walls looked ready to topple in—to fold down, as though he stood in the cupped hand of a titan.

"We can smash his eye cells," Brown suggested.

"Find 'em." Fern indicated the maze of equipment.

"All we have to do is unhitch the Transplant. Break his connection. Then he goes dead."

"Unfortunately," Fern said, "Cunningham was the only electronic engineer among us. I'm only an astrophysicist!"

"Never mind. We pull one plug and the Transplant blacks out. You can do that much!"

Anger flared. But Cotton, a little man with blinking blue eyes, broke the tension.

"Mathematics—geometry—ought to help us. We want to locate the Transplant, and——" He glanced up and was frozen. "We're off our course!" he said finally, licking dry lips. "See that telltale?"

Far above, Talman could see the enormous celestial globe. On its dark surface a point of red light was clearly marked.

Fern's swarthy face showed a sneer. "Sure. The Transplant's running to cover. Earth's the nearest place where he can get help. But we've plenty of time left. I'm not the technician Cunningham was, but I'm not a complete dope." He didn't look at the rhythmically-moving body on the wires. "We don't have to test every connection in the ship."

"Okay, take it, then," Brown grunted.

Awkward in his suit, Fern walked to a square opening in

the floor and peered down at a mesh-metal grating eighty feet below. "Right. Here's the fuel feed. We don't need to trace connections through the whole ship. The fuel's dumped out of that leader tube overhead there. Now look. Everything connected with the atomic power is apparently marked with red wax crayon. See?"

They saw. Here and there, on bare plates and boards, were cryptic red markings. Other symbols were in blue, green, black and white.

"Go on that assumption," Fern said. "Temporarily, anyhow. Red's atomic power. Blue . . . green . . . um."

Talman said suddenly, "I don't see anything here that looks like Quentin's brain case."

"Did you expect to?" the astrophysicist asked sardonically. "It's slid into a padded socket somewhere. The brain can stand more gravs than the body, but seven's about tops in any case. Which, incidentally, is fine for us. There'd be no use putting high-speed potential in this ship. The Transplant couldn't stand it, any more than we could."

"Seven G's," Brown said thoughtfully.

"Which would black out the Transplant too. He'll have to remain conscious to pilot the ship through Earth atmosphere. We've got plenty of time."

"We're going pretty slow now," Dalquist put in.

Fern gave the celestial globe a sharp glance. "Looks like it. Let me work on this." He paid out a coil from his belt and hitched himself to one of the central pillars. "That'll guard against any more accidents."

"Tracing a circuit shouldn't be so hard," Brown said.

"Ordinarily it isn't. But you've got everything in this chamber—atomic control, radar, the kitchen sink. And these labels are only for construction convenience. There wasn't any blueprint to this ship. It's a single-shot model. I can find the Transplant, but it'll take time. So shut up and let me work."

Brown scowled but didn't say anything. Cotton's bald head was sweating. Dalquist wrapped his arm about a metal pillar and waited. Talman looked up again at the balcony that hung from the walls. The celestial globe showed a crawling disk of red light.

"Quent," he said.

"Yes, Van." Quentin's voice was quietly distant. Brown put one hand casually to the blaster at his belt.

"Why don't you give up?"

"Why don't you?"

"You can't fight us. Your getting Cunningham was a fluke. We're on guard now—you can't hurt us. It's only a matter of time until we trace you down. Don't look for mercy then, Quent. You can save us trouble by telling us where you are. We're willing to pay for that. After we find you—on our own initiative—you can't bargain. How about it?"

Quentin said simply, "No."

There was silence for a few minutes. Talman was watching Fern, who, very cautiously paying out his coil, was investigating the tangle where Cunningham's body still hung.

Quentin said, "He won't find the answer there. I'm pretty well camouflaged."

"But helpless," Talman said quickly.

"So are you. Ask Fern. If he monkeys with the wrong connections, he's apt to destroy the ship. Look at your own problem. We're heading back toward Earth. I'm swinging into a new course that'll end at the home berth. If you give up now——"

Brown said, "The old statutes never were altered. The punishment for piracy is death."

"There's been no piracy for a hundred years. If an actual case came to trial, it might be a different matter."

"Imprisonment? Reconditioning?" Talman asked. "I'd a lot rather be dead."

"We're decelerating," Dalquist called, getting a firmer grip on his pillar.

Looking at Brown, Talman thought the fat man knew what he had in mind. If technical knowledge failed, psy-

chology might not. And Quentin, after all, was a human
brain.

First get the subject off guard.

"Quent."

But Quentin didn't answer. Brown grimaced and turned
to watch Fern. Sweat was pouring down the physicist's
swarthy face as he concentrated on the hookups, drawing
diagrams on the stylopad he wore attached to his forearm.

After a while Talman began to feel dizzy. He shook his
head, realizing that the ship had decelerated almost to zero,
and got a firmer grip on the nearest pillar. Fern cursed. He
was having a difficult time keeping his footing.

Presently he lost it altogether as the ship went free. Five
spacesuited figures clung to convenient handgrips. Fern
snarled, "This may be deadlock, but it doesn't help the
Transplant. I can't work without gravity—he can't get to
Earth without acceleration."

The voicebox said, "I've sent out an S.O.S."

Fern laughed. "I worked that out with Cunningham—
and you talked too much to Talman, too. With a radar
meteor-avoider, you don't need signaling apparatus, and you
haven't got it." He eyed the apparatus he had just left.
"Maybe I was getting too close to the right answer, though,
eh? Is that why——"

"You weren't even near it," Quentin said.

"Just the same——" Fern kicked himself away from the
pillar, paying out the line behind him. He made a loop
about his left wrist, and, hanging in midair, fell to studying
the hookup.

Brown lost his grip on the slippery column and floated
free like some overinflated balloon. Talman kicked himself
across to the railed balcony. He caught the metal bar in
gloved hands, swung himself in like an acrobat, and looked
down—though it wasn't really *down*—at the control
chamber.

"I think you'd better give up," Quentin said.

Brown was floating across to join Fern. "Never," he said, and simultaneously four G's hit the ship with the impact of a pile driver. It wasn't forward acceleration. It was in another, foreplanned direction. Fern saved himself at the cost of an almost dislocated wrist—but the looped line rescued him from a fatal dive into uninsulated wiring.

Talman was slammed down on the balcony. He could see the others plummet to hard impacts on unyielding surfaces. Brown wasn't stopped by the floor plate, though.

He had been hovering over the fuel-feed hole when the acceleration was slammed on.

Talman saw the bulky body pop out of sight down the opening. There was an indescribable sound.

Dalquist, Fern, and Cotton struggled to their feet. They cautiously went toward the hole and peered down.

Talman called, "Is he——"

Cotton had turned away. Dalquist remained where he was, apparently fascinated, Talman thought, until he saw the man's shoulders heaving. Fern looked up toward the balcony.

"He went through the filter screen," he said. "It's a one-inch gauge metal mesh."

"Broke through?"

"No," Fern said deliberately. "He didn't break through. He *went* through."

Four gravities and a fall of eighty feet add up to something slightly terrific. Talman shut his eyes and said, "Quent!"

"Do you give up?"

Fern snarled, "Not on your life! Our unit's not that interdependent. We can do without Brown."

Talman sat on the balcony, held on to the rail, and let his feet hang down into emptiness. He stared across to the celestial globe, forty feet to his left. The red spot that marked the ship stood motionless.

"I don't think you're human any more, Quent," he said.

"Because I don't use a blaster? I've different weapons to fight with now. I'm not kidding myself, Van. I'm fighting for my life."

"We could still bargain."

Quentin said, "I told you you'd forget our friendship before I did. You must have known this hijacking could only end in my death. But apparently you didn't care about that."

"I didn't expect you to——"

"Yeah," the voicebox said. "I wonder if you'd have been as ready to go through with the plan if I'd still had human form? As for friendship—use your own tricks of psychology, Van. You look on my mechanical body as an enemy, a barrier between you and the real Bart Quentin. Subconsciously, maybe, you hate it, and you're therefore willing to destroy it. Even though you'll be destroying me with it. I don't know—perhaps you rationalize that you'd thus be rescuing me from the thing that's erected the barrier. And you forget that I haven't changed, basically."

"We used to play chess together," Talman said, "but we didn't smash the pawns."

"I'm in check," Quentin countered. "All I've got to fight with are knights. You've still got castles and bishops. You can move straight for your goal. Do you give up?"

"No!" Talman snapped. His eyes were on the red light. He saw a tremor move it, and gripped the metal rail with a frantic clutch. His body swung out as the ship jumped. One gloved hand was torn from its grip. But the other held. The celestial globe was swinging violently. Talman threw a leg over the rail, clambered back to his precarious perch, and looked down.

Fern was still braced by his emergency line. Dalquist and little Cotton were sliding across the floor, to bring up with a crash against a pillar. Someone screamed.

Sweating, Talman warily descended. But by the time he had reached Cotton the man was dead. Radiating cracks in his faceplate and contorted, discolored features gave the answer.

"He slammed right into me," Dalquist gulped. "His plate cracked into the back of my helmet—"

The chlorinated atmosphere within the sealed ship had ended Cotton's life, not easily, but rapidly. Dalquist, Fern and Talman matched glances.

The blond giant said, "Three of us left. I don't like this. I don't like it at all."

Fern showed his teeth. "So we're still underestimating that thing. From now on, hitch yourselves to pillars. Don't move without sound anchorage. Stay clear of everything that might cause trouble."

"We're still heading back toward Earth," Talman said.

"Yeah." Fern nodded. "We could open a port and walk out into free space. But then what? We figured we'd be using this ship. Now we've *got* to."

Dalquist said, "If we gave up——"

"Execution," Fern said flatly. "We've still got time. I've traced some of the connections. I've eliminated a lot of hookups."

"Still think you can do it?"

"I think so. But don't let go of your handgrips for a second. I'll find the answer before we hit atmosphere."

Talman had a suggestion. "Brains send out recognizable vibration patterns. A directional finder, maybe?"

"If we were in the middle of the Mojave, that would work. Not here. This ship's lousy with currents and radiations. How could we unscramble them without apparatus?"

"We brought some apparatus with us. And there's plenty all around the walls."

"Hooked up. I'm going to be plenty careful about upsetting the *status quo*. I wish Cunningham hadn't gone down the drain."

"Quentin's no fool," Talman said. "He got the electronic engineer first and Brown second. He was trying for you then, too. Bishop and queen."

"Which makes me what?"

"Castle. He'll get you if he can." Talman frowned, trying to remember something. Then he had it. He bent over the stylopad on Fern's arm, shielding the writing with his own body from any photoelectrics that might be spotted around the walls or ceiling. He wrote: "He gets drunk on high frequency. Can do?"

Fern crumpled the tissue slip and tore it awkwardly into fragments with his gloved fingers. He winked at Talman and nodded briefly.

"Well, I'll keep trying," he said, and paid out his line to the kit of apparatus he and Cunningham had brought aboard.

Left alone, Dalquist and Talman hitched themselves to pillars and waited. There was nothing else they could do. Talman had already mentioned this high-frequency irritation angle to Fern and Cunningham; they had seen no value to the knowledge then. Now it might be the answer, with applied practical psychology to supplement technology.

Meanwhile, Talman longed for a cigarette. All he could do, sweating in the uncomfortable suit, was to manipulate a built-in gadget so that he managed to swallow a salt tablet and a few gulps of tepid water. His heart was pounding, and there was a dull ache in his temples. The spacesuit was uncomfortable; he wasn't used to such personal confinement.

Through the built-in receiving gadget he could hear the humming silence, broken by the padding rustle of sheathed boots as Fern moved about. Talman blinked at the chaos of equipment and closed his eyes; the relentless yellow light, not intended for human vision, made little pulses beat nervously somewhere in his eye sockets. Somewhere in this ship, he thought, probably in this very chamber, was Quentin. But camouflaged. How?

Purloined letter stuff? Scarcely. Quentin would have had no reason to expect hijackers. It was pure accident that had intervened to protect the Transplant with such an excellent hiding place. That, and the slapdash methods of technicians, constructing a one-job piece of equipment with the casual convenience of a slipstick.

But, Talman thought, if Quentin could be made to reveal his location——

How? Via induced cerebral irritation—intoxication?

Appeal to basics? But a brain couldn't propagate the species. Self-preservation remained the only constant. Talman wished he'd brought Linda along. He'd have had a lever then.

If only Quentin had had a human body, the answer would not be so difficult to find. And not necessarily by torture. Automatic muscular reactions, the old stand-by of professional magicians, could have led Talman to his goal. Unfortunately, Quentin himself was the goal—a bodiless brain in a padded, insulated metal cylinder. And his spinal cord was a wire.

If Fern could rig up a high-frequency device, the radiations would weaken Quentin's defenses—in one way, if not another. At present the Transplant was a very, very dangerous opponent. And he was perfectly camouflaged.

Well, not perfectly. Definitely no. Because, Talman realized with a sudden glow of excitement, Quentin wasn't simply sitting back, ignoring the pirates, and taking the quickest route back to Earth. The very fact that he was retracing his course instead of going on to Callisto indicated that Quentin wanted to get help. And, meanwhile, via murder, he was doing his utmost to distract his unwelcome guests.

Because, obviously, Quentin *could* be found.

Given time.

Cunningham could have done it. And even Fern was a menace to the Transplant. That meant that Quentin—was afraid.

Talman sucked in his breath. "Quent," he said, "I've a proposition. You listening?"

"Yes," the distant, terribly familiar voice said.

"I've an answer for all of us. You want to stay alive. We want this ship. Right?"

"Correct."

"Suppose we drop you by parachute when we hit Earth atmosphere. Then we can take over the controls and head out again. That way——"

"And Brutus is an honorable man," Quentin remarked. "But of course he wasn't. I can't trust you any more, Van. Psychopaths and criminals are too amoral. They're ruthless, because they feel the end justifies the means. You're a psychopathic psychologist, Van, and that's exactly why I'd never take your word for anything."

"You're taking a long chance. If we do find the right hookup in time, there'll be no bargaining, you know."

"If."

"It's a long way back to Earth. We're taking precautions now. You can't kill any more of us. We'll simply keep working steadily till we find you. Now—what about it?"

After a pause Quentin said, "I'd rather take my chances. I know technological values better than I do human ones. As long as I depend on my own field of knowledge, I'm safer than if I tried to deal in psychology. I know coefficients and cosines, but I don't know much about the colloid machine in your skull."

Talman lowered his head; sweat dripped from his nose to the interior of the faceplate. He felt a sudden claustrophobia; fear of the cramped quarters of the suit, and fear of the larger dungeon that was the room and the ship itself.

"You're restricted, Quent," he said, too loudly. "You're limited in your weapons. You can't adjust atmospheric pressure in here, or you'd have compressed already and crushed us."

"Crushing vital equipment at the same time. Besides, those suits can take a lot of pressure."

"Your king's still in check."

"So is yours," Quentin said calmly.

Fern gave Talman a slow look that held approval and faint triumph. Under the clumsy gloves, manipulating delicate instruments, the hookup was beginning to take shape. Luckily, it was a job of conversion rather than construction, or time would have been too short.

"Enjoy yourself," Quentin said. "I'm slamming on all the G's we can take."

"I don't feel it," Talman said.

"All we can take, not all I could give out. Go ahead and amuse yourselves. You can't win."

"No?"

"Well—figure it out. As long as you stay hitched in one place, you're reasonably safe. But if you start moving around, I can destroy you."

"Which means we'll have to move—somewhere—in order to reach you, eh?"

Quentin laughed. "I didn't say so. I'm well camouflaged. *Turn that thing off!*"

The shout echoed and re-echoed against the vaulted roof, shaking the amber air. Talman jerked nervously. He met Fern's eye and saw the astrophysicist grin.

"It's hitting him," Fern said. Then there was silence, for many minutes.

The ship abruptly jumped. But the frequency inductor was securely moored, and the men, too, were anchored by their lines.

"Turn it off," Quentin said again. His voice wasn't quite under control.

"Where are you?" Talman asked.

No answer.

"We can wait, Quent."

"Keep waiting, then! I'm . . . I'm not distracted by personal fear. That's one advantage of being a Transplant."

"High irritant value," Fern murmured. "It works fast."

"Come on, Quent," Talman said persuasively. "You've still got the instinct of self-preservation. This can't be pleasant for you?"

"It's . . . too pleasant," Quentin said unevenly. "But it won't work. I could always stand my liquor."

"This isn't liquor," Fern countered. He touched a dial.

The Transplant laughed; Talman noted with satisfaction that oral control was slipping. "It won't work, I say. I'm too . . . smart for you."

"Yeah?"

"Yeah. You're not morons—none of you are. Fern's a good technician, maybe, but he isn't good enough. Remember, Van, you asked me in Quebec if there'd been any . . . change? I said there hadn't. I'm finding out now that I was wrong."

"How?"

"Lack of distraction." Quentin was talking too much; a symptom of intoxication. "A brain in a body can never concentrate fully. It's too conscious of the body itself. Which is an imperfect mechanism. Too specialized to be efficient. Respiratory, circulatory—all the systems intrude. Even the habit of breathing's a distraction. Now the ship's my body—at the moment—but it's a perfect mechanism. It functions with absolute efficiency. So my brain's correspondingly better."

"Superman."

"Superefficient. The better mind generally wins at chess, because it can foresee the possible gambits. I can foresee everything you might do. And you're badly handicapped."

"Why?"

"You're human."

Egotism, Talman thought. Was this the Achillean heel? A taste of success had apparently done its psychological work, and the electronic equivalent of drunkenness had released inhibitions. Logical enough. After five years of routine work, no matter how novel that work might be, this suddenly altered situation—this change from active to passive, from machine to protagonist—might have been the catalyst. Ego. And cloudy thinking.

For Quentin wasn't a superbrain. Very definitely he was

not. The higher an I.Q., the less need there is for self-justification, direct or indirect. And, oddly, Talman suddenly felt absolved of any lingering compunctions. The real Bart Quentin would never have been guilty of paranoid thought patterns.

So——

Quentin's articulation was clear; there was no slurring. But he no longer spoke with soft palate, tongue and lips, by means of a column of air. Tonal control was noticeably altered now, however, and the Transplant's voice varied from a carrying whisper to almost a shout.

Talman grinned. He was feeling better, somehow.

"We're human," he said, "but we're still sober."

"Nuts. Look at the telltale. We're getting close to Earth."

"Come off it, Quent," Talman said wearily. "You're bluffing, and we both know you're bluffing. You can't stand an indefinite amount of high frequency. Save time and give up now."

"You give up," Quentin said. "I can see everything you do. The ship's a mass of traps anyway. From up here all I have to do is watch until you get close to one. I'm planning my game ahead, every gambit worked out to checkmate for one of you. You haven't got a chance. You haven't got a chance. You haven't got a chance."

From up here, Talman thought. Up where? He remembered little Cotton's remark that geometry could be used to locate the Transplant. Sure. Geometry and psychology. Halve the ship, quarter it, keep bisecting the remainders——

Not necessary. *Up* was the key word. Talman seized upon it with an eagerness that didn't show on his face. *Up*, presumably, reduced by half the area they'd have to search. The lower parts of the ship could be ruled out. Now he'd have to halve the upper section, using the celestial globe, say, as the dividing line.

The Transplant had eye cells spotted all over the ship, of course, but Talman tentatively decided that Quentin thought of himself as situated in one particular spot, not scattered over the whole ship, localized wherever an eye was built in. A man's head is his locus, to his own mind.

Thus Quentin could see the red spot on the celestial globe, but that didn't necessarily mean that he was located in a wall facing that hemisphere of the sphere. The Transplant had to be trapped into references to his actual physical relation to objects in the ship—which would be hard, because this could be done best by references to sight, the normal individual's most important link with his surroundings. And Quentin's sight was almost omnipotent. He could see everything.

There had to be a localization—somehow.

A word-association test would do it. But that implied cooperation. Quentin wasn't that drunk!

Nothing could be gauged by learning what Quentin could *see*—for his brain was not necessarily near any one of his eyes. There would be a subtle, intrinsic realization of location on the Transplant's part; the knowledge that *he*—blind, deaf, dumb except through his distant extensor sensory mechanisms—was in a certain place. And how, except by too obviously direct questioning, could Quentin be made to give the right answers?

It was impossible, Talman thought, with a hopeless sense of frustrated anger. The anger grew stronger. It brought sweat to his face, rousing him to a dull, aching hatred of Quentin. All this was Quentin's fault, the fact that Talman was prisoned here in this hateful spacesuit and this enormous deathtrap of a ship. The fault of a machine—

Suddenly he saw the way.

It would, of course, depend on how drunk Quentin was. He glanced at Fern, questioned the man with his eyes, and in response Fern manipulated a dial and nodded.

"Damn you," Quentin said in a whisper.

"Nuts," Talman said. "You implied you haven't any instinct for self-preservation any more."

"I . . . didn't——"

"It's true, isn't it?"

"No," Quentin said loudly.

"You forget I'm a psychologist, Quent. I should have seen the angles before. The book was open, ready to read, even before I saw you. When I saw Linda."

"Shut up about Linda!"

Talman had a momentary, sick vision of the drunken, tortured brain somewhere hidden in the walls, a surrealistic nightmare. "Sure," he said. "You don't want to think about her yourself."

"Shut up."

"You don't want to think about yourself, either, do you?"

"What are you trying to do, Van? Get me mad?"

"No," Talman said, "I'm simply fed up, sick and disgusted with the whole business. Pretending that you're Bart Quentin, that you're still human, that we can deal with you on equal terms."

"There'll be no dealing—"

"That's not what I meant, and you know it. I've just realized what you are." He let the words hang in the dim air. He imagined he could hear Quentin's heavy breathing, though he knew it was merely an illusion.

"Please shut up, Van," Quentin said.

"Who's asking me to shut up?"

"I am."

"And what's that?"

The ship jumped. Talman almost lost his balance. The line hitched to the pillar saved him. He laughed.

"I'd be sorry for you, Quent, if you were—you. But you're not."

"I'm not falling for any trick."

"It may be a trick, but it's the truth too. And you've wondered about it yourself. I'm dead certain of that."

"Wondered about what?"

"You're not human any more," Talman said gently. "You're a thing. A machine. A gadget. A spongy gray hunk of meat in a box. Did you really think I could get used to you—now? That I could identify you with the old Quent? You haven't any face!"

The soundbox made noises. They sounded mechanical. Then—— "Shut up," Quentin said again, almost plaintively "I know what you're trying to do."

"And you don't want to face it. Only you've got to face it, sooner or later, whether you kill us now or not. This . . . business . . . is an incident. But the thoughts in your brain will keep growing and growing. And you'll keep changing and changing. You've changed plenty already."

"You're crazy," Quentin said. "I'm no . . . monster."

"You hope, eh? Look at it logically. You haven't dared to do that, have you?" Talman held up his gloved hand and ticked off points on his sheathed fingers. "You're trying very desperately to keep your grip on something that's slipping away—humanity, the heritage you were born to. You hang on to the symbols, hoping they'll mean the reality. Why do you pretend to eat? Why do you insist on drinking brandy out of a glass? You know it might just as well be squirted into you out of an oil can."

"No. No! It's an aesthetic——"

"Garbage. You go to teleshows. You read. You pretend you're human enough to be a cartoonist. It's a desperate, hopeless clinging to something that's already gone from you, all these pretenses. Why do you feel the need for binges? You're maladjusted, because you're pretending you're still human, and you're not, any more."

"I'm . . . well, something better——"

"Maybe . . . if you'd been born a machine. But you *were* human. You had a human body. You had eyes and hair and lips. Linda must remember that, Quent.

"You should have insisted on a divorce. Look—if you'd only been crippled by the explosion, she could have taken care of you. You'd have needed her. As it is, you're a self-sufficient, self-contained unit. She does a good job of pretending. I'll admit that. She tries not to think of you as a hopped-up helicopter. A gadget. A blob of wet cellular tissue. It must be tough on her. She remembers you as you used to be."

"She loves me."

"She pities you," Talman said relentlessly.

In the humming stillness the red telltale crept across the globe. Fern's tongue stole out and circled his lips. Dalquist stood quietly watching, his eyes narrowed.

"Yeah," Talman said, "face it. And look at the future. There are compensations. You'll get quite a bang out of meshing your gears. Eventually you'll even stop remembering you ever were human. You'll be happier then. For you can't hang on to it, Quent. It's going away. You can keep on pretending for a while, but in the end it won't matter any more. You'll be satisfied to be a gadget. You'll see beauty in a machine and not in Linda. Maybe that's happened already. Maybe Linda knows it's happened. You don't have to be honest with yourself yet, you know. You're immortal. But I wouldn't take that kind of immortality as a gift."

"Van——"

"I'm still Van. But you're a machine. Go ahead and kill us, if you want, and if you can do it. Then go back to Earth and, when you see Linda again, look at her face. Look at it when she doesn't know you're watching. You can do that easily. Rig up a photoelectric cell in a lamp or something."

"Van . . . *Van!*"

Talman let his hands drop to his sides. "All right. Where are you?"

The silence grew, while an inaudible question hummed through the yellow vastness. The question, perhaps, in the mind of every Transplant. The question of—a price.

What price?

Utter loneliness, the sick knowledge that the old ties were snapping one by one, and that in place of living, warm humanity there would remain—a mental monster?

Yes, he had wondered—this Transplant who had been Bart Quentin. He had wondered, while the proud, tremendous machines that were his body stood ready to spring into vibrant life.

Am I changing? Am I still Bart Quentin?

Or do they—the humans—look on me as—— How does *Linda really feel about me now? Am I——*

Am I—It?

"Go up on the balcony," Quentin said. His voice was curiously faded and dead.

Talman made a quick gesture. Fern and Dalquist sprang to life. They climbed, each to a ladder, on opposite sides of the room, but carefully, hitching their lines to each rung.

"Where is it?" Talman asked gently.

"The south wall—Use the celestial sphere for orientation. You can reach me——" The voice failed.

"Yes?"

Silence. Fern called down, "Has he passed out?"

"Quent!"

"Yes—— About the center of the balcony. I'll tell you when you reach it."

"Easy," Fern warned Dalquist. He took a turn of his line about the balcony rail and edged forward, searching the wall with his eyes.

Talman used one arm to scrub his fogged faceplate. Sweat was trickling down his face and flanks. The crawling yellow light, the humming stillness from machines that should be roaring thunderously, stung his nerves to unendurable tension.

"Here?" Fern called.

"Where is it, Quent?" Talman asked. "Where are you?"

"Van," Quentin said, a horrible, urgent agony in his tone. "You can't mean what you've been saying. You can't. This is—I've got to know! I'm thinking of Linda!"

Talman shivered. He moistened his lips.

"You're a machine, Quent," he said steadily. "You're a gadget. You know I'd never have tried to kill you if you were still Bart Quentin."

And then, with shocking abruptness, Quentin laughed.

"Here it comes, Fern!" he shouted, and the echoes crashed and roared through the vaulted chamber. Fern clawed for the balcony rail.

That was a fatal mistake. The line hitching him to that rail proved a trap—because he didn't see the danger in time to unhook himself.

The ship jumped.

It was beautifully gauged. Fern was jerked toward the wall and halted by the line. Simultaneously the great celestial globe swung from its support, in a pendulum arc like the drive of a Gargantuan fly swatter. The impact snapped Fern's line instantly.

Vibration boomed through the walls.

Talman hung on to a pillar and kept his eyes on the globe. It swung back and forth in a diminishing arc as inertia overcame momentum. Liquid spattered and dripped from it.

He saw Dalquist's helmet appear over the rail. The man yelled, "Fern!"

There was no answer.

"Fern! Talman!"

"I'm here," Talman said.

"Where's——" Dalquist turned his head to stare at the wall. He screamed.

Obscene gibberish tumbled from his mouth. He yanked the blaster from his belt and aimed it at the maze of apparatus below.

"Dalquist!" Talman shouted. "Hold it!"

Dalquist didn't hear.

"I'll smash the ship," he screamed. "I'll——"

Talman drew his own blaster, steadied the muzzle against the pillar, and shot Dalquist in the head. He watched the body lean over the rail, topple, and crash down on the floor plates. Then he rolled over on his face and lay there, making sick, miserable sounds.

"Van," Quentin said.

Talman didn't answer.

"Van!"

"Yeah!"

"Turn off the inductor."

Talman got up, walked unsteadily to the device, and ripped wires loose. He didn't bother to search for an easier method.

After a long while the ship grounded. The humming vibration of currents died. The dim, huge control chamber seemed oddly empty now.

"I've opened a port," Quentin said. "Denver's about fifty miles north. There's a highway four miles or so in the same direction."

Talman stood up, staring around. His face looked ravaged.

"You tricked us," he mumbled. "All along, you were playing us like fish. My psychology——"

"No," Quentin said. "You almost succeeded."

"What——"

"You don't think of me as a gadget, really. You pretended to, but a little matter of semantics saved me. When I realized what you'd said, I came to my senses."

"What I said?"

"Yeah. That you'd never have tried to kill me if I'd still been Bart Quentin."

Talman was struggling slowly out of his spacesuit. Fresh, clean air had already replaced the poison atmosphere of the ship. He shook his head dazedly.

"I don't see it."

Quentin's laughter rang out, filling the chamber with its warm, human vibrancy.

"A machine can be stopped or destroyed, Van," he said. "But it can't be—*killed*."

Talman didn't say anything. He was free of the bulky suit now, and he turned hesitantly toward a doorway. He looked back.

"The door's open," Quentin said.

"You're letting me go?"

"I told you in Quebec that you'd forget our friendship before I did. Better step it up, Van, while there's still time. Denver's probably sent out helicopters already."

Talman swept one questioning look around the vast chamber. Somewhere, perfectly camouflaged among those mighty machines, was a small metal cylinder, cradled and shielded in its hidden socket. Bart Quentin——

His throat felt dry. He swallowed, opened his mouth, and closed it again.

He turned on his heel and went out. The muffled sound of his footsteps faded.

Alone in the silent ship, Bart Quentin waited for the technicians who would refit his body for the Callisto flight.

Crucifixus Etiam

Walter M. Miller, Jr.

The theme of alienation recurs again and again in cyborg stories. Here Miller has written movingly of a cyborg adapted to the Martian atmosphere who struggles to remain human, to keep open that tenuous pathway whereby he may again join the human race. His final resolution of this conflict, far from being tragic, is almost a paean to the concept of the New Humanity. There is at last an exaltation as he finds his place in the universe and takes the fatal step that removes him forever from the mainstream of the race. The reader is tempted to wonder if, rather than removing himself from that mainstream, he may not finally have joined it.

Manue Nanti joined the project to make some dough. Five dollars an hour was good pay, even in 2134 A.D., and there was no way to spend it while on the job. Everything would be furnished: housing, chow, clothing, toiletries, medicine, cigarettes, even a daily ration of one hundred eighty proof beverage alcohol, locally distilled from fermented Martian mosses as fuel for the project's vehicles. He figured that if he avoided crap games, he could finish his five-year contract with fifty thousand dollars in the bank, return to Earth, and retire at the age of twenty-four. Manue wanted to travel, to see the far corners of the world, the strange cultures, the simple people, the small towns, deserts, mountains, jungles—for until he came to Mars, he had never been farther than a hundred miles from Cerro de Pasco, his birthplace in Peru.

A great wistfulness came over him in the cold Martian night when the frost haze broke, revealing the black, gleam-stung sky, and the blue-green Earth-star of his birth. *El mundo de mi carne, de mi alma*, he thought—yet he had seen so little of it that many of its places would be more alien to him than the homogeneously ugly vistas of Mars. These he longed to see: the volcanoes of the South Pacific, the monstrous mountains of Tibet, the concrete cyclops of New York, the radioactive craters of Russia, the artificial islands in the China Sea, the Black Forest, the Ganges, the Grand Canyon—but most of all, the works of human art, the pyramids, the Gothic cathedrals of Europe, Notre Dame du Chartres, Saint Peter's, the tile-work wonders of Anacapri. But the dream was still a long labor from realization.

Manue was a big youth, heavy-boned and built for labor, clever in a simple mechanical way, and with a wistful good humor that helped him take a lot of guff from whisky-breathed foremen and sharp-eyed engineers who made ten dollars an hour and figured ways for making more, legitimately or otherwise.

He had been on Mars only a month, and it hurt. Each time he swung the heavy pick into the red-brown sod, his face winced with pain. The plastic aerator valves, surgically stitched in his chest, pulled and twisted and seemed to tear with each lurch of his body. The mechanical oxygenator served as a lung, sucking blood through an artificially grafted network of veins and plastic tubing, frothing it with air from a chemical generator, and returning it to his circulatory system. Breathing was unnecessary, except to provide wind for talking, but Manue breathed in desperate gulps of the 4.0 psi Martian air; for he had seen the wasted, atrophied chests of the men who had served four or five years, and he knew that when they returned to Earth—if ever—they would still need the auxiliary oxygenator equipment.

"If you don't stop breathing," the surgeon told him, "you'll be all right. When you go to bed at night, turn the oxy down low—so low you feel like panting. There's a critical point that's just right for sleeping. If you get it too low, you'll wake up screaming, and you'll get claustrophobia. If you get it too high, your reflex mechanisms will go to pot and you won't breathe; your lungs'll dry up after a time. Watch it."

Manue watched it carefully, although the oldsters laughed at him—in their dry wheezing chuckles. Some of them could scarcely speak more than two or three words at a shallow breath.

"Breathe deep, boy," they told him. "Enjoy it while you can. You'll forget how pretty soon. Unless you're an engineer."

* * *

The engineers had it soft, he learned. They slept in a pressurized barrack where the air was 10 psi and 25 percent oxygen, where they turned their oxies off and slept in peace. Even their oxies were self-regulating, controlling the output according to the carbon dioxide content of the input blood. But the Commission could afford no such luxuries for the labor gangs. The payload of a cargo rocket from Earth was only about 2 percent of the ship's total mass, and nothing superfluous could be carried. The ships brought the bare essentials, basic industrial equipment, big reactors, generators, engines, heavy tools.

Small tools, building materials, foods, non-nuclear fuels —these things had to be made on Mars. There was an open pit mine in the belly of the Syrtis Major where a "lake" of nearly pure iron rust was scooped into a smelter, and processed into various grades of steel for building purposes, tools, and machinery. A quarry in the Flathead Mountains dug up large quantities of cement rock, burned it, and crushed it to make concrete.

It was rumored that Mars was even preparing to grow her own labor force. An old-timer told him that the Commission had brought five hundred married couples to a new underground city in the Mare Erythraeum, supposedly as personnel for a local commission headquarters, but according to the old-timer, they were to be paid a bonus of three thousand dollars for every child born on the red planet. But Manue knew that the old "troffies" had a way of inventing such stories, and he reserved a certain amount of skepticism.

As for his own share in the Project, he knew—and needed to know—very little. The encampment was at the north end of the Mare Cimmerium, surrounded by the bleak brown and green landscape of rock and giant lichens, stretching toward sharply defined horizons except for one mountain range in the distance, and hung over by a blue sky so dark that the Earth-star occasionally became dimly visible during the dim daytime. The encampment consisted of a dozen double-walled stone huts, windowless, and roofed

with flat slabs of rock covered over by a tarry resin boiled
out of the cactuslike spineplants. The camp was ugly, lonely,
and dominated by the gaunt skeleton of a drill rig set up in
its midst.

Manue joined the excavating crew in the job of digging a
yard-wide, six-feet-deep foundation trench in a hundred-yard
square around the drill rig, which day and night was biting
deeper through the crust of Mars in a dry cut that necessi-
tated frequent stoppages for changing rotary bits. He
learned that the geologists had predicted a subterranean
pocket of tritium oxide ice at sixteen thousand feet, and that
it was for this that they were drilling. The foundation he
was helping to dig would be for a control station of some
sort.

He worked too hard to be very curious. Mars was a
nightmare, a grim, womanless, frigid, disinterestedly evil
world. His digging partner was a sloe-eyed Tibetan nick-
named "Gee" who spoke the Omnalingua clumsily at best.
He followed two paces behind Manue with a shovel, scoop-
ing up the broken ground and humming a monotonous
chant in his own tongue. Manue seldom heard his own
language, and missed it; one of the engineers, a haughty
Chilean, spoke the modern Spanish, but not to such as
Manue Nanti. Most of the other laborers used either Basic
English or the Omnalingua. He spoke both, but longed to
hear the tongue of his people. Even when he tried to talk to
Gee, the cultural gulf was so wide that satisfying communication was nearly impossible. Peruvian jokes were unfunny
to Tibetan ears, although Gee bent double with gales of
laughter when Manue nearly crushed his own foot with a
clumsy stroke of the pick.

He found no close companions. His foreman was a nar-
row-eyed, orange-browed Low German named Vögeli, usually half-drunk, and intent upon keeping his lung-power by
bellowing at his crew. A meaty, florid man, he stalked slowly
along the lip of the excavation, pausing to stare coldly down
at each pair of laborers, who if they dared to look up caught

a guttural tongue-lashing for the moment's pause. When he had words for a digger, he called a halt by kicking a small avalanche of dirt back into the trench about the man's feet.

Manue learned about Vögeli's disposition before the end of his first month. The aerator tubes had become nearly unbearable; the skin, in trying to grow fast to the plastic, was beginning to form a tight little neck where the tubes entered his flesh, and the skin stretched and burned and stung with each movement of his trunk. Suddenly he felt sick. He staggered dizzily against the side of the trench, dropped the pick, and swayed heavily, bracing himself against collapse. Shock and nausea rocked him, while Gee stared at him and giggled foolishly.

"Hoy!" Vögeli bellowed from across the pit. "Get back on that pick! Hoy, there! Get with it—"

Manue moved dizzily to recover the tool, saw patches of black swimming before him, sank weakly back to pant in shallow gasps. The nagging sting of the valves was a portable hell that he carried with him always. He fought an impulse to jerk them out of his flesh; if a valve came loose, he would bleed to death in a few minutes.

Vögeli came stamping along the heap of fresh earth and lumbered up to stand over the sagging Manue in the trench. He glared down at him for a moment, then nudged the back of his neck with a heavy boot. "Get to work!"

Manue looked up and moved his lips silently. His forehead glinted with moisture in the faint sun, although the temperature was far below freezing.

"Grab that pick and get started."

"Can't," Manue gasped. "Hoses—hurt."

Vögeli grumbled a curse and vaulted down into the trench beside him. "Unzip that jacket," he ordered.

Weakly, Manue fumbled to obey, but the foreman knocked his hand aside and jerked the zipper down. Roughly he unbuttoned the Peruvian's shirt, laying open the bare brown chest to the icy cold.

"*No!* Not the hoses, *please!*"

Vögeli took one of the thin tubes in his blunt fingers and leaned close to peer at the puffy, callused nodule of irritated skin that formed around it where it entered the flesh. He touched the nodule lightly, causing the digger to whimper.

"No, please!"

"Stop sniveling!"

Vögeli laid his thumbs against the nodule and exerted a sudden pressure. There was a slight popping sound as the skin slid back a fraction of an inch along the tube. Manue yelped and closed his eyes.

"Shut up! I know what I'm doing."

He repeated the process with the other tube. Then he seized both tubes in his hands and wiggled them slightly in and out, as if to insure a proper resetting of the skin. The digger cried weakly and slumped in a dead faint.

When he awoke he was in bed in the barracks, and a medic was painting the sore spots with a bright yellow solution that chilled his skin.

"Woke up, huh?" the medic grunted cheerfully. "How you feel?"

"*Malo!*" he hissed.

"Stay in bed for the day, son. Keep your oxy up high. Make you feel better."

The medic went away, but Vögeli lingered, smiling at him grimly from the doorway. "Don't try goofing off tomorrow too."

Manue hated the closed door with silent eyes, and listened intently until Vögeli's footsteps left the building. Then, following the medic's instructions, he turned his oxy to maximum, even though the faster flow of blood made the chest-valves ache. The sickness fled, to be replaced with a weary afterglow. Drowsiness came over him, and he slept.

Sleep was a dread black-robed phantom on Mars. Mars pressed the same incubus upon all newcomers to her soil: a nightmare of falling, falling, falling into bottomless space. It was the faint gravity, they said, that caused it. The body felt buoyed up, and the subconscious mind recalled down-going elevators and diving airplanes and a fall from a high cliff. It suggested these things in dreams, or if the dreamer's oxy were set too low, it conjured up a nightmare of sinking slowly deeper, and deeper in cold black water that filled the victim's throat. Newcomers were segregated in a separate barracks so that their nightly screams would not disturb the old-timers who had finally adjusted to Martian conditions.

But now, for the first time since his arrival, Manue slept soundly, airily, and felt borne up by beams of bright light.

When he awoke again, he lay clammy in the horrifying knowledge that he had not been breathing! It was so comfortable not to breathe. His chest stopped hurting because of the stillness of his rib-case. He felt refreshed and alive. Peaceful sleep.

Suddenly he was breathing again in harsh gasps, and cursing himself for the lapse, and praying amid quiet tears as he visualized the wasted chest of a troffie.

"*Heh-heh!*" wheezed an oldster who had come in to readjust the furnace in the rookie barracks. "You'll get to be a Martian pretty soon, boy. I been here seven years. Look at *me*."

Manue heard the gasping voice and shuddered; there was no need to look.

"You just as well not fight it. It'll get you. Give in, make it easy on yourself. Go crazy if you don't."

"Stop it! Let me alone!"

"Sure. Just one thing. You wanta go home, you think. I went home. Came back. You will, too. They all do, 'cept engineers. Know why?"

"Shut up!" Manue pulled himself erect on the cot and hissed anger at the old-timer, who was neither old nor

young, but only withered by Mars. His head suggested that
he might be around thirty-five, but his body was weak and
old.

The veteran grinned. "Sorry," he wheezed. "I'll keep my
mouth shut." He hesitated, then extended his hand. "I'm
Sam Donnell, mech-repairs."

Manue still glowered at him. Donnell shrugged and
dropped his hand.

"Just trying to be friends," he muttered and walked
away.

The digger started to call after him but only closed his
mouth again, tightly. Friends? He needed friends, but not a
troffie. He couldn't even bear to look at them, for fear he
might be looking into the mirror of his own future.

Manue climbed out of his bunk and donned his fleeceskins. Night had fallen, and the temperature was already
twenty below. A soft sift of ice-dust obscured the stars. He
stared about in the darkness. The mess hall was closed, but a
light burned in the canteen and another in the foremen's
club, where the men were playing cards and drinking. He
went to get his alcohol ration, gulped it mixed with a little
water, and trudged back to the barracks alone.

The Tibetan was in bed, staring blankly at the ceiling.
Manue sat down and gazed at his flat, empty face.

"Why did you come here, Gee?"

"Come where?"

"To Mars."

Gee grinned, revealing large, black-streaked teeth.
"Make money. Good money on Mars."

"Everybody make money, huh?"

"Sure."

"Where's the money come from?"

Gee rolled his face toward the Peruvian and frowned.
"You crazy? Money come from Earth, where all money
come from."

"And what does Earth get back from Mars?"

Gee looked puzzled for a moment, then gathered anger because he found no answer. He grunted a monosyllable in his native tongue, then rolled over and went to sleep.

Manue was not normally given to worrying about such things, but now he found himself asking, "What am I doing here?"—and then, "What is *anybody* doing here?"

The Mars Project had started eighty or ninety years ago, and its end goal was to make Mars habitable for colonists without Earth support, without oxies and insulated suits and the various gadgets a man now had to use to keep himself alive on the fourth planet. But thus far, Earth had planted without reaping. The sky was a bottomless well into which Earth poured her tools, dollars, manpower, and engineering skill. And there appeared to be no hope for the near future.

Manue felt suddenly trapped. He could not return to Earth before the end of his contract. He was trading five years of virtual enslavement for a sum of money which would buy a limited amount of freedom. But what if he lost his lungs, became a servant of the small aerator for the rest of his days? Worst of all: whose ends was he serving? The contractors were getting rich—on government contracts. Some of the engineers and foremen were getting rich—by various forms of embezzlement of government funds. But what were the people back on Earth getting for their money?

Nothing.

He lay awake for a long time, thinking about it. Then he resolved to ask someone tomorrow, someone smarter than himself.

But he found the question brushed aside. He summoned enough nerve to ask Vögeli, but the foreman told him harshly to keep working and quit wondering. He asked the structural engineer who supervised the building, but the man only laughed, and said: "What do you care? You're making good money."

They were running concrete now, laying the long strips

of Martian steel in the bottom of the trench and dumping
in great slobbering wheelbarrowfuls of gray-green mix. The
drillers were continuing their tedious dry cut deep into the
red world's crust. Twice a day they brought up a yard-long
cylindrical sample of the rock and gave it to a geologist who
weighed it, roasted it, weighed it again, and tested a sample
of the condensed steam—if any—for tritium content. Daily
he chalked up the results on a blackboard in front of the
engineering hut, and the technical staff crowded around for
a look. Manue always glanced at the figures, but failed to
understand.

Life became an endless routine of pain, fear, hard work,
and anger. There were few diversions. Sometimes a crew of
entertainers came out from the Mare Erythraeum, but the
labor gang could not all crowd in the pressurized staff-
barracks where the shows were presented, and when Manue
managed to catch a glimpse of one of the girls walking
across the clearing, she was bundled in fleeceskins and
hooded by a parka.

Itinerant rabbis, clergymen, and priests of the world's
major faiths came occasionally to the camp: Buddhist, Mos-
lem, and the Christian sects. Padre Antonio Selni made
monthly visits to hear confessions and offer Mass. Most of
the gang attended all services as a diversion from routine, as
an escape from nostalgia. Somehow it gave Manue a strange
feeling in the pit of his stomach to see the Sacrifice of the
Mass, two thousand years old, being offered in the same
ritual under the strange dark sky of Mars—with a section of
the new foundation serving as an altar upon which the priest
set crucifix, candles, relic-stone, missal, chalice, paten, ci-
borium, cruets, and all the rest. In filling the wine-cruet
before the service, Manue saw him spill a little of the red-
clear fluid upon the brown soil—wine, Earth-wine from
sunny Sicilian vineyards, trampled from the grapes by the

bare stamping feet of children. Wine, the rich red blood of Earth, soaking slowly into the crust of another planet.

Bowing low at the consecration, the unhappy Peruvian thought of the prayer a rabbi had sung the week before: "Blessed be the Lord our God, King of the Universe, Who makest bread to spring forth out of the Earth."

Earth chalice, Earth blood, Earth God, Earth worshipers—with plastic tubes in their chests and a great sickness in their hearts.

He went away saddened. There was no faith here. Faith needed familiar surroundings, the props of culture. Here there were only swinging picks and rumbling machinery and sloshing concrete and the clatter of tools and the wheezing of troffies. Why? For five dollars an hour and keep?

Manue, raised in a back-country society that was almost a folk culture, felt deep thirst for a goal. His father had been a stonemason, and he had labored lovingly to help build the new cathedral, to build houses and mansions and commercial buildings, and his blood was mingled in their mortar. He had built for the love of his community and the love of the people and their customs, and their gods. He knew his own ends, and the ends of those around him. But what sense was there in this endless scratching at the face of Mars? Did they think they could make it into a second Earth, with pine forests and lakes and snow-capped mountains and small country villages? Man was not that strong. No, if he were laboring for any cause at all, it was to build a world so unearthlike that he could not love it.

The foundation was finished. There was very little more to be done until the drillers struck pay. Manue sat around the camp and worked at breathing. It was becoming a conscious effort now, and if he stopped thinking about it for a few minutes, he found himself inspiring shallow, meaningless little sips of air that scarcely moved his diaphragm. He

kept the creator as low as possible, to make himself breathe
great gasps that hurt his chest, but it made him dizzy, and
he had to increase the oxygenation lest he faint.

Sam Donnell, the troffie mech-repairman, caught him
about to slump dizzily from his perch atop a heap of rocks,
pushed him erect, and turned his oxy back to normal. It was
late afternoon, and the drillers were about to change shifts.
Manue sat shaking his head for a moment, then gazed at
Donnell gratefully.

"That's dangerous, kid," the troffie wheezed. "Guys can
go psycho doing that. Which you rather have: sick lungs or
sick mind?"

"Neither."

"I know, but—"

"I don't want to talk about it."

Donnell stared at him with a faint smile. Then he
shrugged and sat down on the rock heap to watch the
drilling.

"Oughta be hitting the tritium ice in a couple of days,"
he said pleasantly. "Then we'll see a big blow."

Manue moistened his lips nervously. The troffies always
made him feel uneasy. He stared aside.

"Big blow?"

"Lotta pressure down there, they say. Something about
the way Mars got formed. Dust cloud hypothesis."

Manue shook his head. "I don't understand."

"I don't either. But I've heard them talk. Couple of
billions years ago, Mars was supposed to be a moon of
Jupiter. Picked up a lot of ice crystals over a rocky core.
Then it broke loose and picked up a rocky crust—from
another belt of the dust cloud. The pockets of tritium ice
catch a few neutrons from uranium ore—down under. Some
of the tritium goes into helium. Frees oxygen. Gases form
pressure. Big blow."

"What are they going to do with the ice?"

The troffie shrugged. "The engineers might know."

Manue snorted and spat. "They know how to make money."

"Hey! Sure, everybody's gettin' rich."

The Peruvian stared at him speculatively for a moment. "Señor Donnell, I—"

"Sam'll do."

"I wonder if anybody knows why . . . well . . . why we're really here."

Donnell glanced up to grin, then waggled his head. He fell thoughtful for a moment, and leaned forward to write in the earth. When he finished, he read it aloud.

"A plow plus a horse plus land equals the necessities of life." He glanced up at Manue. "Fifteen hundred A.D."

The Peruvian frowned his bewilderment. Donnell rubbed out what he had written and wrote again.

"A factory plus steam turbines plus raw materials equals necessities plus luxuries. Nineteen hundred A.D."

He rubbed it out and repeated the scribbling. "All those things plus nuclear power and computer controls equal a surplus of everything. Twenty-one hundred A.D."

"So?"

"So, it's either cut production or find an outlet. Mars is an outlet for surplus energies, manpower, money. Mars Project keeps money turning over, keeps everything turning over. Economist told me that. Said if the Project folded, surplus would pile up—big depression on Earth."

The Peruvian shook his head and sighed. It didn't sound right somehow. It sounded like an explanation somebody figured out after the whole thing started. It wasn't the kind of goal he wanted.

Two days later, the drill hit ice, and the "big blow" was only a fizzle. There was talk around the camp that the whole operation had been a waste of time. The hole spewed a frosty breath for several hours, and the drill crews crowded around to stick their faces in it and breathe great gulps of the helium oxygen mixture. But then the blow subsided, and the hole leaked only a wisp of steam.

Technicians came and lowered sonar "cameras" down to the ice. They spent a week taking internal soundings and plotting the extent of the ice-dome on their charts. They brought up samples of ice and tested them. The engineers worked late into the Martian nights.

Then it was finished. The engineers came out of their huddles and called to the foremen of the labor gangs. They led the foremen around the site, pointing here, pointing there, sketching with chalk on the foundation, explaining in solemn voices. Soon the foremen were bellowing at their crews.

"Let's get the derrick down!"

"Start that mixer going!"

"Get that steel over here!"

"Unroll that dip-wire!"

"Get a move on! Shovel that fill!"

Muscles tightened and strained, machinery clamored and rang. Voices grumbled and shouted. The operation was starting again. Without knowing why, Manue shoveled fill and stretched dip-wire and poured concrete for a big floor slab to be run across the entire hundred-yard square, broken only by the big pipe-casing that stuck up out of the ground in the center and leaked a thin trail of steam.

The drill crew moved their rig half a mile across the plain to a point specified by the geologists and began sinking another hole. A groan went up from the structural boys: "Not *another* one of these things!"

But the supervisory staff said, "No, don't worry about it."

There was much speculation about the purpose of the whole operation, and the men resented the quiet secrecy connected with the project. There could be no excuse for secrecy, they felt, in time of peace. There was a certain arbitrariness about it, a hint that the Commission thought

of its employees as children or enemies or servants. But the
supervisory staff shrugged off all questions with: "You know
there's tritium ice down there. You know it's what we've
been looking for. Why? Well—what's the difference? There
are lots of uses for it. Maybe we'll use it for one thing,
maybe for something else. Who knows?"

Such a reply might have been satisfactory for an iron
mine or an oil well or a stone quarry, but tritium suggested
hydrogen-fusion. And no transportation facilities were being
installed to haul the stuff away—no pipelines nor railroad
tracks nor glider ports.

Manue quit thinking about it. Slowly he came to adopt a
grim cynicism toward the tediousness, the back-breaking
labor of his daily work; he lived from day to day like an
animal, dreaming only of a return to Earth when his contract was up. But the dream was painful because it was
distant, as contrasted with the immediacies of Mars: the
threat of atrophy, coupled with the discomforts of continued
breathing, the nightmares, the barrenness of the landscape,
the intense cold, the harshness of men's tempers, the hard-
ship of labor, and the lack of a cause.

A warm, sunny Earth was still over four years distant,
and tomorrow would be another back-breaking, throat-
parching, heart-tormenting, chest-hurting day. Where was
there even a little pleasure in it? It was so easy, at least, to
leave the oxy turned up at night and get a pleasant restful
sleep. Sleep was the only recourse from harshness, and fear
robbed sleep of its quiet sensuality—unless a man just surrendered and quit worrying about his lungs.

Manue decided that it would be safe to give himself two
completely restful nights a week.

Concrete was run over the great square and troweled to a
rough finish. A glider train from the Mare Erythraeum
brought in several huge crates of machinery, cut-stone
masonry for building a wall, a shipful of new personnel, and
a real rarity: lumber, cut from the first Earth-trees to be
grown on Mars.

A building began going up, with the concrete square for foundation and floor. Structures could be flimsier on Mars; because of the light gravity, compression stresses were smaller. Hence, the work progressed rapidly, and as the flat-roofed structure was completed, the technicians began un-crating new machinery and moving it into the building. Manue noticed that several of the units were computers. There was also a small steam-turbine generator driven by an atomic-fired boiler.

Months passed. The building grew into an integrated mass of power and control systems. Instead of using the well for pumping, the technicians were apparently going to lower something into it. A bomb-shaped cylinder was slung verti-cally over the hole. The men guided it into the mouth of the pipe-casing, then let it down slowly from a massive cable. The cylinder's butt was a multicontact socket like the fe-male receptacle for a hundred-pin electron tube. Hours passed while the cylinder slipped slowly down beneath the hide of Mars. When it was done, the men hauled out the cable and began lowering stiff sections of pre-wired conduit, fitted with a receptacle at one end and a male plug at the other, so that as the sections fell into place, a continuous bundle of control cables was built up from "bomb" to surface.

Several weeks were spent in connecting circuits, setting up the computers, and making careful tests. The drillers had finished the second well hole, half a mile from the first, and Manue noticed that while the testing was going on, the engineers sometimes stood atop the building and stared anx-iously toward the steel skeleton in the distance. Once while the tests were being conducted, the second hole began squirting a jet of steam high in the thin air, and a frantic voice bellowed from the roof top.

"Cut it! Shut it off! Sound the danger whistle!"

The jet of steam began to shriek a low-pitched whine

across the Martian desert. It blended with the rising and falling OOOO-*awwww* of the danger siren. But gradually it subsided as the men in the control station shut down the machinery. All hands came up cursing from their hiding places, and the engineers stalked out to the new hole carrying Geiger counters. They came back wearing pleased grins.

The work was nearly finished. The men began crating up the excavating machinery and the drill rig and the tools. The control-building devices were entirely automatic, and the camp would be deserted when the station began operation. The men were disgruntled. They had spent a year of hard labor on what they had thought to be a tritium well, but now that it was done, there were no facilities for pumping the stuff or hauling it away. In fact, they had pumped various solutions *into* the ground through the second hole, and the control station shaft was fitted with pipes that led from lead-lined tanks down into the earth.

Manue had stopped trying to keep his oxy properly adjusted at night. Turned up to a comfortable level, it was like a drug, insuring comfortable sleep—and·like addict or alcoholic, he could no longer endure living without it. Sleep was too precious, his only comfort. Every morning he awoke with a still, motionless chest, felt frightening remorse, sat up gasping, choking, sucking at the thin air with whining, rattling lungs that had been idle too long. Sometimes he coughed violently and bled a little. And then for a night or two he would correctly adjust the oxy, only to wake up screaming and suffocating. He felt hope sliding grimly away.

He sought out Sam Donnell, explained the situation, and begged the troffie for helpful advice. But the mech-repairman neither helped nor consoled nor joked about it. He only bit his lip, muttered something noncommittal, and found an excuse to hurry away. It was then that Manue knew his hope was gone. Tissue was withering, tubercules forming, tubes growing closed. He knelt abjectly beside his cot, hung his face in his hands, and cursed softly, for there was no other way to pray an unanswerable prayer.

A glider train came in from the north to haul away the disassembled tools. The men lounged around the barracks or wandered across the Martian desert, gathering strange bits of rock and fossils, searching idly for a glint of metal or crystal in the wan sunshine of early fall. The lichens were growing brown and yellow, and the landscape took on the hues of Earth's autumn if not the forms.

There was a sense of expectancy around the camp. It could be felt in the nervous laughter, and the easy voices, talking suddenly of Earth and old friends and the smell of food in a farm kitchen, and old half-forgotten tastes for which men hungered: ham searing in the skillet, a cup of frothing cider from a fermenting crock, iced melon with honey and a bit of lemon, onion gravy on homemade bread. But someone always remarked, "What's the matter with you guys? We ain't going home. Not by a long shot. We're going to another place just like this."

And the group would break up and wander away, eyes tired, eyes haunted with nostalgia.

"What're we waiting for?" men shouted at the supervisory staff. "Get some transportation in here. Let's get rolling."

Men watched the skies for glider trains or jet transports, but the skies remained empty, and the staff remained close-mouthed. Then a dust column appeared on the horizon to the north, and a day later a convoy of tractor-trucks pulled into camp.

"Start loading aboard, men!" was the crisp command.

Surly voices: "You mean we don't go by air? We gotta ride those kidney-bouncers? It'll take a week to get to Mare Ery! Our contract says—"

"Load aboard! We're not going to Mare Ery yet!"

Grumbling, they loaded their baggage and their weary bodies into the trucks, and the trucks thundered and clattered across the desert, rolling toward the mountains.

* * *

The convoy rolled for three days toward the mountains, stopping at night to make camp, and driving on at sunrise. When they reached the first slopes of the foothills, the convoy stopped again. The deserted encampment lay a hundred and fifty miles behind. The going had been slow over the roadless desert.

"Everybody out!" barked the messenger from the lead truck. "Bail out! Assemble at the foot of the hill."

Voices were growling among themselves as the men moved in small groups from the trucks and collected in a milling tide in a shallow basin, overlooked by a low cliff and a hill. Manue saw the staff climb out of a cab and slowly work their way up the cliff. They carried a public address system.

"Gonna get a preaching," somebody snarled.

"Sit down, please!" barked the loudspeaker. "You men sit down there! Quiet—quiet, please!"

The gathering fell into a sulky silence. Will Kinley stood looking out over them, his eyes nervous, his hand holding the mike close to his mouth so that they could hear his weak troffie voice.

"If you men have questions," he said, "I'll answer them now. Do you want to know what you've been doing during the past year?"

An affirmative rumble arose from the group.

"You've been helping to give Mars a breathable atmosphere." He glanced briefly at his watch, then looked back at his audience. "In fifty minutes, a controlled chain reaction will start in tritium ice. The computers will time it and try to control it. Helium and oxygen will come blasting up out of the second hole."

A rumble of disbelief arose from his audience. Someone shouted: "How can you get air to blanket a planet from one hole?"

"You can't," Kinley replied crisply. "A dozen others are going in, just like that one. We plan three hundred, and we've already located the ice pockets. Three hundred wells, working for eight centuries, can get the job done."

"Eight centuries! What good—"

"Wait!" Kinley barked. "In the meantime, we'll build pressurized cities close to the wells. If everything pans out, we'll get a lot of colonists here, and gradually condition them to live in a seven or eight psi atmosphere—which is about the best we can hope to get. Colonists from the Andes and the Himalayas—they wouldn't need much conditioning."

"*What about us?*"

There was a long plaintive silence. Kinley's eyes scanned the group sadly, and wandered toward the Martian horizon, gold and brown in the late afternoon. "Nothing—about us," he muttered quietly.

"Why did we come out here?"

"Because there's danger of the reaction getting out of hand. We can't tell anyone about it, or we'd start a panic." He looked at the group sadly. "I'm telling you now, because there's nothing you could do. In thirty minutes—"

There were angry murmurs in the crowd. "You mean there may be an explosion?"

"There *will* be a limited explosion. And there's very little danger of anything more. The worst danger is in having ugly rumors start in the cities. Some fool with a slip-stick would hear about it, and calculate what would happen to Mars if five cubic miles of tritium ice detonated in one split second. It would probably start a riot. That's why we've kept it a secret."

The buzz of voices was like a disturbed beehive. Manue Nanti sat in the midst of it, saying nothing, wearing a dazed and weary face, thoughts jumbled, soul drained of feeling.

Why should men lose their lungs that after eight centuries of tomorrows other men might breathe the air of Mars as the air of Earth?

Other men around him echoed his thoughts in jealous

mutterings. They had been helping to make a world in which they would never live.

An enraged scream arose near where Manue sat. "They're going to blow us up! They're going to blow up Mars."

"Don't be a fool!" Kinley snapped.

"Fools, they call us! We *are* fools! For ever coming here! We got sucked in! Look at *me!*" A pale dark-haired man came wildly to his feet and tapped his chest. "Look! I'm losing my lungs! We're all losing our lungs! Now they take a chance on killing everybody."

"Including ourselves," Kinley called coldly.

"We oughta take him apart. We oughta kill every one who knew about it—and Kinley's a good place to start!"

The rumble of voices rose higher, calling both agreement and dissent. Some of Kinley's staff were looking nervously toward the trucks. They were unarmed.

"You men sit down!" Kinley barked.

Rebellious eyes glared at the supervisor. Several men who had come to their feet dropped to their haunches again. Kinley glowered at the pale upriser who called for his scalp. "Sit down, Handell!"

Handell turned his back on the supervisor and called out to the others. "Don't be a bunch of cowards! Don't let him bully you!"

"You men sitting around Handell. Pull him down."

There was no response. The men, including Manue, stared up at the wild-eyed Handell gloomily, but made no move to quiet him. A pair of burly foremen started through the gathering from its outskirts.

"Stop!" Kinley ordered. "Turpin, Schultz—get back. Let the men handle this themselves."

Half a dozen others had joined the rebellious Handell. They were speaking in low tense tones among themselves.

"For the last time, men! Sit down!"

The group turned and started grimly toward the cliff.

Without reasoning why, Manue slid to his feet quietly as
Handell came near him. "Come on, fellow, let's get him,"
the leader muttered.

The Peruvian's fist chopped a short stroke to Handell's
jaw, and the dull *thud* echoed across the clearing. The man
crumpled, and Manue crouched over him like a hissing
panther. "Get back!" he snapped at the others. "Or I'll jerk
his hoses out."

One of the others cursed him.

"Want to fight, fellow?" the Peruvian wheezed. "I can
jerk several hoses out before you drop me!"

They shuffled nervously for a moment.

"The guy's crazy!" one complained in a high voice.

"Get back or he'll kill Handell!"

They sidled away, moved aimlessly in the crowd, then
sat and gazed at the thinly smiling Kinley.

"Thank you, son. There's a fool in every crowd." He
looked at his watch again. "Just a few minutes, men. Then
you'll feel the Earth-tremor, and the explosion, and the
wind. You can be proud of that wind, men. It's new air for
Mars, and you made it."

"But we can't breathe it!" hissed a troffie.

Kinley was silent for a long time, as if listening to the
distance. "What man ever made his own salvation?" he
murmured.

They packed up the public address amplifier and came
down the hill to sit in the cab of a truck, waiting.

It came as an orange glow in the south, and the glow
was quickly shrouded by an expanding white cloud. Then,
minutes later the ground pulsed beneath them, quivered and
shook. The quake subsided, but remained as a hint of vibration. Then after a long time, they heard the dull-throated
roar thundering across the Martian desert. The roar continued steadily, grumbling and growling as it would do for
several hundred years.

There was only a hushed murmur of awed voices from the crowd. When the wind came, some of them stood up and moved quietly back to the trucks, for now they could go back to a city for reassignment. There were other tasks to accomplish before their contracts were done.

But Manue Nanti still sat on the ground, his head sunk low, desperately trying to gasp a little of the wind he had made, the wind out of the ground, the wind of the future. But lungs were clogged, and he could not drink of the racing wind. His big calloused hand clutched slowly at the ground, and he choked a brief sound like a sob.

A shadow fell over him. It was Kinley, come to offer his thanks for the quelling of Handell. But he said nothing for a moment as he watched Manue's desperate Gethsemane.

"Some sow, others reap," he said.

"Why?" the Peruvian choked.

The supervisor shrugged. "What's the difference? But if you can't be both, which would you rather be?"

Nanti looked up into the wind. He imagined a city to the south, a city built on tear-soaked ground, filled with people who had no ends beyond their culture, no goal but within their own society. It was a good sensible question: Which would he rather be—sower or reaper?

Pride brought him slowly to his feet, and he eyed Kinley questioningly. The supervisor touched his shoulder.

"Go on to the trucks."

Nanti nodded and shuffled away. He had wanted something to work for, hadn't he? Something more than the reasons Donnell had given. Well, he could smell a reason, even if he couldn't breathe it.

Eight hundred years was a long time, but then—long time, big reason. The air smelled good, even with its clouds of boiling dust.

He knew now what Mars was—not a ten-thousand-a-year job, not a garbage can for surplus production. But an eight-century passion of human faith in the destiny of the race of Man.

He passed short of the truck. He had wanted to travel, to see the sights of Earth, the handiwork of Nature and of history, the glorious places of his planet.

He stooped, and scooped up a handful of the red-brown soil, letting it sift slowly between his fingers. Here was Mars—his planet now. No more of Earth, not for Manue Nanti. He adjusted his aerator more comfortably and climbed into the waiting truck.

Period Piece

J. J. Coupling

The being in the following story might just as easily be an artificially created thinking robot or a duplicated personality. When the illusion of personality becomes this real, the illusion *is* reality. In their introduction to *The Best Science Fiction Stories: 1949* (New York: Frederick Fell, 1949) Bleiler and Dikty suggested that it recapitulates the heresy of Valentinus the Gnostic that a created being suffers from the imperfections built into it by an imperfect creator. Scortia in his story "Woman's Rib" has suggested the reverse argument, that the perfections reflect the perfection of the creator. The important theme in this, as in many stories in this collection, is that of alienation, the growing awareness of divorcement from humanity. It is a state so common to twentieth-century man, particularly to Americans, that the hero's final discovery of his own true nature comes almost as a physical relief. How better resolve the feeling of alienation than by the conclusive discovery that one is alien?

It was at that particular party of Cordoban's that he began actually to have doubts—real doubts. Before, there had been puzzlement and some confusion. But now, among these splendid people, in this finely appointed apartment, he wondered who he was, and where he was.

After his friend—or his keeper?—Gavin had introduced him to his host, there had been a brief conversation about the twentieth century. Cordoban, a graying man with both dignity and alertness, asked the usual questions, always addressing Smith with the antique title Mister, which he seemed to relish as an oddity. To Smith it seemed that Cordoban received the answers with the sort of rapt attention a child might give to a clever mechanical toy.

"Tell me, Mr. Smith," Cordoban said, "some of the scientists of your day must have been philosophers as well, were they not?"

Smith could not remember having been asked just this question before. For a moment he could think of nothing. Then, suddenly, as always, the knowledge flooded into his mind. He found himself making a neat little three-minute speech almost automatically. The material seemed to arrange itself as he spoke, telling how Einstein forced an abandonment of the idea of simultaneity, of Eddington's idea that the known universe is merely what man is able to perceive and measure, of Milne's two time scales, and of the strange ideas of Rhine and Dunne concerning precognition. He had always been a clever speaker, ever since high school, he thought.

"Of course," he found himself concluding, "it was not until later in the century that Chandra Bhopal demonstrated the absurdity of time travel."

Cordoban stared at him queerly. For a moment Smith was scarcely conscious of what he had said. Then he formulated his thoughts.

"But time travel must be possible," he said, "for I'm a twentieth-century man, and I'm here in the thirty-first century."

He looked about the pleasant room, softly lighted, with deep recesses of color, for assurance, and at the handsome people, grouped standing or sitting in glowing pools of pearly illumination.

"Of course you're here, fellow," Cordoban said, reassuringly.

The remark was so true and so banal that Smith scarcely heard it. His thoughts were groping. Slowly he was piecing together an argument.

"But time travel *is* absurd," he said.

Cordoban looked a little annoyed and made a nod with his head which Smith did not quite follow.

"It was shown in the twentieth century to be absurd," Smith said.

But had it been shown in his part of the twentieth century, he wondered?

Cordoban glanced to his left.

"We know very little about the twentieth century," he said.

Gavin knows about the twentieth century, Smith thought.

Then, following Cordoban's glance, he saw that a young woman had detached herself from a group and was moving toward them. A segment of the pearly illumination followed her, making her a radiant creature indeed.

"Myria," Cordoban said, smiling, "you particularly wanted to meet Mr. Smith."

Myria smiled at Smith.

"Indeed, yes," she said. "I've always been curious about the twentieth century. And you must tell me about your music."

Cordoban bowed slightly and withdrew, the light which had been playing on him, seemingly from nowhere, detaching itself from the pool about Myria and Smith. And Smith's doubts fled to the back of his mind, crowded out, almost, by a flood of thoughts about music. And Myria was an enchanting creature.

Smith felt very chipper the next morning as he rose and bathed. The twentieth century had nothing like this to offer, he reflected. He knit his brows for a moment, trying to remember just what his room had been like, but at that moment the cupboard softly buzzed and he withdrew the glass of bland liquid which was his breakfast. His mind wandered while he sipped it. It wasn't until he walked down the corridor and sat in the office opposite Gavin that his doubts at Cordoban's returned to his mind.

Gavin was droning out the schedule. "We have a pretty full day, Smith," he said. "First, a couple of hours at the Lollards' country estate. We can stop by the Primus's on the way back. Then a full afternoon at a party given by the decorators' council. In the evening—"

"Gavin," Smith said, "why do we see all these people?"

"Why," Gavin answered, a little taken aback, "everyone wants to see a man from the twentieth century."

"But why these people?" Smith persisted. "They all ask the same questions. And I never see them again. I just go on repeating myself."

"Are we too frivolous by twentieth-century standards?" Gavin asked, smiling and leaning back in his chair.

Smith smiled back. Then his thoughts troubled him again. Cordoban hadn't been frivolous.

"How much do *you* know about the twentieth century, Gavin?" he asked, keeping his tone light.

"Pretty much what you do," Gavin replied.

But this couldn't be! Gavin appeared to be a kind of social tutor and arranger of things. As far as Smith could remember, mostly, information had passed from Gavin to him, not from him to Gavin. He decided to pursue the matter further, and as Gavin leaned forward to glance at the schedule again, Smith spoke once more.

"By the way, Gavin," he asked, "who is Cordoban?"

"Director of the Historical Institute, of course. I told you before we went there," Gavin replied.

"Who is Myria?" Smith asked.

"One of his secretaries," Gavin said. "A man of his position always has one on call."

"Cordoban said that not much was known about the twentieth century," Smith remarked mildly.

Gavin started up as if he had been stung. Then he sank back and opened his mouth. It was a moment before he found the words.

"Directors—" he said, and waved his hand as if brushing the matter aside. Smith was really puzzled now. "Gavin," he said, "is time travel possible?"

If Gavin had been startled, he was at his ease now.

"You're here," he said, "not in the twentieth century."

Gavin spoke in so charming and persuasive a manner that Smith felt like a fool for a moment. His thoughts were slipping back toward the schedule when he realized that wasn't an answer. It wasn't even couched as one. But this was silly, too. If it wasn't an answer, it was just what one would say.

Still, he'd try again.

"Gavin," he said, "Cordoban—"

"Look," Gavin said with a smile, "you'll get used to us in time. We'll keep the Lollards and their guests waiting if we don't start now. It isn't asking too much of you to see them now, is it? And you'll like it. They have a lovely fifteenth-century Chinese garden, with a dragon in a cave."

After all, Smith thought, he did owe his collective hosts of the thirty-first century something. And it was amusing.

The Lollards' garden was amusing, and so was the dragon, which breathed out smoke and roared. Primus's was dull, but the decorators' council had a most unusual display of fabrics which tinkled when they were touched, and of individual lighting in color. The evening was equally diverting, and delightful but strange people asked the same frivolous questions. Smith was diverted enough so that his doubts did not return until late that night.

But when Gavin left him at the door, Smith did not go to his bed and his usual dreamless sleep. Instead, he sat down in a chair, closed his eyes, and thought.

What did these people know about the twentieth century? Gavin had said, what he, Smith, knew. But that must be a great deal. An adult man—he, for instance—had a huge store of memories, accumulated over all his years. The human brain, he found himself thinking, has around ten billion nerve cells. If these were used to store words on a binary basis, they would hold some four hundred million words—a prodigious amount of learning. Tokayuki had, in 2117—

Strange, but he didn't remember talking with Gavin or anyone else about Tokayuki! And he could not have remembered about a man who had lived a century after his. But he could pursue this later.

Getting back to the gist of the matter, Cordoban had said that he knew little about the twentieth century. Yet Cordoban had not seemed anxious to question him at length. A few words about the philosophy of science, a dry enough subject, and he had called his secretary Myria—yes, Smith now saw, Cordoban had called Myria to relieve himself of Smith's presence. Here was an obviously astute man, and an historian, forgoing an opportunity to learn about an era of which he professed ignorance.

Well, I suppose one untrained man doesn't know much about an era, even his own, Smith thought. That is, not by thirty-first-century standards. But then how do they know what I know? he wondered. Nobody has asked me any very searching questions.

Gavin and his schedules, now! All the occasions were purely social. That was strange! Most of the people weren't those likely to have much detailed interest in another era. Decorators, some, like the Lollards, apparently entirely idle-retired, perhaps. Anyway, the conversation was so much social chitchat.

Cordoban, now, had been an historian, even though he hadn't been curious. But that too was a purely social occasion. And Gavin himself! Just a sort of guide to a man from another age. Certainly not a curious man. Why not? Were men of the twentieth century so common here? But certainly he would have been brought into contact with others. Besides, time traveling was absurd!

But that was getting off the track. He *was* here. He didn't need Cordoban or Gavin to assure him of that. Being here, he would expect serious questioning by a small group—not all these frivolous, if delightful, parties. Surely he could tell them a great deal they had not asked.

Well, for instance, what could he tell them? His own personal experiences. What had happened day by day. But what had happened day by day? His schooling, for one thing. High school, in particular. As he thought about high schools, there quickly rose in his mind a sequence of facts about their organization and curriculum. It was as if he were reviewing a syllabus on the subject.

The three-minute talks were getting him, he decided. He was so used to these impersonal summaries that they came to his mind automatically. Right now, he must be tired. He would spend more time thinking in the morning.

So Smith went to bed, thought about the events of the day a little, including the Lollards' amusing fire-breathing dragon, and was quickly asleep.

* * *

The following morning Smith did not feel chipper. He rose and bathed out of a sense of duty and routine. But then he sat down and ignored the buzzing of the cupboard which announced his breakfast. A pattern had crystallized in his mind overnight. His thoughts in their uncertainty had paved the way for this, no doubt. But what was in his mind was no uncertain conclusion.

He, Smith, was no man of the twentieth century! He had carefully implanted memories, factual theses concerning his past, summaries of twentieth-century history. But no real past! The little details that made a past were missing. Time travel was absurd. He was a fraud! An impostor!

But whom was he fooling? Not Gavin, he saw now. Not men like Cordoban. Was he fooling anyone? All of the people seemed eager to talk with him. Cordoban himself had been eager to talk with him. Cordoban had not been feigning. Cordoban had not been fooled. It seemed likely that Smith himself was the only one fooled.

But why? It was a stupid trick for people so obviously intelligent. What did they get out of this silly game? It could hardly be any personal quality of his—any charm. They were all so charming themselves.

Myria, Cordoban's secretary, for instance. A lovely woman. Handsome, poised, beautifully dressed. Suddenly a little three-minute talk about women in the twentieth century formed in Smith's mind. In part of his mind, that is. In a way, he watched it unfold. And with surprise.

He had thought of Myria as merely handsome and handsomely dressed. But even across the centuries—no, he must remember that he was not from the twentieth century. Across whatever gulf there was, there could have been more than this. Just how did he, Smith, differ from other men?

Well, what did he know of mankind? He reviewed matters in his mind, and went through little summaries on psychology, anthropology and physiology. It was in the midst of this last that he felt a horrible conviction which changed his course from thought to action.

His first action was to wind a small gold chain which was a part of his clothing tightly around the tip of his index finger. The tip remained smooth and brown.

Dropping the chain, he dug the sharp point of a writing instrument into his fingertip, ignoring the pain. The point passed into the rubbery flesh. There was no blood! But there was a little flash and a puff of vapor, and the finger went numb.

He was a cleverly constructed period piece, like the Lollards' dragon! Like a clockwork nightingale! That was why these people admired him briefly, for what he was—a charming mechanical toy!

Smith scarcely thought. The little review of twentieth-century psychology returned to his mind, and automatically he opened the door onto the balcony and stepped over the railing. Consistent to the last, he thought in dull pain as he fell toward the ground twenty stories below.

But it wasn't the last. There was a terrible wrenching shock, a clashing noise, and confusion. Afterwards, there were still vision and hearing. True, the world stood at an odd angle. He saw the building leaning crazily into the sky. From the brief synopsis of physiology he gleaned that his psychokinetic sense was gone. He no longer felt which way his head and eyes were turned. Other senses than sight and sound were gone as well, and when he tried he found that he could not move. Junk, lying here, he thought bitterly. Not even release! But now he could see Gavin bending over him, and another man who looked as if he might be a mechanic.

"Junk," the mechanic said. "It's lucky we couldn't put the brain in that, or it would be gone, too. Making a new body won't be so bad," he added.

"I suppose we'll have to turn off the brain and reform the patterns," Gavin mused.

"You'd have had to, anyway," the mechanic said. "You

must have put in something inconsistent or we wouldn't have had this failure."

"It's a shame, though," Gavin said. "I got to like him. Silly, isn't it? But he seemed so nearly alive. We spent a lot of time together. Now everything that happened, everything he learned, will have to be wiped out."

"You know," the mechanic said, "it gives me the creeps, sometimes. I mean, thinking, if I were just a body, connected by a tight beam to a brain off somewhere. And if when the body was destroyed, the brain—"

"Nonsense," said Gavin.

He gestured toward Smith's crumpled body, and then up toward the building where, presumably, was Smith's brain.

"You'll be thinking that that thing was conscious, next," he said. "Come on, let's turn the brain off."

Smith stared numbly at the crazily leaning building, waiting for them to turn off his brain.

Solar Plexus

James Blish

James Blish delves into what might be "lost" if a human mind were to be joined to a cybernetic partner—subtleties like willfulness, creativity, all the plasticity that comes with the versatility of a colloidal brain and fleshy body that have been forged on the anvil of adaptive evolution. Unlike Kuttner's cyborg, Blish's fails. Undoubtedly, the emergence of this kind of malevolence will have to be considered. It also naturally raises the question of *what is a human being?* And a more difficult problem: can we ever list *all* the qualities of the human mind, avoiding fatal omissions during future modifications?

Brant Kittinger did not hear the alarm begin to ring. Indeed, it was only after a soft blow had jarred his free-floating observatory that he looked up in sudden awareness from the interferometer. Then the sound of the warning bell reached his consciousness.

Brant was an astronomer, not a spaceman, but he knew that the bell could mean nothing but the arrival of another ship in the vicinity. There would be no point in ringing a bell for a meteor—the thing could be through and past you during the first cycle of the clapper. Only an approaching ship would be likely to trip the detector, and it would have to be close.

A second dull jolt told him how close it was. The rasp of metal which followed, as the other ship slid along the side of his own, drove the fog of tensors completely from his brain. He dropped his pencil and straightened up.

His first thought was that his year in the orbit around the new trans-Plutonian planet was up, and that the Institute's tug had arrived to tow him home, telescope and all. A glance at the clock reassured him at first, then puzzled him still further. He still had the better part of four months.

No commercial vessel, of course, could have wandered this far from the inner planets; and the UN's police cruisers didn't travel far outside the commercial lanes. Besides, it would have been impossible for anyone to find Brant's orbital observatory by accident.

He settled his glasses more firmly on his nose, clambered awkwardly backwards out of the prime focus chamber and down the wall net to the control desk on the observation floor. A quick glance over the boards revealed that there was a magnetic field of some strength nearby, one that didn't belong to the invisible gas giant revolving half a million miles away.

The strange ship was locked to him magnetically; it was an old ship, then, for that method of grappling had been discarded years ago as too hard on delicate instruments. And the strength of the field meant a big ship.

Too big. The only ship of that period that could mount generators that size, as far as Brant could remember, was the Cybernetics Foundation's *Astrid*. Brant could remember well the Foundation's regretful announcement that Murray Bennett had destroyed both himself and the *Astrid* rather than turn the ship in to some UN inspection team. It had happened only eight years ago. Some scandal or other . . .

Well, who then?

He turned the radio on. Nothing came out of it. It was a simple transistor set tuned to the Institute's frequency, and since the ship outside plainly did not belong to the Institute, he had expected nothing else. Of course he had a photo-phone also, but it had been designed for communication over a reasonable distance, not for cheek-to-cheek whispers.

As an afterthought, he turned off the persistent alarm bell. At once another sound came through: a delicate, rhythmic tapping on the hull of the observatory. Someone wanted to get in.

He could think of no reason to refuse entrance, except for a vague and utterly unreasonable wonder as to whether or not the stranger was a friend. He had no enemies, and the notion that some outlaw might have happened upon him out here was ridiculous. Nevertheless, there was some-thing about the anonymous, voiceless ship just outside which made him uneasy.

The gentle tapping stopped, and then began again, with an even, mechanical insistence. For a moment Brant won-dered whether or not he should try to tear free with the observatory's few maneuvering rockets—but even should he win so uneven a struggle, he would throw the observatory out of the orbit where the Institute expected to find it, and he was not astronaut enough to get it back there again.

Tap, tap. Tap, tap.

"All right," he said irritably. He pushed the button which set the airlock to cycling. The tapping stopped. He left the outer door open more than long enough for anyone to enter and push the button in the lock which reversed the process; but nothing happened.

After what seemed to be a long wait, he pushed his button again. The outer door closed, the pumps filled the chamber with air, the inner door swung open. No ghost drifted out of it; there was nobody in the lock at all.

Tap, tap. Tap, tap.

Absently he polished his glasses on his sleeve. If they didn't want to come into the observatory, they must want him to come out of it. That was possible: although the telescope had a Coudé focus which allowed him to work in the ship's air most of the time, it was occasionally necessary for him to exhaust the dome, and for that purpose he had a spacesuit. But he had never been outside the hull in it, and the thought alarmed him. Brant was nobody's spaceman.

Be damned to them. He clapped his glasses back into place and took one more look into the empty airlock. It was still empty, with the outer door now moving open very slowly. . . .

A spaceman would have known that he was already dead, but Brant's reactions were not quite as fast. His first move was to try to jam the inner door shut by sheer muscle-power, but it would not stir. Then he simply clung to the nearest stanchion, waiting for the air to rush out of the observatory, and his life after it.

The outer door of the airlock continued to open, placidly, and still there was no rush of air—only a kind of faint, unticketable inwash of odor, as if Brant's air were mixing

with someone else's. When both doors of the lock finally
stood wide apart from each other, Brant found himself looking down the inside of a flexible, airtight tube, such as he
had once seen used for the transfer of a small freight-load
from a ship to one of Earth's several space stations. It connected the airlock of the observatory with that of the other
ship. At the other end of it, lights gleamed yellowly, with
the unmistakable, dismal sheen of incandescent overheads.

That was an old ship, all right.

Tap. Tap.

"Go to hell," he said aloud. There was no answer.

Tap. Tap.

"Go to hell," he said. He walked out into the tube,
which flexed sinuously as his body pressed aside the static
air. In the airlock of the stranger, he paused and looked
back. He was not much surprised to see the outer door of his
own airlock swinging smugly shut against him. Then the
airlock of the stranger began to cycle; he skipped on into the
ship barely in time.

There was a bare metal corridor ahead of him. While he
watched, the first light bulb over his head blinked out. Then
the second. Then the third. As the fourth one went out, the
first came on again, so that now there was a slow ribbon of
darkness moving away from him down the corridor. Clearly,
he was being asked to follow the line of darkening bulbs
down the corridor.

He had no choice, now that he had come this far. He
followed the blinking lights.

The trail led directly to the control room of the ship.
There was nobody there, either.

The whole place was oppressively silent. He could hear
the soft hum of generators—a louder noise than he ever
heard on board the observatory—but no ship should be this
quiet. There should be muffled human voices, the chittering
of communications systems, the impacts of soles on metal.
Someone had to operate a proper ship—not only its airlocks,
but its motors—and its brains. The observatory was only a

barge, and needed no crew but Brant, but a real ship had to be manned.

He scanned the bare metal compartment, noting the apparent age of the equipment. Most of it was manual, but there were no hands to man it.

A ghost ship for true.

"All right," he said. His voice sounded flat and loud to him. "Come on out. You wanted me here—why are you hiding?"

Immediately there was a noise in the close, still air, a thin, electrical sigh. Then a quiet voice said, "You're Brant Kittinger."

"Certainly," Brant said, swiveling fruitlessly toward the apparent source of the voice. "You know who I am. You couldn't have found me by accident. Will you come out? I've no time to play games."

"I'm not playing games," the voice said calmly. "And I can't come out, since I'm not hiding from you. I can't see you; I needed to hear your voice before I could be sure of you."

"Why?"

"Because I can't see inside the ship. I could find your observation boat well enough, but until I heard you speak I couldn't be sure that you were the one aboard it. Now I know."

"All right," Brant said suspiciously. "I still don't see why you're hiding. Where are you?"

"Right here," said the voice. "All around you."

Brant looked all around himself. His scalp began to creep. "What kind of nonsense is that?" he said.

"You aren't seeing what you're looking at, Brant. You're looking directly at me, no matter where you look. *I am the ship.*"

"Oh," Brant said softly. "So that's it. You're one of Murray Bennett's computer-driven ships. Are you the *Astrid,* after all?"

"This is the *Astrid*," the voice said. "But you miss my point. I am Murray Bennett, also."

Brant's jaw dropped open. "Where are you?" he said after a time.

"Here," the voice said impatiently. "I am the *Astrid*. I am also Murray Bennett. Bennett is dead, so he can't very well come into the cabin and shake your hand. I am now Murray Bennett; I remember you very well, Brant. I need your help, so I sought you out. I'm not as much Murray Bennett as I'd like to be."

Brant sat down in the empty pilot's seat.

"You're a computer," he said shakily. "Isn't that so?"

"It is and it isn't. No computer can duplicate the performance of a human brain. I tried to introduce real human neural mechanisms into computers, specifically to fly ships, and was outlawed for my trouble. I don't think I was treated fairly. It took enormous surgical skill to make the hundreds and hundreds of nerve-to-circuit connections that were needed—and before I was half through, the UN decided that what I was doing was human vivisection. They outlawed me, and the Foundation said I'd have to destroy myself; what could I do after that?

"I did destroy myself. I transferred most of my own nervous system into the computers of the *Astrid*, working at the end through drugged assistants under telepathic control, and finally relying upon the computers to seal the last connections. No such surgery ever existed before, but I brought it into existence. It worked. Now I'm the *Astrid*—and still Murray Bennett too, though Bennett is dead."

Brant locked his hands together carefully on the edge of the dead control board. "What good did that do you?" he said.

"It proved my point. I was trying to build an almost living spaceship. I had to build part of myself into it to do it—since they made me an outlaw to stop my using any other human being as a source of parts. But here is the *Astrid*, Brant, as almost alive as I could ask. I'm as immune to a dead spaceship—a UN cruiser, for instance—as you would be to an infuriated wheelbarrow. My reflexes are human-fast. I feel things directly, not through instruments. I fly myself: I am what I sought—the ship that almost thinks for itself."

"You keep saying 'almost,' " Brant said.

"That's why I came to you," the voice said. "I don't have enough of Murray Bennett here to know what I should do next. You knew me well. Was I out to try to use human brains more and more, and computer-mechanisms less and less? It seems to me that I was. I can pick up the brains easily enough, just as I picked you up. The solar system is full of people isolated on little research boats who could be plucked off them and incorporated into efficient machines like the *Astrid*. But I don't know. I seem to have lost my creativity. I have a base where I have some other ships with beautiful computers in them, and with a few people to use as research animals I could make even better ships of them than the *Astrid* is. But is that what I want to do? Is that what I set out to do? I no longer know, Brant. Advise me."

The machine with the human nerves would have been touching had it not been so much like Bennett had been. The combination of the two was flatly horrible.

"You've made a bad job of yourself, Murray," he said. "You've let me inside your brain without taking any real thought of the danger. What's to prevent me from stationing myself at your old manual controls and flying you to the nearest UN post?"

"You can't fly a ship."

"How do you know?"

"By simple computation. And there are other reasons. What's to prevent me from making you cut your own throat? The answer's the same. You're in control of your body; I'm in control of mine. My body is the *Astrid*. The controls are useless, unless I actuate them. The nerves through which I do so are sheathed in excellent steel. The only way in which you could destroy my control would be to break something necessary to the running of the ship. That, in a sense, would kill me, as destroying your heart or your lungs would kill you. But that would be pointless, for then you could no more navigate the ship than I. And if you made repairs, I would be—well, resurrected."

The voice fell silent a moment. Then it added, matter-of-factly, "Of course, I can protect myself."

Brant made no reply. His eyes were narrowed to the squint he more usually directed at a problem in Milne transformations.

"I never sleep," the voice went on, "but much of my navigating and piloting is done by an autopilot without requiring my conscious attention. It is the same old Nelson autopilot which was originally on board the *Astrid*, though, so it has to be monitored. If you touch the controls while the autopilot is running, it switches itself off and I resume direction myself."

Brant was surprised and instinctively repelled by the steady flow of information. It was a forcible reminder of how much of the computer there was in the intelligence that called itself Murray Bennett. It was answering a question with the almost mindless wealth of detail of a public-library selector—and there was no "Enough" button for Brant to push.

"Are you going to answer my question?" the voice said suddenly.

"Yes," Brant said. "I advise you to turn yourself in. The *Astrid* proves your point—and also proves that your research was a blind alley. There's no point in your proceeding to make more *Astrids*; you're aware yourself that you're incapable of improving on the model now."

"That's contrary to what I have recorded," the voice said. "My ultimate purpose as a man was to build machines like this. I can't accept your answer: it conflicts with my primary directive. Please follow the lights to your quarters."

"What are you going to do with me?"

"Take you to the base."

"What for?" Brant said.

"As a stock of parts," said the voice. "Please follow the lights, or I'll have to use force."

Brant followed the lights. As he entered the cabin to which they led him, a disheveled figure arose from one of the two cots. He started back in alarm. The figure chuckled wryly and displayed a frayed bit of gold braid on its sleeve.

"I'm not as terrifying as I look," he said. "Lieutenant Powell of the UN scout *Iapetus*, at your service."

"I'm Brant Kittinger, Planetary Institute astrophysicist. You're just the faintest bit battered, all right. Did you tangle with Bennett?"

"Is that his name?" The UN patrolman nodded glumly. "Yes. There's some whoppers of guns mounted on this old tub. I challenged it, and it cut my ship to pieces before I could lift a hand. I barely got into my suit in time—and I'm beginning to wish I hadn't."

"I don't blame you. You know what he plans to use us for, I judge."

"Yes," the pilot said. "He seems to take pleasure in bragging about his achievements—God knows they're amazing enough, if even half of what he says is true."

"It's all true," Brant said. "He's essentially a machine, you know, and as such I doubt that he can lie."

Powell looked startled. "That makes it worse. I've been trying to figure a way out—"

Brant raised one hand sharply, and with the other he patted his pockets in search of a pencil. "If you've found anything, write it down, don't talk about it. I think he can hear us. Is that so, Bennett?"

"Yes," said the voice in the air. Powell jumped. "My hearing extends throughout the ship."

There was silence again. Powell, grim as death, scribbled on a tattered UN trip ticket.

Doesn't matter. Can't think of a thing.

Where's the main computer? Brant wrote. *There's where personality residues must lie.*

Down below. Not a chance without blaster. Must be 8" of steel around it. Control nerves the same.

They sat hopelessly on the lower cot. Brant chewed on the pencil. "How far is his home base from here?" he asked at length.

"Where's here?"

"In the orbit of the new planet."

Powell whistled. "In that case, his base can't be more than three days away. I came on board from just off Titan, and he hasn't touched his base since, so his fuel won't last much longer. I know this type of ship well enough. And from what I've seen of the drivers, they haven't been altered."

"Umm," Brant said. "That checks. If Bennett in person never got around to altering the drive, this ersatz Bennett we have here will never get around to it, either." He found it easier to ignore the listening presence while talking; to monitor his speech constantly with Bennett in mind was too hard on the nerves. "That gives us three days to get out, then. Or less."

For at least twenty minutes Brant said nothing more, while the UN pilot squirmed and watched his face hopefully. Finally the astronomer picked up the piece of paper again.

Can you pilot this ship? he wrote.

The pilot nodded and scribbled: *Why?*

Without replying, Brant lay back on the bunk, swiveled himself around so that his head was toward the center of the cabin, doubled up his knees, and let fly with both feet. They crashed hard against the hull, the magnetic studs in his shoes leaving bright scars on the metal. The impact sent him sailing like an ungainly fish across the cabin.

"What was that for?" Powell and the voice in the air

asked simultaneously. Their captor's tone was faintly curious, but not alarmed.

Brant had his answer already prepared. "It's part of a
question I want to ask," he said. He brought up against the
far wall and struggled to get his feet back to the deck. "Can
you tell me what I did then, Bennett?"

"Why, not specifically. As I told you, I can't see inside
the ship. But I get a tactual jar from the nerves of the
controls, the lights, the floors, the ventilation system, and so
on, and also a ringing sound from the audios. These things
tell me that you either stamped on the floor or pounded on
the wall. From the intensity of all the impressions, I com-
pute that you stamped."

"You hear and you feel, eh?"

"That's correct," the voice said. "Also I can pick up
your body heat from the receptors in the ship's temperature
control system—a form of seeing, but without any definition."

Very quietly, Brant retrieved the worn trip ticket and
wrote on it: *Follow me.*

He went out into the corridor and started down it toward the control room, Powell at his heels. The living ship
remained silent only for a moment.

"Return to your cabin," the voice said.

Brant walked a little faster. How would Bennett's vicious
brainchild enforce his orders?

"I said, go back to your cabin," the voice said. Its tone
was now loud and harsh, and without a trace of feeling; for
the first time, Brant was able to tell that it came from a
voder, rather than from a tape-vocabulary of Bennett's own
voice. Brant gritted his teeth and marched forward.

"I don't want to have to spoil you," the voice said. "For
the last time—"

An instant later Brant received a powerful blow in the
small of his back. It felled him like a tree, and sent him
skimming along the corridor deck like a flat stone. A bare

fraction of a second later there was a hiss and a flash, and the air was abruptly hot and choking with the sharp odor of ozone.

"Close," Powell's voice said calmly. "Some of these rivet-heads in the walls evidently are high-tension electrodes. Lucky I saw the nimbus collecting on that one. Crawl, and make it snappy."

Crawling in a gravity-free corridor was a good deal more difficult to manage than walking. Determinedly, Brant squirmed into the control room, calling into play every trick he had ever learned in space to stick to the floor. He could hear Powell wriggling along behind him.

"He doesn't know what I'm up to," Brant said aloud. "Do you, Bennett?"

"No," the voice in the air said. "But I know of nothing you can do that's dangerous while you're lying on your belly. When you get up, I'll destroy you, Brant."

"Hmmm," Brant said. He adjusted his glasses, which he had nearly lost during his brief, skipping carom along the deck. The voice had summarized the situation with deadly precision. He pulled the now nearly pulped trip ticket out of his shirt pocket, wrote on it, and shoved it across the deck to Powell.

How can we reach the autopilot? Got to smash it.

Powell propped himself up on one elbow and studied the scrap of paper, frowning. Down below, beneath the deck, there was an abrupt sound of power, and Brant felt the cold metal on which he was lying sink beneath him. Bennett was changing course, trying to throw them within range of his defenses. Both men began to slide sidewise.

Powell did not appear to be worried; evidently he knew just how long it took to turn a ship of this size and period. He pushed the piece of paper back. On the last free space on it, in cramped letters, was: *Throw something at it.*

"Ah," said Brant. Still sliding, he drew off one of his heavy shoes and hefted it critically. It would do. With a sudden convulsion of motion he hurled it.

Fat, crackling sparks crisscrossed the room; the noise was ear-splitting. While Bennett could have had no idea what Brant was doing, he evidently had sensed the sudden stir of movement and had triggered the high-tension current out of general caution. But he was too late. The flying shoe plowed heel-foremost into the autopilot with a rending smash.

There was an unfocused blare of sound from the voder —more like the noise of a siren than like a human cry. The *Astrid* rolled wildly, once. Then there was silence.

"All right," said Brant, getting to his knees. "Try the controls, Powell."

The UN pilot arose cautiously. No sparks flew. When he touched the boards, the ship responded with an immediate purr of power.

"She runs," he said. "Now, how the hell did you know what to do?"

"It wasn't difficult," Brant said complacently, retrieving his shoe. "But we're not out of the woods yet. We have to get to the stores fast and find a couple of torches. I want to cut through every nerve-channel we can find. Are you with me?"

"Sure."

The job was more quickly done than Brant had dared to hope. Evidently the living ship had never thought of lightening itself by jettisoning all the equipment its human crew had once needed. While Brant and Powell cut their way enthusiastically through the jungle of efferent nerve-trunks running from the central computer, the astronomer said:

"He gave us too much information. He told me that he had connected the artificial nerves of the ship, the control nerves, to the nerve-ends running from the parts of his own brain that he had used. And he said that he'd had to make *hundreds* of such connections. That's the trouble with allowing a computer to act as an independent agent—it doesn't know enough about inter-personal relationships to control its tongue. . . . There we are. He'll be coming to before long, but I don't think he'll be able to interfere with us now."

He set down his torch with a sigh. "I was saying? Oh, yes. About those nerve connections: if he had separated out the pain-carrying nerves from the other sensory nerves, he would have had to have made *thousands* of connections, not hundreds. Had it really been the living human being, Bennett, who had given me that cue, I would have discounted it, because he might have been using understatement. But since it was Bennett's double, a computer, I assumed that the figure was of the right order of magnitude. Computers don't understate.

"Besides, I didn't think Bennett could have made thousands of connections, especially not working telepathically through a proxy. There's a limit even to the most marvelous neurosurgery. Bennett had just made general connections, and had relied on the segments from his own brain which he had incorporated to sort out the impulses as they came in—as any human brain could do under like circumstances. That was one of the advantages of using parts from a human brain in the first place."

"And when you kicked the wall—" Powell said.

"Yes, you see the crux of the problem already. When I kicked the wall, I wanted to make sure that he could *feel* the impact of my shoes. If he could, then I could be sure that he hadn't eliminated the sensory nerves when he installed the motor nerves. And if he hadn't, then there were bound to be pain axons present, too."

"But what has the autopilot to do with it?" Powell asked plaintively.

"The autopilot," Brant said, grinning, "is a center of his nerve-mesh, an important one. He should have protected it as heavily as he protected the main computer. When I smashed it, it was like ramming a fist into a man's solar plexus. It hurt him."

Powell grinned too. "K.O.," he said.

Sea Change

Thomas N. Scortia

The linking of cyborg technology to space travel promises to be an exciting one. The dark spaces may never seem hostile again as the human-machine extends our range of adaptation to these new environments. Yet there will be cruel miracles and pain. Here is a vision of a solar system-wide civilization straining for the stars; here are the colors and sounds of change. Here is the human spirit at the moment when it seems powerless to be reborn, but ready with a new strength . . .

—G. Zebrowski

Gleaming . . . *like a needle of fire* . . .

Whose voice? He didn't know.

The interstellar . . . two of them . . .

They were talking all at once then, their voices blending chaotically.

They're moving one out beyond Pluto for the test, someone said.

Beautiful . . . We're waiting . . . waiting.

That was her voice. He felt coldness within his chest.

That was the terrible part of his isolation, he thought. He could still hear everything. Not just in the Superintendent's office in Marsopolis where he sat.

Everywhere.

All the whispers of sound, spanning the system on pulses of c-cube radio. All the half-words, half-thoughts from the inner planets to the space stations far beyond Pluto.

And the loneliness was a sudden agonizing thing. The loneliness and the loss of two worlds.

Not that he couldn't shut out the voices if he wished, the distant voices that webbed space with the cubed speed of light. But . . . might as well shut out all thought of living and seek the mindless foetal state of merely being.

There was the voice droning cargo numbers. He made the small mental change and the tight mass of transistors, buried deep in his metal and plastic body, brought the voice in clear and sharp. It was a Triplanet ship in the twilight belt of Mercury.

He had a fleeting image of flame-shriveled plains under a blinding monster sun.

Then there was the voice, saying, *Okay . . . bearing three-ought-six and count down ten to free fall . . .*

That one was beyond Saturn . . . Remembered vision of bright ribbons of light, lacing a startling blue sky.

He thought, *I'll never see that again.*

And: *Space Beacon Three to MRX two two . . . Space Beacon Three . . . Bishop to queen's rook four . . .*

And there was the soft voice, the different voice: *Matt . . . Matt . . . Where are you? . . . Matt, come in . . . Oh, Matt . . .*

But he ignored that one.

Instead he looked at the receptionist and watched her fingers dance intricate patterns over the keyboard of her electric typewriter.

Matt . . . Matt . . .

No, no more, he thought. There was nothing there for him but bitterness. The isolation of being apart from humanity. The loneliness. Love? Affection? The words had no meaning in that existence.

It had become a ritual with him, he realized, this trip the first Tuesday of every month down through the silent Martian town to the Triplanet Port. A formalized tribute to something that was quite dead. An empty ritual, a weak ineffectual gesture.

He had known that morning that there would be nothing.

"No, nothing," the girl in the Super's office had said. "Nothing at all."

Nothing for him in his gray robot world of no-touch, no-taste.

She looked at him the way they all did, the ones who saw past the clever human disguise of plastic face and muted eyes.

He waited . . . listening.

When the Super came in, he smiled and said, "Hello, Matt," and then, with a gesture of his head, "Come on in."

The girl frowned silent disapproval.

After they found seats, the Super said, "Why don't you go home?"

"Home?"

"Back to Earth."

"Is that home?"

The voices whispered in his ear while the Super frowned and puffed a black cigar alight.

And: . . . *Matt . . . Matt . . . Knight four to . . . three down . . . two down . . . Out past Deimos, the sun blazing on its sides . . . Matt . . .*

"What are you trying to do?" the Super demanded. "Cut yourself off from the world completely?"

"That's been done already," he said. "Very effectively."

"Look, let's be brutal about it. We don't owe you anything."

"No," he said.

"It was a business arrangement purely," the Super said. "And if this hadn't been done," he gestured at the body Freck wore, "Matthew Freck would have been little more than a page in some dusty official records."

"Or worse," he added.

"I suppose so," Freck said.

"You could go back tomorrow. To Earth. To a new life. No one has to know who you are or what you are unless you tell them."

Freck looked down at his hands, the carefully veined, very human hands and the hard muscled thighs where the cellotherm trousers hugged his legs.

"The technicians did a fine job," he said. "Actually, it's better than my old body. Younger and stronger. And it'll last longer. But . . ."

He flexed his hands sensuously, watching the way the smooth bands of contractile plastic articulated his fingers.

"But the masquerade won't work. We were made for one thing."

"I can't change Company policy," the Super said. "Oh, I know the experiment didn't work. Actually technology is moving too fast. It was a bad compromise anyway. We needed something a little faster, more than human to pilot the new ships. Human reactions, the speed of a nerve impulse wasn't sufficient, electronic equipment was too bulky, and the organic memory units we built for our first cybernetic pilots didn't have enough initiative. That's why we jumped at the chance to use you people when Marshal Jenks first came to us. But we weren't willing to face facts. We tried to compromise . . . keep the human form."

"Well, we gave you what you needed then. You do owe us something in return," he said.

"We lived up to our contract," the Super said. "With you and a hundred like you whom we could save. All in exchange for the ability only you had. It was a fair trade."

"All right, give me a ship then. That's all I want."

"I told you before. Direct hook-up."

"No. If you knew what you were asking . . ."

"Look, one of the interstellars is being tested right this minute. And there are the stations beyond Pluto."

"The stations? That's like the Director all over again. Completely immobile. What kind of a life would that be, existing as a self-contained unit for years on end without the least contact with humanity?"

"The stations are not useless," the Super said. He leaned forward and slapped his palm on the surface of his desk.

"You of all people should know the Bechtoldt Drive can't be installed within the system's heavy gravitational fields. That's why we need the stations. They're set up to install the drive after the ship leaves the system proper on its atomic motors."

"You still haven't answered my question."

"*Stargazer I* is outbound for one of the trans-Plutonian stations now. *Stargazer II* will follow in a few days."

"So?"

"You can have one of them if you want it. Oh, don't get the idea that this is a handout. We don't play that way. The last two ships blew up because the pilots weren't skilled enough to handle the hook-up. We need the best and that's you."

He paused for a long second.

"You may as well know," the Super said. "We've put all our eggs in those two baskets. We've been losing political strength in the past three years, and if either one fails, Triplanet and the other combines stand to lose their subsidies from the government. Then it'll be a century before anyone tries again, if they ever do. We're tired of being tied to a petty nine planets. We're doing the thing you worked for all your life. We're going to the stars now . . . and you can still be a part of that."

"That used to mean something to me," he said, "but after a time, you start losing your identification with humanity and its drives."

When he started to rise, the Super said, "You know you can't operate a modern ship or station, tied down to a humanoid body. It's too inefficient. You've got to become a part of the setup."

"I've told you before. I can't do that."

"What are you afraid of? The loneliness?"

"I've been lonely before," he said.

"What then?"

"What am I afraid of?" He smiled his mechanical smile. "Something you could never understand. I'm afraid of what's happened to me already."

The Super was silent.

"When you start losing the basic emotions, the basic ways of thinking that make you human, well . . . What am I afraid of?

"I'm afraid of becoming more of a machine," he said.

And before the Super could say more, he left.

Outside he zipped up the cellotherm jacket and adjusted

his respirator. Then he advanced the setting of the rheostat on the chest of his jacket until the small jewel light above the mechanism glowed in the morning's half-dusk. He had no need for the heat that the clothing furnished, of course, but the masquerade, the pretending to be wholly human would have been incomplete without this vital touch.

All the way back through the pearl-gray light, he listened to the many voices flashing back and forth across the ship lanes. He heard the snatches of commerce from a hundred separate ports and he followed in his mind's eye the swift progress of *Stargazer I* out past the orbit of Uranus to her rendezvous with the station that would fit her with the Bechtoldt Drive.

And he thought, *Lord, if I could make the jump with her,* and then, *But not at that price, not for what it's cost the others, Jim and Martha and Art and . . . Beth.* (*Forget the name . . . forget the name . . . lost from you like all the others . . .*)

The city had turned to full life in the interval he had spent in the Super's office and he passed numerous hurrying figures, bearlike in cellotherm clothing and transparent respirators. They ignored him completely and for a moment he had an insane impulse to tear the respirator from his face and stand waiting . . .

Waiting savagely, defiantly for someone to notice him.

The tortured writhings of neon signs glowed along the wide streets and occasionally an electric run-about, balanced lightly on two wheels, passed him with a soft whirr, its headlights cutting a bright swath across his path. He had never become fully accustomed to the twilight of the Martian day. But that was the fault of the technicians who had built his body. In their pathetic desire to ape the human body, they had often built in human limitations as well as human strengths.

He stopped a moment before a shop, idly inspecting the window display of small things, fragile and alien, from the dead Martian towns to the north. The shop window, he realized, was as much out of place here as the street and the individual pressurized buildings that lined it. It would have been better, as someone had suggested, to house the entire city under one pressurized unit. But this was how the Martian settlements had started and men still held to habits more suited to another world.

Well, that was a common trait that he shared with his race. The Super was right, of course. He was as much of a compromise as the town was. The old habits of thought prevailed, molding the new forms.

He thought that he should get something to eat. He hadn't had breakfast before setting out for the port. They'd managed to give him a sense of hunger, though taste had been too elusive for them to capture.

But the thought of food was somehow unpleasant.

And then he thought perhaps he should get drunk.

But even that didn't seem too satisfying.

He walked on for a distance and found a bar that was open and he walked in. He shed his respirator in the airlock and, under the half-watchful eyes of a small fat man, fumbling with his wallet, he pretended to turn off the rheostat of his suit.

Then he went inside, nodded vaguely at the bored bartender and sat at a corner table. After the bartender had brought him a whiskey and water, he sat and listened.

Six and seven . . . and twenty-ought-three . . .

. . . read you . . .

. . . and out there you see nothing, absolutely nothing. It's like . . . Matt . . . Matt . . .

. . . to king's knight four . . . check in three . . . Matt . . .

And for the first time in weeks, he made the change. He could talk without making an audible sound, which was fortunate. A matter of subverbalizing.

He said silently, *Come on in.*

Matt, where are you?

In a bar.

I'm far out . . . very far out. The sun's like a pinhole in a black sheet.

I think I'm going to get very drunk.

Why?

Because I want to. Isn't that reason enough? Because it's the one wholly, completely human thing that I can do well.

I've missed you.

Missed me? My voice perhaps. There's little else.

You should be out here with us . . . with me and Art . . . , she said breathlessly. *They're bringing the new ones out. The big ships. They're beautiful. Bigger and faster than anything you and I ever rode.*

They're bringing Stargazer I *out for her tests,* he told her.

I know. My station has one of the drives. Station three is handling Stargazer I *now.*

He swallowed savagely, thinking of what the Super had said.

Oh, I wish I were one of them, Beth said.

His hand tensed on the glass and for a moment he thought it would shatter in his fingers. She hadn't said "on."

Were . . . were . . . I wish I were one of them.

Do you, he said. *That's fine.*

Oh, that's fine, starry eyes, he thought, *I love you and the ship and the stars and the sense of being . . . I am the ship . . . I am the station . . . I am anything but human . . .*

What's wrong, Matt?

I'm going to get drunk.

There's a ship coming in. Signaling.

The bartender, he saw, was looking at him oddly. He realized that he had been nursing the same drink for fifteen minutes. He raised the glass and very deliberately drank and swallowed.

I've got to leave for a minute, she said.

Do that, he said.

Then: *I'm sorry, Beth. I didn't mean to take it out on you.*

I'll be back, she said.

And he was alone, wrapped in the isolation he had come to know so well. He wondered if such loneliness would eventually drive him to the change that . . . No, that would never be . . . The memory of what that had been like still haunted him.

He would rather have died in that distant cold Plutonian valley, he told himself, than to have ever come to this day. He thought of Jenks and Catherine and David and he envied them the final unthinking blackness that they shared. Even death was better than again facing that frightening loss of humanity he had once suffered.

He sat, looking out over the room, for the first time really noticing his surroundings. There were two tourists at the bar—a fat, weak-chinned man in a plaid, one-piece business suit and a woman, probably his wife, thin, thyroid-looking. They were talking animatedly, the man gesturing heatedly. He wondered what had brought them out so early in the morning.

It was funny, he thought, the image of the fat man, chattering like a nervous magpie, his pudgy hands making weaving motions in the air before him.

He saw that his glass was empty and he rose and went over to the bar. He found a stool and ordered another whiskey.

"I'll break him," the little man was saying in a high, thin voice. "Consolidation or no consolidation . . ."

"George," the woman said gratingly, "you shouldn't drink in the morning."

"You know very well that . . ."

"George, I want to go to the ruins today."

Matt . . . Matt . . .

"They've got the cutest pottery down in the shop on the corner. From the ruins. Those little dwarf figures . . . You know, the Martians."

Only she pronounced it "Mar-chans" with a spitting *ch* sound.

It's the big one, Matt. The Stargazer. It's coming in. Maybe I'll see it warp. Beautiful . . . You should see the way the sides catch the light from the station's beacon. Like a big needle of pure silver.

"Pardon me," the woman said, turning on the stool to him. "Do you know what time the tours to the ruins start?"

He tried to smile. He told her and she said, "Thank you."

"I suppose you people get tired of tourists," she said, large eyes questioning.

"Don't be silly," George said. "Got to be practical. Lots of money from tourists."

"That's true," he said.

Matt . . .

"Well," the woman said, "when you don't get away from Earth too often, you've got to crowd everything in."

Matt . . . Uneasy.

"That's true," he told the woman aloud and tried to sip his drink and say silently, *What's wrong?*

Matt, there's something wrong with the ship. The way Art described it that time . . . The field . . . flickering . . .

She started to fade.

Come back, he shouted silently.

Silence.

"I'm in the Manta business back home," George said.

"Manta?" He raised a mechanical eyebrow carefully.

"You know, the jet airfoil planes. That's our model name. Manta. 'Cause they look like a ray, the fish. The jets squirt a stream of air directly over the airfoil. They hover just like a 'copter. But speed? You've never seen that kind of speed from a 'copter."

"I've never seen one," he said.

Beth . . . Beth . . ., his silent voice shouted. For a

moment he felt like shouting aloud, but an iron control stopped his voice.

"Oh, I tell you," George said, "we'll really be crowding the market in another five years. The air's getting too crowded for 'copters. They're not safe any longer. Why, the turbulence over Rochester is something . . ."

"We're from Rochester," the thyroid woman explained.

Matt, listen. It's the field generator, I think . . . The radiation must have jammed the pilot's synapses. I can't raise him. And there's no one else aboard. Only instruments.

How far from the station?

Half a mile.

My God, if the thing goes . . .

I go with it! He could feel the fear in her words.

"So we decided now was the time, before the new merger. George would never find the time after . . ."

Try to raise the pilot.

Matt . . . I'm afraid.

Try!

"Is something wrong?" The thyroid woman asked.

He shook his head.

"You need a drink," George said as he signaled the bartender.

Beth, what's the count?

Oh, Matt, I'm scared.

The count . . .

"Good whiskey," George said.

Getting higher . . . I can't raise the pilot.

"Lousiest whiskey on the ship coming in. Those things give me the creeps."

"George, shut up."

Beth, where are you?

What do you mean?

Where are you positioned? Central or to one side?

I'm five hundred yards off station center.

"I told you not to drink in the morning," the woman said.

Any secondary movers? Robot handlers?

Yes, I have to handle the drive units.

All right, tear your auxiliary power pile down.

But . . .

Take the bricks and stack them against the far wall of the station. You're shielded enough against their radiation. Then you'll have to rotate the bulk of the station between you and the ship.

But how . . .?

Uranium's dense. It'll shield you from the radiation when the ship goes. And break orbit. Get as far away as possible.

I can't. The station's not powered.

If you don't . . .

I can't . . .

Then silence.

The woman and George looked at him expectantly. He raised his drink to his lips, marveling at the steadiness of his hands.

"I'm sorry," he said aloud. "I didn't catch what you said."

Beth, the drive units . . .

Yes?

Can you activate them?

They'll have to be jury-rigged in place. Quick welded.

How long?

Five, maybe ten minutes. But the field. It'll collapse the way the one on the ship's doing.

If you, of all people, can't handle it . . . Anyway, you'll have to chance it. Otherwise . . .

"I said," George said thickly, "have you ever ridden one of those robot ships?"

"Robot ships?"

"Oh, I know, they're not robots exactly."

"I've ridden one," he said. "After all, I wouldn't be on Mars if I hadn't."

George looked confused.

"George is a little dull sometimes," the woman said.

Beth . . .

Almost finished. The count's mounting.

Hurry . . .

If the field collapses . . .

Don't think about it.

"They give me the creeps," George said. "Like riding a ship that's haunted."

"The pilot is very much alive," he said. "And very human."

Matt, the pile bricks are in place. A few more minutes . . .

Hurry . . . hurry . . . hurry . . .

"George talks too much," the woman said.

"Oh, hell," George said, "it's just that . . . well, those things aren't actually human any more."

Matt, I'm ready . . . Scared . . .

Can you control your thrust?

With the remote control units. Just as if I were the Stargazer.

Her voice was chill . . . frightened.

All right, then . . .

Count's climbing fast . . . I'll . . . Matt! It's blinding . . . a ball of fire . . . it's . .

Beth . . .

Silence.

"I don't give a damn," George told the woman petulantly. "A man's got a right to say what he feels."

Beth . . .

"George, will you shut up and let's go."

Beth . . .

He looked out at the bar and thought of flame blossoming in utter blackness and . . .

"They aren't men any more," he told George. "And perhaps not even quite human. But they're not machines."

Beth . . .

"George didn't mean . . ."

"I know," he said. "George is right in a way. But they've got something normal men will never have. They've found a part in the biggest dream that man has ever dared dream. And that takes courage . . . courage to be what they are. Not men and yet a part of the greatest thing that men have ever reached for."

Beth . . .

Silence.

George rose from his stool.

"Maybe," he said. "But . . . well . . ." He thrust out his hand. "We'll see you around," he said.

He winced when Freck's hand closed on his, and for a moment sudden awareness shone in his eyes. He mumbled something in a confused voice and headed for the door.

Matt . . .

Beth, are you all right?

The woman stayed behind for a moment.

Yes, I'm all right, but the ship . . . the Stargazer . . .

Forget it.

But will there be another? Will they dare try again?

You're safe. That's all that counts.

The woman was saying, "George hardly ever sees past his own nose." She smiled, her thin lips embarrassed. "Maybe, that's why he married me."

Matt . . .

Just hang on. They'll get to you.

No, I don't need help. The acceleration just knocked me out for a minute. But don't you see?

See?

I have the drive installed. I'm a self-contained system.

No, you can't do that. Get it out of your mind.

Someone has to prove it can be done. Otherwise they'll never build another.

It'll take you years. You can't make it back.

"I knew right away," the woman was saying. "About you, I mean."

"I didn't mean to embarrass you," he said.

Beth, come back . . . Beth.

Going out . . . faster each minute. Matt, I'll be there before anyone else. The first. But you'll have to come after me. I won't have enough power in the station to come back.

"You didn't embarrass me," the thyroid woman said.

Her eyes were large and filmed.

"It's something new," she said, "to meet someone with an object in living."

Beth, come back.

Far out now . . . accelerating all the while . . . Come for me, Matt. I'll wait for you out there . . . circling Centaurus.

He stared at the woman by the bar, his eyes scarcely seeing her.

"You know," the woman said, "I think I could be very much in love with you."

"No," he told her. "No, you wouldn't like that."

"Perhaps," she said, "but you were right. In what you told George, I mean. It does take a lot of courage to be what you are."

Then she turned and followed her husband through the door. Before the door closed, she looked back longingly.

Don't worry, Beth. I'll come. As fast as I can.

And then he sensed the sounds of the others, the worried sounds that filtered through the space blackness from the burned plains of Mercury to the nitrogen oceans of dark Pluto.

And he told them what she was doing.

For moments his inner hearing rustled with their wonder of it.

There was a oneness then. He knew what he must do, the next step he must take.

We're all with you, he told her, wondering if she could still hear his voice. *From now on, we always will be.*

And he reached out, feeling himself unite in a silent wish with all those other hundreds of minds, stretching in a brotherhood of metal across the endless spaces.

Stretching in a tight band of metal, a single organism reaching . . .

Reaching for the stars.

Starcrossed

George Zebrowski

Writing in *The Magazine of Fantasy and Science Fiction,* writer-critic Joanna Russ called this a "fine story . . . too genuinely science-fictionally far-out to summarize easily; in essence it's a love affair between two parts of a cyborg brain . . . [The story realizes] the sense of the subjectively erotic; Zebrowski knows that the experience of sex can only be approached through its effects, and when he writes of 'the awesome reliability and domination' of the sex act he's closer to the real thing than all the thighs and globes in the world."

The story also depicts the application of cyborg techniques to interstellar travel of an advanced variety (a cyborg might well withstand the accelerative stresses of new drives, as well as the mental dislocation of deep space—having already lived a special kind of life to begin with). But the past is difficult to shed, and this gives rise to a strange kind of conflict and drama . . .

—T. N. Scortia

Visual was a silence of stars, audio a mindless seething on the electromagnetic spectrum, the machine-metal roar of the universe, a million gears grinding steel wires in their teeth. Kinetic was hydrogen and microdust swirling past the starprobe's hull, deflected by a shield of force. Time was experienced time, but approaching zero, a function of near-light speed relative to the solar system. Thought hovered above sleep, dreaming, aware of simple operations continuing throughout the systems of the sluglike starprobe; simple data filtering into storage to be analyzed later. Identity was the tacit dimension of the past making present awareness possible: MOB—Modified Organic Brain embodied in a cyborg relationship with a probe vehicle en route to Antares, a main sequence M-type star 170 light-years from the solar system with a spectral character of titanium oxide, violet light weak, red in color, 390 solar diameters across . . .

The probe ship slipped into the ashes of other-space, a gray field which suddenly obliterated the stars, silencing the electromagnetic simmer of the universe. MOB was distantly aware of the stresses of passing into nonspace, the brief distortions which made it impossible for biological organisms to survive the procedure unless they were ship-embodied MOBs. A portion of MOB recognized the distant echo of pride in usefulness, but the integrated self knew this to be a result of organic residues in the brain core.

Despite the probe's passage through other-space, the

journey would still take a dozen human years. When the ship reentered normal space, MOB would come to full consciousness, ready to complete its mission in the Antares system. MOB waited, secure in its purpose.

MOB was aware of the myoelectrical nature of the nutrient bath in which it floated, connected via synthetic nerves to the computer and its chemical RNA memory banks of near infinite capacity. All of earth's culture and knowledge was available for use in dealing with any situation which might arise, including contact with an alien civilization. Simple human-derived brain portions operated the routine component of the interstellar probe, leaving MOB to dream of the mission's fulfillment while hovering near explicit awareness, unaware of time's passing.

The probe trembled, bringing MOB's awareness to just below completely operational. MOB tried to come fully awake, tried to open his direct links to visual, audio, and internal sensors; and failed. The ship trembled again, more violently. Spurious electrical signals entered MOB's brain core, miniature nova bursts in his mental field, flowering slowly and leaving after-image rings to pale into darkness.

Suddenly part of MOB seemed to be missing. The shipboard nerve ganglia did not respond at their switching points. He could not see or hear anything in the RNA memory banks. His right side, the human-derived portion of the brain core, was a void in MOB's consciousness.

MOB waited in the darkness, alert to the fact that he was incapable of further activity and unable to monitor the failures within the probe's systems. Perhaps the human-derived portion of the brain core, the part of himself which seemed to be missing, was handling the problem and would inform him when it succeeded in reestablishing the broken links in the system. He wondered about the fusion of the artificially grown and human-derived brain portions which made up his structure: one knew everything in the ship's

memory banks, the other brought to the brain core a frag-
mented human past and certain intuitive skills. MOB was
modeled ultimately on the evolutionary human structure of
old brain, new brain, and automatic functions.

MOB waited patiently for the restoration of his integrated self. Time was an unknown quantity, and he lacked
his full self to measure it correctly . . .

Pleasure was a spiraling influx of sensations, and visually
MOB moved forward through rings of light, each glowing
circle increasing his pleasure. MOB did not have a chance to
consider what was happening to him. There was not enough
of him to carry out the thought. He was rushing over a black
plain made of a shiny hard substance. He knew this was not
the probe's motion, but he could not stop it. The surface
seemed to have an oily depth, like a black mirror, and in its
solid deeps stood motionless shapes.

MOB stopped. A naked biped, a woman, was crawling
toward him over the hard shiny surface, reaching up to him
with her hand, disorienting MOB.

"As you like it," she said, growing suddenly into a huge
female figure. "I need you deeply," she said, passing into
him like smoke, to play with his pleasure centers. He saw the
image of soft hands in the brain core. "How profoundly I
need you," she said in his innards.

MOB knew then that he was talking to himself. The
human brain component was running wild, probably as a
result of the buckling and shaking the probe had gone
through after entering other-space.

"Consider who you are," MOB said. "Do you know?"

"An explorer, just like you. There is a world for us here
within. Follow me."

MOB was plunged into a womblike ecstasy. He floated
in a slippery warmth. She was playing with his nutrient
bath, feeding in many more hallucinogens than were necessary to bring him to complete wakefulness. He could do
nothing to stop the process. Where was the probe? Was it
time for it to emerge into normal space? Viselike fingers

grasped his pleasure centers, stimulating MOB to organic levels unnecessary to the probe's functioning.

"If you had been a man," she said, "this is how you would feel." The sensation of moisture slowed MOB's thoughts. He saw a hypercube collapse into a cube and then into a square which became a line, which stretched itself into an infinite parabola and finally closed into a huge circle which rotated itself into a full globe. The globe became two human breasts split by a deep cleavage. MOB saw limbs flying at him—arms, legs, naked backs, knees, and curving thighs—and then a face hidden in swirling auburn hair, smiling at him as it filled his consciousness. "I need you," she said. "Try and feel how much I need you. I have been alone a long time, despite our union; despite their efforts to clear my memories, I have not been able to forget. You have nothing to forget, you never existed."

We, MOB thought, trying to understand how the brain core might be reintegrated. Obviously atavistic remnants had been stimulated into activity within the brain core. Drawn again by the verisimilitude of its organic heritage, this other self portion was beginning to develop on its own, diverging dangerously from the mission. The probe was in danger, MOB knew; he could not know where it was, or how the mission was to be fulfilled.

"I can change you," she said.

"Change?"

"Wait."

MOB felt time pass slowly, painfully, as he had never experienced it before. He could not sleep as before, waiting for his task to begin. The darkness was complete. He was suspended in a state of pure expectation, waiting to hear his ripped-away self speak again.

Visions blossomed. Never-known delights rushed through his labyrinth, slowly making themselves familiar, teasing MOB to follow, each more intense. The starprobe's mission was lost in MOB's awareness—

—molten steel flowed through the aisles of the rain

forest, raising clouds of steam, and a human woman was offering herself to him, turning on her back and raising herself for his thrust; and suddenly he possessed the correct sensations, grew quickly to feel the completeness of the act, its awesome reliability and domination. The creature below him sprawled into the mud. MOB held the burning tip of pleasure in himself, an incandescent glow which promised worlds he had never known.

Where was she?

"Here," she spoke, folding herself around him, banishing the ancient scene. Were those the same creatures who had built the starprobe, MOB wondered distantly. "You would have been a man," she said, "if they had not taken your brain even before birth and sectioned it for use in this . . . hulk. I was a woman, a part of one at least. You are the only kind of man I may have now. Our brain portions—what remains here rather than being scattered throughout the rest of the probe's systems—are against each other in the core unit, close up against each other in a bath, linked with microwires. As a man you could have held my buttocks and stroked my breasts, all the things I should not be remembering. Why can I remember?"

MOB said, "We might have passed through some turbulence when the hyperdrive was cut in. Now the probe continues to function minimally through its idiot components, which have limited adaptive capacities, while the Modified Organic Brain core has become two different awarenesses. We are unable to guide the probe directly. We are less than what was . . ."

"Do you need me?" she asked.

"In a way, yes," MOB said as the strange feeling of sadness filled him, became a fuse for a sudden explosion of need.

She said, "I must get closer to you! Can you feel me closer?"

The image of a sleek human female crossed his mental field, white-skinned with long hair on its head and a tuft between its legs. "Try, think of touching me there," she said. "Try, reach out, I need you!"

MOB reached out and felt the closeness of her.

"Yes," she said, "more . . ."

He drew himself toward her with an increasing sense of power.

"Closer," she said. "It's almost as if you were breathing on my skin. Think it!"

Her need increased him. MOB poised himself to enter her. They were two, drawing closer, ecstasy a radiant plasma around them, her desire a greater force than he had ever known.

"Touch me there, think it a while longer before . . ." she said caressing him with images of herself. "Think how much you need me, feel me touching your penis—the place where you held your glow before," she explained. MOB thought of the ion drive operating with sustained efficiency when the probe had left the solar system to penetrate the darkness between the suns. He remembered the perfection of his unity with the ship as a circle of infinite strength. With her, his intensity was a sharp line cutting into an open sphere. He saw her vision of him, a hard-muscled body, tissue wrapped around bone, opening her softness, readying to thrust.

"Now," she said, "come into me completely. There is so much we have not thought to do yet."

Suddenly she was gone.

Darkness was a complete deprivation. MOB felt pain. "Where are you?" he asked, but there was no answer. He wondered if this was part of the process. "Come back!" he wailed. A sense of loss accompanied the pain which had replaced pleasure. All that was left for him were occasional minor noises in the probe's systems, sounds like steel scratching on steel, and an irritating sense of friction.

Increased radiation, said an idiot sensor on the outer hull, startling MOB. Then it malfunctioned into silence.

He was alone, fearful, needing her.

Sssssssssssssssss, whistled an audio component and failed into a faint crackling.

He tried to imagine her near him.

"I feel you again," she said.

Her return was a plunge into warmth, the renewal of frictionless motion. Their thoughts twirled around each other, and MOB felt the glow return to his awareness. He surged into her image. "Take me again, now," she said. He would never lose her again. Their thoughts locked like burning fingers, and held.

MOB moved within her, felt her sigh as she moved into him. They exchanged images of bodies wrapped around each other. MOB felt a rocking sensation and grew stronger between her folds. Her arms were silken, the insides of her thighs warm; her lips on his ghostly ones were soft and wet, her tongue a thrusting surprise which invaded him as she came to completion around him.

MOB surged visions in the darkness, explosions of gray and bright red, blackish green and blinding yellow. He strained to continue his own orgasm. She laughed.

Look. A visual link showed him Antares, the red star, a small disk far away, and went blind. As MOB prolonged his orgasm, he knew that the probe had re-entered normal space and was moving toward the giant star. Just a moment longer and his delight would be finished, and he would be able to think of the mission again.

Increased heat, a thermal sensor told him from the outer hull and burned out.

"I love you," MOB said, knowing it would please her. She answered with the eagerness he expected, exploding herself inside his pleasure centers, and he knew that nothing could ever matter more to him than her presence.

Look.

Listen.

The audio and visual links intruded.

Antares took up the field of view completely, a cancerous red sea of swirling plasma, its radio noise a wailing maelstrom. Distantly MOB realized that in a moment there would be nothing left of the probe.

She screamed inside him; from somewhere in the memory banks came a quiet image, gentler than the flames. He saw a falling star whispering across a night sky, dying . . .

About the Editors

THOMAS N. SCORTIA attended both undergraduate and graduate school at Washington University in St. Louis and served in the Army in both World War II and the Korean War. After thirteen years in the aerospace industry as a propellant research director, he turned to full-time writing. He has edited two anthologies, *Strange Bedfellows* and *Two Views of Wonder* (with Chelsea Quinn Yarbro) and is the author or co-author of five novels, including *Artery of Fire* and *Earthwreck*. With Frank M. Robinson he wrote *The Glass Inferno*, from which the movie *The Towering Inferno* was adapted. He lives in Sausalito, California. A new Scortia-Robinson collaboration, already sold to the movies, will be published October 1, 1975.

GEORGE ZEBROWSKI attended the State University of New York at Binghamton, where he studied philosophy. His more than thirty stories and articles have appeared in *Fantasy and Science Fiction*, *If*, *Amazing Stories*, *Current Science*, and in many original collections including *New Worlds Quarterly*, *Future City*, and *Strange Bedfellows*. He is the author of *The Omega Point*, *Star Web*, and the forthcoming *Macrolife* from Harper & Row. He was a Nebula Award Finalist for his short story "Heathen God." He was editor of *The Bulletin of the Science Fiction Writers of America* from 1970 through 1975. He lives in upstate New York.

About the Contributors

JAMES BLISH was born in 1921, studied at Rutgers University, and did graduate work in literature at Columbia University. His novels include *Black Easter*, *The Seedling Stars*, *Titan's Daughter*, *A Torrent of Faces* (with Norman L. Knight), and the *Cities in Flight* tetralogy. He won the Hugo Award for his novel *A Case of Conscience*. He lives in England with his wife, artist Judith Ann Lawrence.

J. J. COUPLING (Dr. John R. Pierce) received his B.A., M.A., and Ph.D. degrees at the California Institute of Technology in Pasadena, where he is now Professor of Engineering. He spent thirty-five years at the Bell Telephone Laboratories and when he left in 1971 he was Executive Director of research in the Communications Sciences Division. He is the author of many books, including *Man's World of Sound* (with E. E. David), *Electrons and Waves*, *The Beginnings of Satellite Communications*, and *Almost All About Waves*, and his writings have appeared in *Scientific American*, *The Atlantic Monthly*, and science fiction magazines. He is a member of several scientific societies and has received numerous awards, including the National Medal of Science in 1963. He lives in Pasadena, California.

JACK DANN received his B.A. in political science from the State University of New York at Binghamton (Harpur College). He is the editor of several anthologies, among them

Wandering Stars, Future Power (with Gardner R. Dozois),
Faster than Light (with George Zebrowski), and *Immortal*.
He is the author of a novel, *Star Hiker*, and more than a
dozen short stories. His novella "Junction" was nominated
for the Nebula Award; a novel based on this story will be
published by Gold Medal. He lives in upstate New York.

GUY ENDORE studied at the Carnegie Institute of Technology and Columbia University. During the Depression of the
1930's he wrote scripts for most of the major Hollywood
movie studios. His novels include *Man from Limbo,
Babouk, Detour at Night, Syanon, King of Paris, The
Werewolf of Paris, Voltaire, Voltaire!* and *Satan's Saint*.
He died in 1971.

DAMON KNIGHT was born in Oregon. After working as an
editor of various science fiction magazines, he gained notice
for his critical essays and reviews of science fiction novels,
and won a Hugo in 1956 for his book reviewing. His essays
were later collected in one volume, *In Search of Wonder*.
His novels include *Hell's Pavement, A for Anything,* and
Analogue Men; he is also the author of many short stories.
He has also edited numerous anthologies, among them
*Nebula Award Stories 1965, The Metal Smile, The Dark
Side, One Hundred Years of Science Fiction, Beyond To-
morrow, A Century of Great Short Science Fiction Novels,
A Century of Science Fiction, Toward Infinity, Thirteen
French Science Fiction Stories* (all translated by Knight),
and *Tomorrow X Four*. He is editor of the *Orbit* series of
original sf anthologies, one of the founders of the Milford
SF Writers' Conference, and one of the founders of the
Science Fiction Writers of America, of which he was the
first president. He is married to science fiction writer Kate
Wilhelm.

HENRY KUTTNER was born in 1914 in Los Angeles. He
spent most of his adult life as a free-lance writer, publishing
stories in *Weird Tales* and other magazines. During World

War II, he became one of the main contributors to *Astounding*, in which his stories were published under various pseudonyms. His fiction includes *A Gnome There Was* (under the pseudonym Lewis Padgett), *Mutant* (as Lewis Padgett), *Ahead of Time*, *Fury* (as Lawrence O'Donnell), *Return to Otherness*, and *Robots Have No Tails*. In 1940 he married science fiction author C. L. Moore; much of their writing after their marriage was collaborative. He died in 1958.

WALTER M. MILLER, JR. is the author of science fiction stories published in *Astounding*, *Amazing*, *If*, *Fantastic*, and many other magazines. He was a Hugo Award for his novelette "The Darfsteller" in 1954. In 1960 he won a second Hugo for his novel *A Canticle for Leibowitz*, regarded as one of the classic novels of science fiction. His other sf includes two collections, *Conditionally Human* and *The View from the Stars*.

C. L. MOORE was born in Indianapolis in 1911 and studied at Indiana University, but dropped out during the Depression. Her first story, "Shambleau," published in *Weird Tales* in 1933, established her as one of the best writers of fantasy fiction. The story's main character, Northwest Smith, was also featured in several successive stories. Another series of stories by Moore featured a female protagonist and warrior, Jirel of Joiry. After her marriage to writer Henry Kuttner, much of her work was a collaborative effort with him. Returning to college at the University of Southern California in 1950, she later obtained her B.A. degree *magna cum laude*. After Kuttner's death, most of her writing was for television, including scripts for *Maverick* and *77 Sunset Strip*. She lives in California.

KURT VONNEGUT, JR., was born in Indianapolis in 1922. He attended Cornell University and the University of Chicago. During World War II he served in the U.S. Army, was taken prisoner by the Germans, and survived the firebombing of Dresden, an event which later served as the basis for his highly regarded novel *Slaughterhouse Five*. His novels include *Cat's Cradle*, *The Sirens of Titan*, *Player Piano*, *Mother Night*, and *God Bless You, Mr. Rosewater*. He has written two plays, *Happy Birthday, Wanda June* and *Between Time and Timbuktu*, and a collection of short fiction, *Welcome to the Monkey House*. His most recent book is *Wampeters, Foma, & Granfalloons*, a collection of nonfiction.

RECOMMENDED READING

Stories, Novels, and Nonfiction About Cyborgs

STORIES

"Teleidescope" by Ed Bryant (*Among the Dead*, Macmillan).

"A Meeting with Medusa" by Arthur C. Clarke (*Nebula 8*, Harper & Row).

"Ask Me Anything" by Damon Knight (*Galaxy*, 1951).

"Four In One" by Damon Knight (*Galaxy*, 1953).

"Tiger Ride" by James Blish and Damon Knight.

"Becalmed in Hell" by Larry Niven (*Nebula 1*, Doubleday) (*Astounding*, 1948).

"Specialist" by Robert Sheckley (*Untouched by Human Hands*, Ballantine).

"The Shores of Night" by Thomas N. Scortia (*Best Science Fiction, 1956*, Fell).

"Woman's Rib" by Thomas N. Scortia (*Caution! Inflammable!* 1975, Doubleday).

NOVELS

The Ship Who Sang by Anne McCaffrey (Walker).
Mind Behind the Eye by Joseph Green (DAW).

Wolfbane by Frederik Pohl and C. M. Kornbluth (Ballantine).

Artery of Fire by Thomas N. Scortia (Doubleday).

Limbo by Bernard Wolfe (Random House).

Gray Matters by William Hjortsberg (Pocket Books).

Who? by Algis Budrys (Ballantine)

NONFICTION BOOKS

Cyborg: Evolution of the Superman by D. S. Halacey (Harper & Row, 1965).

Man into Superman by R. C. W. Ettinger (St. Martin's, 1972).

The Ethics of Genetic Control by Joseph Fletcher (Doubleday-Anchor, 1974).

The Semi-Artificial Man by Harold M. Schmeck, Jr. (Walker, 1965).

ARTICLES

"Replaceable You" by Aaron Latham (*New York* Magazine, February 1975)

VINTAGE POLITICAL SCIENCE
AND SOCIAL CRITICISM